HINTERLAND

LOGAN SPURGEON

Quill & Crow

Hinterland
written by Logan Spurgeon
published by Quill & Crow Publishing House

This book is a work of fiction. All incidents, dialogue, and characters, except for some well-known historical and public figures, are either products of the author's imagination or used in a fictitious manner. Any resemblance to actual persons, living or dead, or actual events is purely coincidental.

Copyright © 2025 Logan Spurgeon

All rights reserved. Published in the United States by Quill & Crow Publishing House, Ohio. No portion of this book may be reproduced in any form without permission from the publisher, except as permitted by U.S. copyright law.

Printed in the United States of America

Cover Design by Fay Lane

Edited by Lisa Morris, Tiffany Putenis

ISBN: 978-1-958228-90-6

ISBN: 978-1-958228-89-0 (ebook)

Publisher's Website: quillandcrowpublishinghouse.com

For my father, I wish you could be here to see this
or
For my father, thank you for making this possible
or
For my father, thank you for teaching me the peace of wild things
or
For my father, from whom I learned to love the wilderness

or simply,

For my father

PUBLISHER'S NOTE

This book contains scenes of graphic cannibalism. Please be advised.

FOREWORD

In early October 2023, I was sitting in a cafe thinking about the next book I would write. I had recently finished my forthcoming Gothic novel, *The House on Garnet Hill,* and had to get away from haunted houses for a bit. I always wanted to do a wilderness survival story—I loved reading *Hatchet, Lord of the Flies,* and *The Most Dangerous Game* as a kid—and began to outline a rough premise for what would become *Hinterland.*

November was right around the corner, and I planned to attempt the daunting challenge of writing a novel in a month. I had a vague premise in place and a few names picked out, but I wasn't sure where the story would lead. I put *Hinterland* on the shelf until I could start writing on November 1st.

Just days before I was set to write the novel, I started receiving innumerable phone calls and messages from friends asking if I had heard the news about a former Christian ministry I was in and the allegations against the founder. Story after story broke detailing spiritual manipulation, clergy abuse, sexual misconduct, and "prophetic" falsehoods.

Needless to say, I was shocked, but not entirely surprised. For years, there had been allegations of cultish behaviors within the organization, but I brushed those off because I couldn't see behind the curtain. Once it was pulled back, it was clear that it was indeed a cult.

How did I end up in this situation?

In my teenage and early adult years, I struggled to reconcile my religious upbringing with my sexuality. The two seemed to be at odds with each other, and I was caught in the middle. I would often hear sermons about LGBT+ people and how they were destined for hell. I prayed every night for God to take my desires from me, but they never went away. When people asked about my sexuality, I would lie. I told them it was wrong to be gay, but all the while I was falling in love with one of my friends. I was living a double life, and I needed to find a solution.

Enter IHOPKC—the International House of Prayer of Kansas City—an evangelical Christian ministry devoted to 24/7 prayer and worship until the return of Jesus. Their sole mission is to run a prayer and worship room 24/7 and "change the understanding and expression of Christianity in a generation" into ushering in the end times and the return of Jesus Christ within our lifetimes.

How could they possibly solve my perceived problem? First, one of my friends in our church's youth group attended a conference put on by IHOPKC. When he returned, he spoke of miracles—vision being restored, people in wheelchairs walking, and others being "set free" from homosexuality. Second, I believed my sexuality was partially due to a lack of faith or wholeheartedness. IHOPKC was a ministry where thousands of other young adults sacrificed their 20s to read the Bible, study theology, and spend forty hours a week in the prayer room. If I could be like those *radical* Christians, then I wouldn't be gay.

That wasn't all. While attending a conference put on by IHOPKC, someone from their "university" (I say "university" because, despite their promise to get accredited, they never did) approached me, claiming that God told them to tell me that I was supposed to come and attend classes there. Further, several messages and "prophetic words" were given, saying that my friendships, my family, school, and society were keeping me from a vibrant relationship with God.

What was I to say? I was struggling with college life, depressed, and tormented by my sexuality. My life was falling apart, and the ministry seemed to have all the answers. So I made the choice to quit school, give up my full-ride scholarship, and do a six-month internship in Kansas City. After all, it was what God wanted, right?

I lied during my intake interview and claimed that God healed me from being gay—only because I didn't want that to disqualify me from the internship. I got in. Six months of prayer, worship, and reading the Bible. We lived in overcrowded apartments and ate cafeteria food. We took classes and spent six hours every night from 6 pm to midnight in the prayer room.

Afterward, I considered my options and decided to remain at the ministry and complete a four-year certificate at the "university." At first, everything seemed great, but slowly the truth came out again. I tried dating girls only to end up crying in my car after a date. I was still attracted to men, and I couldn't understand why when I was doing everything "right." So I took the next step and joined a program offered by the ministry.

It was the closest you could get to conversion therapy without being actual conversion therapy. I joined the program, lied my way through it, avoided the "g" word, and hoped that if I fixed other problems in my life, the gay thing would go away. It didn't. After a horrible senior year in my program, I decided to leave Kansas City and return home.

My problems followed me. I was dating a girl who was my best friend, teaching Sunday school at my church, working at a great job, and about to head off to Seminary to get my M.A. in Theology. Everything looked great on paper, but I was depressed, struggling, and caught in an endless cycle of shame and hiding.

Finally, with the help of my best friend and cousin—and some therapy—I decided to be honest with myself. I was gay. That was never going away. I had to accept myself, tell others, and figure out what my life would look like.

Ignoring my sexuality for over a decade for the sake of religious dogma was detrimental. I lost so much of myself throughout the years. Eventually, I stepped back and realized that I was unknown—no one close to me knew the *real* me, and I barely knew myself. I was a shell of a person, carved out so that others would accept me.

It was during this time that I started distancing myself from IHOPKC. I had been casually following them and attending some conferences or visiting the prayer room when I was back in town, but coming out to my friends from the ministry was a rough experience. Further, several leaders started promoting right-wing conspiracy theories that did not align with their previous beliefs. I could see that the organization was going in a similar direction to the church I grew up in. I started to disengage, untangle my own beliefs from what I was taught, and deconstruct my faith. I started writing again after years of abandoning my long-held desire to craft stories.

From 2018 to 2023, I did my own thing—rediscovering myself and learning what I wanted from life. Deconstructing my faith and figuring out what I believed. I reignited my passion for storytelling and wrote two books and numerous short stories. I dated, fell in love, had my heart broken, found my best friends, and lived my life.

That brings us back to October 2023 and the unfolding allegations. It turns out that ushering in the end times is a telltale sign of a doomsday cult. Who knew? The entire "ministry" was predicated on delusion and lies. Our lives, our money, our bodies, and our time were sacrificed on the altar to uphold the ego of one man.

As I began to process my own feelings, I reconnected with old friends and met new ones who had similar experiences to my own. The whirlwind of scandal ignited a firestorm within me. I had to channel all those feelings into something. In the chaos of my fury, sorrow, frustration, and despondency, *Hinterland* was born.

Kestrel's story is, in a way, my own story. I lost the core of who I was and found myself among strangers. I struggled against nature and religion, belief and doubt, truth and lies. I had to lean on others when I lost my way, and in the end, I found myself again.

I survived.

- Logan Spurgeon, 2025

ONE

THE DEVOURERS

"Kestrel. That is your name."

Kestrel, Kestrel, Kestrel.

He said it over and over in his head, trying to memorize the word before he attempted to speak it. It didn't come out at first—his lips were cracked, his tongue dry. His teeth tasted of iron when he licked them. A hoarse voice uttered from his desiccated throat as he spoke the name that was not his own. "Kestrel."

"Can you hear me?"

Kestrel looked up. Though she stood only a few feet away from him, the woman who spoke was a blur. He strained to focus. Her face was grainy, and her edges shimmered.

"He hit his head hard." A shadowy, bulky body emerged from the indistinguishable world behind the woman.

It was all becoming too much. Kestrel turned his attention back to the woman, looked for where her eyes should be, and narrowed his until they vanquished the filmy glaze preventing his sight.

"Look, he's coming to!"

Kestrel tried to find who had spoken, but there were too many of them. They stood loosely arranged around him, some low to the ground, others half-hidden behind the nearby trees. The torches and little fires scattered around them illuminated their figures, throwing shadows across their faces. The woods were dense and quiet, save for the sound of their breath and distant leaves falling to the wet earth. The wind pressed the trees, and Kestrel heard what sounded like archaic wind chimes above him. Their bleak, graceless music grated his ears.

A strong, gentle hand touched his cheek and guided him back. The woman who spoke earlier examined Kestrel with bright yellow eyes—the color of digested bile, catlike. Her hair fell along her round face in jagged strands as if cut with a rusted knife.

"Where am I?" Kestrel asked.

"You are with us," she said joyously, the words falling from salivating lips.

"Who are you?" Kestrel's head throbbed with pain. His hair felt wet and heavy, and the air around him smelled of blood. When he tried to lift his hand to touch his head, a tremor wormed through his skull and into the soft flesh of his forgetful mind. Too soon to move quickly.

"Don't you remember?" a timid voice asked from somewhere along the tree line.

Kestrel shot his gaze toward the sound. It took him a moment to gain focus again; when he did, he saw a little girl peer from behind a tree. She was young—no more than seven or eight. Her clothes were tattered, her faded blue jeans and pale pink shirt contrasted with her otherwise drab outfit—a practical brown coat and gray sneakers. On her head, she wore fur rabbit ears that looked to be part of an old Halloween costume.

Something hung around her neck. Kestrel couldn't tell what it was, but the girl held on to it carefully before she concealed it in her coat like a prized possession. Her eyes were big and curious, but heartbroken. Clean streaks ran down her face where the dirt had been washed away by tears.

"Not now, Cottontail," the woman said, pulling Kestrel's focus back to her.

Cottontail. Like the rabbit ears she wears.

"Who are you?" Kestrel repeated.

"We are your people. You belong to us now," the catlike woman said. She smiled and leaned forward to kiss his forehead. Kestrel recoiled from the stranger, wishing he could wipe her saliva from his skin. He stared up at her with disgust.

"No. Who are *you?*" Kestrel asked pointedly.

"Ah." The woman stood upright. She wore old, ripped blue jeans and the remnants of a white collared shirt. It was partially covered by a grayish-brown wool vest that was frayed at the bottom seam. Around her neck hung a sort of tie Kestrel hadn't seen before.

He stared.

"*You* are Kestrel." She reaffirmed the strange name. "And I am Lynx, the leader of our people. You've been chosen, and soon you'll be initiated. Do you know where you are?"

When he shook his head, Lynx smirked. His answer pleased her.

Lynx adjusted the object that hung around her neck. It glinted in the forest's scant light and refracted a gleam that almost matched her eyes. It was a bolo tie, and in the center, a warm amber stone shone as bright as honey.

"He's the one," the high-pitched voice from before called out.

Kestrel tried to find the owner of the voice, but his sight was blocked by a towering monstrosity of a man. His eyes were hidden behind a matted fur mask that made him look like an ox, and his chin and mouth were obscured by an unruly beard. Horns jutted from the mask and twisted around his ears. He stood tall and immovable, watching.

"What's happening?" Kestrel cried, suddenly alarmed. His heart raced, and blood pounded behind his eyes, drumming in his ears and turning his stomach.

"You hit your head. Hard. You will be fine," the intimidating man assured him.

It was not quite the comfort Kestrel needed. It was only then, in the blistering chill, that he realized his hands and feet were tied, his hiking boots wrapped in rope.

"Don't be afraid. You've been with us a long time. You've forgotten us, but it will all come back to you soon. I promise," Lynx said. She turned back toward the hiding girl. "Cottontail, please get Kestrel a canteen of water."

Cottontail. Lynx. Kestrel.

It felt like he was collecting names like trinkets.

The girl hopped out of sight, returning with a silver bottle. She carefully unscrewed the cap and handed it to Lynx, who held it to Kestrel's lips. He gulped down the water, but he couldn't get enough. It was lukewarm and tasted like metal, but he didn't mind.

Lynx pulled the canteen from his lips, and Kestrel caught his breath. Small dribbles ran down his chin; he wished he could drink them up. He wanted more, but the bottle was almost empty.

Lynx handed it back to Cottontail, who peered into the mostly depleted void. She sighed and screwed the cap back on. The pendant hanging around her neck fell forward, and the swinging appendage made Kestrel's stomach flip. Cottontail noticed his queasy look and hid it away behind her brown coat once more.

It was a foot.

Not just any foot—a child's foot.

Her foot.

Kestrel looked down and saw a series of bandages wrapped around her small leg where her foot should have been.

What the—what's happening?

The masked man with horns, the woman with the bolo tie and catlike eyes, and the girl with her own foot hanging around her neck. How did he end up here?

"It's a charm." Cottontail scrunched her face as she tried to close up her coat. Her efforts were futile, and the bulky necklace fell out once again. She held her own foot in her hand and stared at it. It was the steel gray of death, cold and hardened, the edges blackened and bruised purple.

"Frostbite," the large man said, answering the question Kestrel was too afraid to ask.

Shock coiled around Kestrel, struck by the horror that the little girl kept a prize of her agony, a charm to ward away further mutilation, a pound of flesh. Water and acid—the only thing his belly had to offer—spewed from his mouth onto the autumn-dusted earth. The leaves caught his nausea and held it there, like Cottontail held her foot, a reflecting pool of revulsion. At the mere thought of it, Kestrel heaved once more.

"It'll be okay." Cottontail put a small, dirt-stained hand on his shoulder, patting him twice before Lynx asked her to get another bottle of water. She hopped away in obedience, her rabbit ears bouncing as she disappeared behind the group.

Kestrel's lungs faltered. He needed to slow the speed of his heart. Too much was happening. The woods around him began to spin, and his eyes lost their strength. He teetered on his knees, rocking back and forth as the ground threatened to jump up toward him.

"I got him," the man said as he stabilized Kestrel.

The feel of the strange man's hands on his shoulders made Kestrel recoil. He gasped as the man cut the cords binding him, then lifted and leaned him against a nearby stone.

Cottontail returned with another bottle and gave it to Lynx, making sure to keep her distance this time. Lynx approached, touching his forehead with the back of her hand like his mother had when he had a fever as a child. She shook her head and gave him another drink.

My mother.

A distant memory, alive but flickering out, reminding him he once had a life far from this place. He knew these strangers were not his people, these woods were not his home, and his name was not Kestrel. He had a mother out there, and maybe a father, too.

If only he could remember.

There was no evidence of how long he'd been in the woods, how or why he was there in the first place—if it was of his own volition or if he'd been taken by these people. There had to be a logical explanation. The water settled in his stomach, slowing the terror inside him as it alleviated his thirst.

With newfound clarity, he looked around to see more people. Cottontail, Lynx, the unnamed man, and *others*. Nine. He counted nine others. There could be even more beyond, hiding among the shapes and shadows of the trees and rocks around him. He was surrounded.

The clinking from above resumed as the wind picked up—a wicked chorus that sounded like rocks rolling down the hill, of trees shattering upon rapids, or the breaking of bodies. He looked up, and his hopes were quickly dashed. Hanging above him weren't stones or sticks. Bones from broken, dismantled bodies hung from the branches of the high canopy, cracking against each other as they swayed.

There were crimson strings around them, rope stained red. They resembled veins intertwined, sinew and bowels, wrapped around ashen white, burnt black, aged gray, and sickly yellow bones—tibia and femur, rib and radius, sternum and jaw. Instead of chimes to celebrate spring, their ungodly death rattle brought forth the chill of autumnal air that precedes the winter dark.

"Don't be afraid," Cottontail said in her soft voice. "You are not one of them."

Kestrel could not hide his eyes, the sweat beading his brow, nor the tremble of his jaw as he watched a mandible smack against a spinal column, scattering teeth upon the earth. He wondered how many had fallen and been lost, barren seeds unable to yield the fruit of their former hosts. How many people died to decorate these trees?

Kestrel looked back down to see flames rising behind Lynx's head. Smoke rose and swirled among the bones above, joining in their dance. A large bonfire was set up beyond where Lynx stood; it smelled acrid, metallic, and foul, like hair and flesh crisping. Above the burning body, little glimmers of dust sparkled.

No, no, no.

Lynx stepped aside, and Kestrel saw the makeshift altar, wood stacked neatly in blocks. A slab of bark—like a mortician's table—held the body of a young man. The body had recently been laid out on the pyre; the extremities were not yet blemished by blisters and black char. For a moment, he swore he saw the hand of the burning man writhing. He dismissed the thought as much as he could.

"Muskox, are we ready?" Lynx turned to the large man, who nodded.

Kestrel said the name to himself, a growing call sheet of strangers who shouldn't be allowed to continue their rituals. The atrocities warned him to get up, to run as fast as he could and find a way home. But there was no home to run to.

Not that Kestrel didn't have one. He supposed he did, though he couldn't remember where it was. He wasn't even sure of his current location. A forest, to be sure—but where? When? The trees were tall above the ribbons and bones, dense leaves turning shades of brown, red, orange, and yellow in the dying autumn.

Death surrounded him. At least he knew that.

"This is the sacrifice," Lynx said. She moved out of the way and gestured toward the bonfire.

The others began to chant and howl, their vocalizations strange.

The smell, the sight, the very idea of it made Kestrel want to jump into the fire himself—to burn away to cinder, lift up as ash upon the wind, and drift high above and far away from this place and its barbaric people. At least he wouldn't have to endure whatever was about to happen.

Muskox, along with two other men, began shoveling dirt onto the fire. The tendrils of flame retracted, the smell of smoke littered with earth and flesh. The wooden structure that held up the body was no longer like a mortician's slab—it was now a banquet table being readied for a feast.

"The time is now!" a woman shouted. A flowing cloth draped her body, making her look like a vulture wrapped in its wings, a hungry scavenger above a carcass. She wore a patinated leather mask with a plume of feathers springing from the top. Her eyes were hidden, but her mouth and nose had been left uncovered. She waved the others over, and they gathered around the body.

"Hoatzin," Lynx addressed the woman. "Have you prepared the spirits?"

Hoatzin. The vulture-like woman is Hoatzin.

Kestrel knew he must memorize all of their names and mentally made a list of those who were about to commit this heinous act.

"It is ready," Hoatzin shrilled. She stirred a vat of liquid that splashed at the edges. It reminded him of a witch's brew, a glowing, sinister cauldron. She pulled out a beat-up ladle and took a long sip.

The group looked at the spread body. One licked his lips, another quieted her stomach with a hand, and a few bowed their heads, but one—a woman—stared directly at Kestrel. She smiled at Kestrel and put her wool hood over her head. She checked those around her and looked back at him.

"Friend." She mouthed the words to him. He couldn't trust her—he couldn't trust anyone here—but something stirred within him. She guaranteed no one was looking for a third time and mouthed an apology.

What was she sorry for? He thought about what was about to happen, what he was about to see, and he knew the answer. Kestrel grimaced at the thought of it.

"Thank you, Grouse, for your sacrifice," Lynx said as she raised her arms high in the air. "We are able to go on because of your death. Your blood will be our blood, your flesh our flesh, your life our life. We are one."

"No, don't do this!" Kestrel stood, but his head swelled, and the land beneath him went sideways. He stumbled and caught himself on a nearby tree as the world swirled; he felt his awareness fade.

Bark scraped his hands and arms, peeling skin from his palms. The scent of sap and blood was sharp and nauseating. He looked away from the altar, from the people gathering around the burnt remains, searching for the little girl.

"Can I have a bite of the thigh?" Cottontail asked as she peered up at the body.

Kestrel was losing his battle to stay conscious. The darkness swirling over his body was a welcome gift. He no longer had to witness the charred man being devoured, the twelve rejoicing in their meal as they picked his bones clean to hang up by crimson threads in the trees.

He was lucky, for now, that he was not among the devourers.

TWO
SALT HILL

There was no path through the woods, no trail to follow, and no clear way forward, at least to Kestrel. If there was, he wasn't privy to the knowledge. As he followed the group blindly, a man behind him swept a broom made of branches across the ground, hiding their tracks as much as possible. From what, Kestrel did not know.

He had awoken that morning to an empty canopy. The bones hanging above him were gone, and the altar transformed to ash, the evidence scattered among the fallen leaves. He had hoped to wake from this nightmare, to find himself startled in bed and the gruesome visions just a conjuring of fear and warning. But all of it was real.

Two men had wrapped the bones in their stained ropes and placed them in large canvas backpacks, which they carried on their backs with ease. The weight of their hunger for flesh didn't seem to bother them either.

Cannibals.

The word gnawed at him. He was walking in the company of cannibals who had feasted on a young man last night and seemed to enjoy it deeply. Spared of the savagery, Kestrel had been given a small bundle of dried fruits and foraged nuts by Cottontail. She smiled when she handed it to him, but he hadn't been able to focus on anything beyond the foot hanging around her neck.

Kestrel winced as the forest floor dug at his bare feet. He looked down at his ripped blue jeans and green plaid shirt. Still, he found no memories. He tried to remember his home—the kind of house he lived in, the sort of bed he slept in, the clothes he wore. Was this what he wore every day, or was it the outfit he chose when he wandered into the wilderness? He wasn't even sure what his own face looked like. He ran his hand over his features and through his matted hair.

The fall.

They said he had fallen and hit his head. That's when the memories fled his mind, gone to roost somewhere distant, waiting for him to build a nest so they might return safely. There was no way of knowing if he fell or if he was pushed, but he didn't want to ask the others. He knew doubt would poison every word they spoke.

"Halt," Lynx commanded before she sniffed the air.

The two men carrying the bones, whom Lynx called Pronghorn and Thinhorn, stopped. Thinhorn licked his arm, and Pronghorn nudged him to quit. *Brothers.* Kestrel was sure of it. They had such similar features and mannerisms that they had to be related.

Up to that point, the twelve had been in a single-file line behind Lynx, marching toward an unknown destination. Lynx exchanged words with Hoatzin—the birdlike woman—and a short man with scales on his face and shoulders. Kestrel shuddered at their appearances in the daylight, each one more uncanny than the other. The older ones seemed to have taken on the guise of their name.

Cottontail peeked out from behind Muskox to look at the three talking. Pronghorn shifted his pack, and the remains softly rattled. Goosebumps rose along Kestrel's arm at the sound of the bones.

He turned to see the woman who had spoken to him during the sacrifice. "Who are you?" he asked.

"Stoat," she said, without fully turning around.

"Last night..." Kestrel couldn't finish.

Stoat stared at him with ebony eyes that matched her skin. She lowered her hood, releasing her salt-and-pepper braids to fall over her shoulders. She put a hand on his shoulder, signaling for him to hush with her other hand. "I'll explain later," she whispered. "They're too close."

Kestrel searched her deep eyes. Nothing made sense, and he wasn't getting any closer to finding out the truth of what was going on or who these people were. He longed for any bit of information, scrambling as if he were trying to catch sunbeams in his hand.

"That's Bowhead." Stoat gestured for Kestrel to turn around.

Kestrel watched as the man—Bowhead—worked to erase their trail.

Bowhead paused and leaned against his wide broom to catch his breath. It was made of what appeared to be an old mop handle, twigs, and evergreen branches. "Nice to meet you," he said. His voice was heavy, deep, and powerful—not stern, but confident. Assured. His mouth was wide and grimly set. The man loomed large, bulkier and more muscular than Muskox, which was quite a feat. Age had worn down his face, giving his dark skin a gray hue, but his hair was so black, it shone blue. His eyes were the opposite of Stoat's—tired, drained of life.

"You too," Kestrel said, and tried to size up the only one who could potentially stop him from running back into the woods and hiding away. "Why are we stopping?" he asked.

"Lynx senses something," Stoat explained.

"She can see the unseen. That's why she leads us," Bowhead added.

It was not the explanation Kestrel wanted, but it seemed to be the only one they would offer.

"Have some water." Stoat passed her bottle to Kestrel without any hint of a smile. "You can trust me."

If it was an offering or appeasement, it fell short. Kestrel needed more. More information about where he was, *who* he was, who he was with, and where they were going. Stoat was the only one to offer anything to him thus far. The water felt good in his throat—a mercy. He was grateful for the drink, but suspicion bubbled up in him as he handed the water bottle back to her. "Who are the others?" he asked, pointing ahead.

"Gannet, Cottontail, Cross Fox, Thinhorn, Pronghorn, Muskox, Hoatzin, Caiman, Lynx," Stoat answered while putting the bottle back in her pack. "In that exact order."

"Always in order," Bowhead said.

"How old is she?" Kestrel couldn't stop staring at the little girl with a foot around her neck. She was playing a clapping game with Gannet, who looked too old to be a boy but not old enough to be a man.

Neither Bowhead nor Stoat responded. He tapped Stoat on the shoulder, but she raised her hood and adjusted her pack. Before he could get an answer, Lynx addressed them.

"Let's move!"

Hoatzin and the scaly man fell back in line, and everyone started to trod in a new direction. The trees and landscape seemed to blend together, a mirage of waypoints leading the pack to their destination, a labyrinth without walls.

"Do you know where we're going?" Kestrel asked out loud.

"We head to Salt Hill," Bowhead told him.

"What is Salt Hill?"

No one replied.

Lynx led the group further into the woods, climbing until they came to a small stream. The water rumbled over the rocks, stealing leaves from the shore and sky, and carrying them down the slight slope. The group stopped to drink—some slowly and deeply, others quickly and repeatedly—but Kestrel hesitated. He knew to be wary of drinking from streams, but his mouth was so dry. He knelt and leaned over the rapidly moving surface, sipping the water despite his worry.

"Cross Fox," Lynx called to the woman with dusky brown, bushy hair. A dark stripe ran along her mask. It looked like a black lightning bolt on the burnt orange fur.

"Fill everything," Cross Fox said to the rest of the group after the two spoke. She crouched down to fill a hydration pack, the kind a camper might carry with them. Her torso was long, but her limbs seemed unusually short. "It will be heavy, but we will need it until we reach the river."

Cottontail filled up two plastic water bottles as Thinhorn took a large military canteen and dipped it below the surface. Muskox took his turn with an old milk jug that still had its label on it. Kestrel realized he didn't have anything to fill.

"Here," Stoat said as she tossed him a water bottle. "I have two."

"Thank you."

"You were blessed to be chosen," Stoat said with watery eyes. Her mouth stayed open as if she had more to say.

"Was I?"

"Yes." Hoatzin said as she peered at him from across the river. Her body was stooped low, her arms spread out to the side like great wings, and her wild hair stuck up in all directions. Her eyes were red. "The gods have chosen you for their purpose."

Hoatzin removed the canister strapped across her chest before tilting her head too far to the right—unnatural and leering. There was a sort of wandering in her gaze, an examination of the unseen that lingered around the forest. She scooped up some water with the canister and mixed it in a chipped mug with some sort of mash. Then she took a sip, savoring it.

Stoat and Kestrel stood and stepped away from the stream.

"You were saved by the gods. Otherwise—" Stoat did not finish her sentence.

Kestrel knew.

Eaten.

He was saved from being eaten by the people who now called him blessed.

He felt grateful, but he also felt a tinge of guilt. If he hadn't been saved, would the other man have been spared? It could've been him on that altar, burned and torn up for a meal, his liver charred, hair singed, and flesh sitting in the bellies of the twelve others around him. He shuddered at the thought.

"We will reach Salt Hill by nightfall," Lynx said to the group, her catlike eyes gleaming, the amber gemstone in her bolo tie refracting light on the stream.

All eyes turned to her.

"We will camp there for the night, collect the bounty, then move on."

The bounty.

Kestrel wondered what that could be and why the place was called Salt Hill. He opened his mouth to ask, but Stoat gave him a warning glance. To save or to silence him, he wasn't sure.

The party finished filling their bottles and packed up. Bowhead ensured the footprints by the water had turned to mud—nothing left to trace them. It occurred to Kestrel that he would have to leave something behind in case someone was looking for him, but he would have to get it past Bowhead and the others first.

If there was anyone looking for him.

The remainder of the journey up to Salt Hill was uneventful. Everyone walked in an ordered pace, keeping up with Lynx, even Cottontail. The little rabbit girl walked on a tilt. Her missing foot made her stature uneven, but she used a sturdy stick to keep her balance. When she grew tired, Muskox carried her on his back.

Finally, the sun dipped below the mountainous horizon, and an abundance of shadows bloomed—the perfect hideaway for predators and prey alike. Even the trees, once so full of life—evergreen—became sinister spires. They grew farther apart as the group approached their destination, their cover becoming increasingly sparse.

They reached a clearing at the edge of Salt Hill, and Kestrel's eyes went wide. Rocks jutted up from the earth like an exposed spinal column, an unearthed giant. The fading sunlight blessed the salt rock formation with a yellow glow, bright and vivid like a hundred precious stones glinting in the night. An open wound of darkness, the start of a cave, was the only break in the shimmering stone.

"Rest up for the night," Lynx commanded as she stood at the entrance of the small cave in the salt rock. The other eleven set down their gear, relieving themselves from the weight of their packs and unrolling makeshift sleeping mats.

"I will make a fire," Muskox said.

"I can help," Cottontail chirped as she followed him off into the nearby woods to gather twigs and kindling.

Kestrel noticed Bowhead watching everyone with intense care. The man muttered to himself as if he were taking notes so he could erase any trace of them once morning came.

"Cross Fox, with me," Lynx commanded as she headed into a nearby cave.

"What's in there?" Kestrel asked Stoat who was setting out her water bottle and a thick wool blanket she used for a bed. She took a breath but didn't respond.

"This is for you." Cross Fox appeared behind him to give him a folded blanket and a wrapped package. "This is a small provision of fruits and nuts until tomorrow night. Ration it out, or you'll have to forage tomorrow if you're hungry. I see you already have a bottle. Once you're initiated, I'll give you your own pack." She didn't wait for a reply. Her short legs quickly carried her to the cave entrance and down into the salty darkness.

"That belonged to Grouse," Stoat said. "His sacrifice meant you got to live. Don't take it for granted."

Kestrel nodded and unfolded his blanket. The smell of dead leaves, autumn wind, and musk stirred up from the fabric. Was that the last trace of Grouse, besides what remained in the guts of those around him? Kestrel set the blanket down with care as if it were a sacred thing. His life—his survival—was only due to the death of the stranger. He felt sick.

"Play along until it's time," Stoat whispered and walked off.

Her words sent him spiraling. What did she mean by that? It seemed she was not the same as the others—a double agent of sorts. She was looking out for him, and if that was the case, then maybe she was truly his friend. She returned after speaking with Hoatzin and sat next to him, facing the opposite way.

"You'll be initiated once we cross the river." She did not speak directly to him but faced the woods, her eyes searching, her voice hushed. "You'll eat and drink what you're given. If you refuse, you'll be sacrificed next. Don't throw up, or you'll have to keep eating and drinking until your body accepts it."

"What is it?"

"The drink is fermented fruit. You already know what you'll be eating. Just accept it now, and that'll make stomaching it easier. Eat the fruit and nuts tonight."

Flesh. They were going to make him eat human flesh.

Kestrel tried not to think about it, but the words ripped through the mental curtain and let the sickening light in. He was hungry, but not starving. Certainly not enough for *that*. He also wondered where the body might come from since Grouse was picked clean last night. Would it be another of the pack?

"What's going on?" Tears came to Kestrel's eyes. The phrase felt tired on his tongue.

"I don't know," Stoat admitted, her voice unsteady. "But we will get out of here."

Muskox and Cottontail returned by the time Kestrel steeled himself, and his eyes had dried. The small campfire would be enough to warm them for the night. Bowhead disappeared with his branch down the path they had come from, looking solely at the ground. When he reemerged, he was sweeping the ground like a big tail moving to and fro.

Once the fire was lit, Lynx emerged from the cave to sit in front of the blaze. Her eyes glowed in the flicks of fire that painted her face. Cross Fox appeared shortly after and distributed something to each person. When Cross Fox handed Stoat her portion, Kestrel realized it was a bundle of cured meat.

Kestrel held his breath as Stoat tore into the preserved flesh. She ate without a second thought. He, too, would have to eat it—eat *someone*—tomorrow night. She continued to devour the food as he struggled against his nausea. Cross Fox passed him over and handed the next portion to Thinhorn, who began licking all of the salt from the dried flesh.

Cottontail ate her small bite quickly, and Muskox picked off a piece to give her more.

Kestrel's little parcel of nuts and dried fruit was a delight. Not enough by any means, but better than the alternative. Everyone ate their portions and carefully drank from their bottles. Above them, bats flitted between the salt stones and the forest. Warmth radiated from the fire to fight the blistering wind.

At least bones weren't jingling in the trees tonight.

"There will be a sleeping bag in your pack," Stoat said as she set up her own. That was all she said to him for the rest of the night. The others went about their routine, but Kestrel was too exhausted to pay attention. There was enough to worry about—his memories, his whereabouts, the people who surrounded him, figuring out a way to escape, starvation...

His head spun, and he couldn't focus. He lay down and watched the firelight dance upon the trees. He wished he had something soft on which he could rest his head, but the remnants of grass were better than the hard ground.

The frost of night kept him awake for hours, even as those around him seemed to sleep. Every sound, every movement made him startle. Somewhere in the harrowing night, branches were breaking and leaves were rustling. Kestrel could've sworn footsteps were coming toward him. He opened his eyes. If there were something in the dark woods, then he would face it head-on. But fear wrapped around his bones like the red cords he saw in the trees last night.

Thump.

Kestrel rolled over, eyes wide. Someone had dropped a new log on the flames. The wood crackled and shifted, sending embers into the air. A shadow moved against the darkness. He sat up, squinting to see what it was.

Scales glinted in the light—flecks of green and black and orange. A face with sickening eyes. The man keeping watch removed his mask and stared at him. Kestrel didn't look away as the lizard man ripped a piece of dried flesh with his sharp teeth and grinned, flecks of shredded meat stuck in his teeth.

What was his name again?

Kestrel lay back down slowly. The crackle of the fire and the sound of chewing were drowned out by his heartbeat—a traitor to his senses. He thought of last night, of the horrors he'd seen—the fire, the altar, the body, the hunger.

Would he be next?

The smell of last night returned to him—the perfume of roasting meat, the depravity.

His stomach groaned.

THREE
COLD WATERS

Sleep hadn't welcomed him once in the night. In fact, it turned him away from its door, refusing to see him. Kestrel hoped he could get some shut-eye in the early hours, but the sound of lapping kept him up. When the sun rose, he turned over to see Thinhorn licking the wall of salt rocks. His tongue rubbed against the stone, eyes closed to savor the taste.

"Knock it off," Pronghorn called out. "Get some sleep."

Chastised, Thinhorn returned to the thick cot he shared with his brother.

Kestrel snacked on the rest of the fruit and nuts in the early morning, then wandered off to relieve himself in the dense brush to his left. No one stirred from their sleep. As he emptied his bladder, he realized no one had followed him. Maybe they knew there was nowhere to run, nowhere to hide, no memories to reclaim.

When he returned to the campsite, Bowhead was standing by his mat, asking him if he had buried his waste and how far he had gone into the woods. He hadn't gone far, and he hadn't buried it.

"Leave no trace. Travel quietly. Stay together. Tread lightly," Bowhead said as if it were a poem he'd written and recited a hundred times. Then he sighed, took his makeshift rake, and disappeared.

Kestrel wondered what would happen if evidence were left behind. Then the thought of Bowhead as a housemaid with a feather duster, cleaning dust from old vases and mantels, came to mind. He stifled a laugh before he remembered the man was erasing all traces of him.

KESTREL WASN'T sure how long he'd been out. No one told him. His head still throbbed, but eating and drinking had helped. His memories were still lost, like wisps of fog that meandered on the dewed grass around him. Fleeting vapors that floated just before him but would vanish if he tried to grab hold of them.

Bowhead arrived back at the camp moments later, leaned his branch against a tree, and lay back down. The fire had dwindled to embers, taking the warmth along with it. Morning larks sang, and the sound of Stoat breathing gave the birds a steady drum beat, but a dissonance struck the little melody—Thinhorn was licking the salt rocks again.

Within the hour, the entire group had risen and begun packing up what little belongings they had. While Bowhead crushed the remnants of the fire back into the earth, they rolled their mats, lifted the packs they'd used for pillows off the ground, and stored their water bottles. Before they set out, Cross Fox portioned out more cured flesh, and the twelve ate their breakfast.

Kestrel wondered if it were the last time he would be skipped over. *There's no way out,* he thought. Not until his memories returned or they came across other, saner people. And that was if they returned at all. Even then, he wasn't sure he could survive alone without food or gear.

Pronghorn and Thinhorn carried their pack of bones, and Kestel wondered if what was left of the young man—Grouse—was neatly tucked away with the other bones and strings. It was a mystery why they even carried the remains with them and didn't bury the evidence. Or why they used them as decorations.

Cross Fox left the group at some point and returned from the cave with a small bundle and a backpack that looked like it belonged to a little girl. The purple fabric was dusted with salt, and the straps were tattered. She put the pack on Cottontail's back and asked Muskox to carry both of them. He agreed, bending down to collect the girl.

Cross Fox gave the bundle to Shrew, a young man with a long nose, crooked glasses, shaggy hair, and a thin frame. Kestrel thought he looked as skeletal as the bone chimes they hung from the treetops.

"Don't let Gannet touch the food," Cross Fox warned Shrew as she shot a sideways glance at the young man. Gannet was younger than Shrew—likely a teenager—and had puffy red cheeks. He walked with his feet turned out.

"I'm not an idiot," Gannet protested.

"You're selfish," Cross Fox said, dismissing him. "You take things that don't belong to you. It's like you can't control yourself."

"Not true!" Gannet scoffed. "You're being rude."

"I still haven't found those matches that went missing last week," Cross Fox fired back, but before she could say more, Lynx stepped into their squabble.

"Remember two winters ago when you ate a quarter of our cache in two days?" she chastised him. "That season was incredibly harsh, and we had to scavenge for more food in the freezing snow."

Gannet hung his head.

Shrew patted Gannet on the shoulder with a sympathetic smile. When he showed his teeth, Kestrel saw that one was red. Not coated in blood as if he chewed his gums or had just taken a bite of flesh or a berry, but dyed a deep crimson color. The root was still yellowed, but it faded into the dark color—a sanguine gradient.

Shrew and Gannet. Names to add to his running list. Though he'd figured out most of their names came from animals, he had never heard of some of them. He didn't even know what type of animal a kestrel was.

"We're heading to the Snake. From there, we will make our way through the valley, then up to the sacred mountains," Lynx said as she put her bag on her back and pointed off in a direction.

"It's a few days' journey," Cross Fox informed the group. "Ready yourselves."

"What's the Snake?" Kestrel whispered to Stoat.

"The Snake is a wide river near the valley." She leaned her head toward him. "Caiman conquered the Snake years before our time and threw its slithering body to the ground. Out of it flowed water that hasn't ceased to this day."

Caiman. The man with scales who kept the first watch. Kestrel thought of his creepy yellow eyes staring right at him before he turned over. Ever since he awoke, Kestrel felt Caiman's eyes on him throughout the day. The story about the Snake sounded like a legend, something from antiquity—certainly not how rivers form.

Then the realization hit him. Gannet had eaten too much of their food stash two winters ago, and Caiman supposedly slayed the river a while back. *Years.* These people, these *cannibals*, had been living out here for years.

Kestrel swallowed and steadied his breath so the others wouldn't notice. "What are we doing out here?"

"We are heading to the sacred mountains," Stoat said, echoing Lynx's words. As if it meant something to him. "After your initiation tonight, we will continue our journey upwards."

Kestrel took a step back. "What happens when we get to the sacred mountains?"

Stoat looked around her.

While Lynx discussed a matter with Caiman and Hoatzin, Bowhead set to work ensuring their erasure. Cottontail tugged at the hair on Muskox's head, and Pronghorn tried to stop Thinhorn from licking the walls of Salt Hill. Cross Fox double-checked the supplies while Gannet and Shrew laughed at something Gannet had done.

The coast was clear. There were no listening ears—at least ones not close enough to hear.

"I don't know," Stoat admitted quietly. "Not entirely. They say there are Eidolons on the mountains—ancient gods—but I don't know what happens when we meet them."

"Idol ons?"

"One word." Stoat bent down and traced the word in the dirt. *Eidolons.*

It was not what Kestrel was expecting. From her need to certify there were no eavesdroppers, he assumed she was going to reveal a larger, more important secret. Not the absence of knowledge. They were heading to a mountain to find myths.

There was fear in her eyes.

"You don't know what will happen on the mountain?" Kestrel asked.

"They won't say. I've been here a few months, and they won't say. Not yet."

"A few months?"

"At least. It's hard to tell. The last time I saw you, before we both ended up here, it was early spring, maybe." Stoat said.

Kestrel whipped his head around to look at her. She hid her emotions like they were buried deep inside the earth to await the first thaw of spring, her face barren as if what she had just said wasn't shattering.

"What?" Kestrel winced. His voice was louder than even he expected. He looked around furtively.

Caiman, Lynx, and Hoatzin turned their attention to him and Stoat, their eyes searching intently. The rest of the group slowly followed, and soon all eyes were locked on him and his question. He cursed the volume of his response and prayed they hadn't heard the full conversation.

"I was telling Kestrel of the Snake, how Caiman slayed the serpent—that the waters flowed from its belly and gave us life. He was impressed." Stoat gave them half a lie, as cool as the air around them.

They seemed to buy it.

"We owe Caiman our gratitude." Lynx gestured toward him.

Bowhead and Muskox thanked him, the others nodding along.

"I had the same reaction when I first heard the tale," Pronghorn declared.

"It's time to head out," Lynx said, effectively silencing the group.

The single-file line formed. Kestrel fell behind Stoat quickly, wiping the sweat from his forehead. She pulled up her fur hood and did not look at him when he whispered his thanks. Bowhead watched the group move out, then began his work.

Kestrel was bursting to ask Stoat about the last time she saw him. Where were the two of them? How long had they known each other? As far as he could tell, they had just met the other day when Grouse was sacrificed to make room for him. He wondered if she was one of his missing memories. If she was, as she said, a friend.

A real friend. A friend from before, he thought.

She did not speak to him on the journey to the Snake; there was no way she could without being overheard.

The trees of the old-growth forest parted as what remained of the high grass spiked through the soil of the lowlands. The river grew in the distance, winding from a distant plain down to the banks they approached. Cottontail climbed down from Muskox, wanting to walk the rest of the way to the river.

Hop, not walk, Kestrel thought.

Muskox kept an eye on Cottontail as if a bird of prey might snatch her up in its claws. The grass, despite its state of decay, was enough to shield her from anything hunting above. Kestrel wondered if there were predators lurking in the thigh-high threads of grass, ready to pounce.

The roar of the water sounded like it belonged to an ancient beast. The river tumbled down rocks, beating the stone smooth, breaking down the fragments of soil and root, tearing at the banks, and claiming the earth as its own. Slithering and churning scales of water that devoured as it went.

Lynx surveyed the area with Caiman and Hoatzin.

"All clear!" Lynx shouted.

The line relaxed into a gaggle of bodies approaching the water's edge. Everyone refilled their canteens and bottles before some took sips from the rushing water; others washed their faces or stripped down to swim in the shallow pools that strayed off from the river's course.

"Not a word about what we discussed," Stoat whispered. Then she took off her shirt, tied up her hair, and walked into the river to bathe.

Kestrel dropped his pack and went to the bank to fill his bottle and wash off. As he approached the gently turning water, he saw himself for the first time. His eyes were narrow, his jaw lean, and his head looked smaller than he expected. The pain had made it feel like a swelling balloon. His hair was a dark orangish brown—distinct enough that he considered it might have been dyed—and feathered around his face.

He couldn't look away. Kestrel's face was wounded but oddly familiar. He touched his features again, considering how unusual it was to forget one's appearance and rediscover it through a reflection.

Cottontail jumped in the water nearby and sent ripples across the reflected image. Kestrel abandoned the shimmering ghost of his face and decided to wash. He stripped, then cautiously dipped his feet in the water.

Ice cold tendrils infiltrated his veins as he felt the frigid sensation in his bones. The chill was almost too much. Kestrel shouldn't have expected any less—the sun was high, but not enough to warm the earth's autumnal breath. He shuddered and let out little bursts of air.

Kestrel marveled at how easily the others jumped in. Gannet had submerged his head and was swimming underneath the chilled flow of the Snake. When he reemerged, his full cheeks burned red, and he held a stone. Then he dove back down, his legs flopping lazily in the air, toes webbed.

Cottontail washed the foot that hung from her neck as if it were precious jewelry.

Animals.

Each person embodied their given names—or maybe it was the other way around. It was possible that Lynx assigned names based on their characteristics. He wondered what she saw in him that would cause her to bestow upon him the strange word.

Lynx left the water after bathing and dried off as best she could before putting her clothes back on. She never took off her bolo tie with its amber stone. She lay on the shore of the Snake and looked up to the gray vault above them.

She was tracking something. It was as if she was following a fly flitting from spot to spot, watching the sun move or the clouds alter their shape on the winds. Kestrel watched her from his spot in the cold waters. Then, in catlike quickness, she locked eyes with him. He turned away, not as fast as she moved, and continued to scrub the dirt from his body with his hands.

"Hey," a glasses-less Shrew swam by him and waded by the embankment across from him. Then Shrew lifted his naked body out of the water and onto the grassy slope. He kept his gaze set on Kestrel and smirked. He shook his hair and winked at Kestrel, then lay out on the ground to take a nap.

Kestrel submerged his head slowly, feeling the cold, fresh current tumble against him until he could get out of the water without embarrassment. By this time, the air was slightly warmer, but the warmth of the sun was still unable to compete with the coming winter.

After a few hours of washing, swimming, and relaxing, the group dried off, repacked, and prepared to leave the Snake. They regrouped into their line as Lynx double-checked the sky.

The sound of rocks falling, a distant echo of danger, came from the valley and mountains ahead. Without hesitation, the group ducked behind the boulders at the edge of the river. Caiman went into motion, touching his belt, and scanned around them. Lynx and Hoatzin did the same until a second thunder resounded.

Kestrel crouched and pressed his body against the frigid stone. Someone put a hand on his shoulder, and he recoiled at the touch. His eyes darted to Bowhead behind him and the others who were scattered among the large rocks by the river.

Gunshots. Kestrel realized they were coming from up in the valley. His breath caught in his throat as he looked to the three leading.

"Pronghorn, Muskox—with me!" Caiman commanded.

Muskox set down Cottontail, and Pronghorn dropped his bag of bones against the stone he and Thinhorn hid behind. Pronghorn whipped out a folding shotgun from his pack while Muskox brandished an axe. Caiman unholstered the small handgun strapped to his right side.

"It sounds like it's coming from the west," Pronghorn said.

"A hunter?" Muskox asked.

"Scout the source," Lynx demanded. "I'll lead the others up to the right side of the valley. We rendezvous at the burnt cabin tomorrow night."

"Be safe," Hoatzin said, and bowed her head to bless them.

Caiman nodded and led the two others away from their cover. A third shot rang out, and Kestrel shuddered. The three split from the pack, and the thirteen were now ten.

Lynx spat out hurried commands. "Gannet, take Pronghorn's pack. Stoat, watch Cottontail. We'll stay low until we reach the tree line." She pointed toward the ridge ahead. "There may be others."

Kestrel peeled away from the rock, his shoulders tight, his body cautious of every movement. Gannet picked up Pronghorn's pack despite it appearing too large for him to wield. As the line began to move, Stoat looked back at him and nodded for him to follow. It took him a minute to take his first step away from safety, but staying in the open was dangerous.

Onward he went, as low as he could go, cautious and keeping close to the others as they headed to the burnt cabin.

FOUR

PUSH!

There were more things to fear than the cannibals, though the fear of the hunters wasn't as worrisome as the thought of being eaten. Kestrel's ears still rang with the sound of distant gunshots as he hurried to keep up with the rest of the group. The sun above seemed intent on speeding through the sky, the shadows quickly lengthening, and they mirrored its haste.

"Who are they?" Kestrel huffed when he caught his breath.

"Hunters," Stoat said coldly.

"They're hunting...us?"

The word tasted bitter in his mouth. There was no *us*. There was only survival until he could escape, but someone hunting the others put him in harm's way. Down the barrel of a rifle, in the center of a scope. A sudden crack made him flinch. Gannet jumped away from the branch he stepped on.

"Easy," Stoat commanded. "We'll be safe. For now."

"Why are they hunting...us?" Kestrel asked hesitantly.

She didn't answer, and that made his head spin.

The line staggered as the group grew tired. Lynx ran ahead, climbed to the top of a rock, and removed her mask. Her breath came out in a thin vapor. The air grew colder the farther they went into the wilderness.

"I know you're tired, but we must move as fast as we can. The burnt cabin is a day away, but if we hurry, we can make it there in time," Lynx looked at each of them one by one. Her eyes locked with Kestrel and held them for a moment longer.

"Don't fall behind." Cross Fox bit at Gannet.

"Say a prayer to the gods for the safety of the others," Hoatzin said. "Two members of our family were lost when a hunter came upon us without warning. We had ventured too close to the human lands and lost a vital part of our group. That cannot happen again."

"Kestrel must be initiated," Lynx said.

"We are still two days out from the burnt cabin," Cross Fox reminded her.

Hoatzin smiled. "Then we roll the Gambit Stones to initiate Kestrel into our fold."

"What if they bring back a hunter?" Gannet scratched his head.

"The stones will tell us the desires of the Eidolons. If Caiman returns with another, their fate will be decided then. This is the way they speak to us." Hoatzin shook the container around her neck.

"We have to move," Lynx called.

Everyone readied themselves, and they resumed their trek.

Kestrel had no idea what Gambit Stones were, but he couldn't quite get his mind around the human lands. Isn't that what he was? A human? He closed his eyes and tried to squeeze out the fragments of his life before. There were some things he faintly remembered. The faint outline of a house and the curve of a road, people bustling about. He saw them as though through a glass darkly—their faces obscured.

How far could they be from here? Kestrel wasn't sure, but he knew they were headed away from any sort of civilization and toward the mountains.

"The burnt cabin will keep us safe," Stoat said.

Kestrel wasn't sure if she was trying to comfort Cottontail with her words or if she was letting him know offhand. Either way, he was lucky that his initiation—and what he had to do—was delayed until they reached their destination. His mind drifted to the hunters, wondering if they were the key to his escape. He could see himself at the end of a distant scope, unaware of the bullet readied for him, but would they pull the trigger if they knew he was not a part of the pack?

"The hunters are a danger," Bowhead said quietly, as if he could sense Kestrel's desire to use them as a means to escape. He offered nothing more, continuing his work in preventing anyone from tracking them. Precise, invisible, and silent. He never seemed to stop. Day and night. Did he ever sleep?

Kestrel frowned. Although he had been spared tonight, the ritual would still take place at the burnt cabin. Stoat told him to play along, to eat and drink whatever they gave him, to participate in their brutality, to consume. He shuddered at the thought of becoming like them, insensitive to the atrocities they were committing and serene in their violence.

I am not like them.

He almost believed it.

They walked on until a well-trodden path appeared along the rocky side of a low mountain. Kestrel wondered how many animals had walked this way, keeping close to the craggy wall, avoiding predators hunting them. He no longer heard gunshots, and he wasn't sure if he felt relief or worry.

Stoat slowed in front of him, and he peered around her. The path began to curve and compress—a rock face on both sides with an ancient pathway in between. It looked as if the mountain had been cracked in two.

A gateway to the unknown.

Kestrel stopped as a thought hit him.

Gannet squeezed between the sides, sucking in as he sidestepped his way. Kestrel looked behind him at Bowhead, who lingered behind, broom in hand. The others were already ahead of them.

"We could run," Kestrel whispered to Stoat. "While they're on the other side."

"No."

"This might be our only chance to get away. We have to get out of here while we can. The two of us can take him."

"It's not safe," Stoat said between her teeth. "You have to trust me."

Kestrel couldn't decide if he should. There was an opportunity now to escape. Bowhead was distracted, and the two of them could overpower him. The others would be stuck between the walls. The coin flipped in his head. Trust Stoat or trust his gut. Follow or flee. Tails or heads. Spinning, spinning, spinning.

He looked behind him and saw the sun had begun to set, the horizon glowing with the fiery warmth of the vanishing sun. Above them, the silver moon rose over the ridge of the mountains against the dusky plum sky. It was going to be dark soon, and he feared wandering out in the wilderness without a clear direction.

The sound of gunfire pierced the air in the distance. Kestrel winced, his eyes immediately darting around to find Shrew, who met his gaze with a worried look. *At least he's okay.* The thought came to him unbidden.

Bowhead hurried up the path as another round of gunshots rang, faint but sure. From the crevice of the rock, Cottontail yelped, and someone shushed her. He couldn't leave the little girl, could he? Bowhead stepped behind Kestrel and turned to look at Stoat. She was already shimmying through the gap.

The coin landed in his head. He would have to trust her.

As he slipped between the rock faces, his hands scraped against the rough stone. Stoat was just ahead, almost out of sight as the narrowing passage turned. He squeezed past the bend, finally seeing the opening. Hoatzin and Cottontail waited in front of him, while Bowhead tried to make it through the final turn. Kestrel looked up and saw a large boulder sitting precariously on a little ledge, Cross Fox testing the rock with her hand. Lynx pointed down to where he stood while Thinhorn, Shrew, and Stoat readied themselves. Gannet looked confused, but Kestrel knew what they were about to do.

"Come help us push," Thinhorn said as he set his feet firmly against the mountainside. He shoved the rock with his arm and shoulder. Little pebbles and loose dirt rolled to Kestrel's feet as it began to move.

"Won't it draw them to us?" Gannet asked.

"Rocks fall all the time," Hoatzin said. "The hunters won't suspect us."

Kestrel thought the same thing as Gannet—too much noise would get their attention and block the only way back to the river. Lynx stared at him, and he knew he had no choice. He climbed up the slope to meet the others.

As soon as Bowhead cleared the exit, they began to push against the boulder. Kestrel's hands and arms burned against the frigid stone, his skin tearing from the friction. The stone wasn't budging.

"Gods!" Hoatzin shrieked. "Hide us beyond the cleft in the rock. Protect us from the hunters so that we might ascend to your mountain and fulfill your desire. Great Eidolons, cast the stone to the earth!"

Bowhead joined the effort. He planted next to Kestrel and put all his weight against it. They heaved, sweat dripping down their faces, until there was a slight shake and the rock began to teeter back and forth. More rocks slid out from under it as the cliff gave way.

"Push!" Lynx commanded.

Kestrel stopped putting in the effort, but it was too late. There was already enough momentum. The boulder rolled down, clamoring as it went, until it crashed against the opening and blocked it. His stomach sank. That might have been his only exit—his only chance at escape.

His ears rang as the sound of the rock crashing against the mountain echoed around him. He put his hands on them and winced as if it had been an explosion.

When he got his bearings, Kestrel stood back to look at the scene.

Gannet had collapsed to the ground, huffing. Cross Fox and Stoat gave each other pats on the back. Bowhead sat, but Lynx stood tall with pride. Hoatzin seemed to be cheering with Cottontail. Only Shrew looked at the result with any sort of confusion. When their eyes met, Kestrel noted something akin to awe in the other's expression. He smiled uncertainly back at him.

There would be no going back to the human lands for now.

"We'll camp here," Lynx said. "Rest as much as you can. We must reach the burnt cabin by tomorrow night. I'll take the first hour watch; Thinhorn after me, then Cross Fox, Stoat, Shrew, and Bowhead."

Kestrel climbed down from the cliff face along with the others. He turned and extended a hand to Shrew to help him down, and Shrew took his hand. He felt a jolt in his body, as if something had snapped into place—a warmth, a shift in the air. Shrew smiled at him as he made it back down. Their eyes met for a moment and lingered longer.

"We need a fire," Gannet interrupted.

"No fire tonight. We don't want to draw any unwanted attention this way, in case they can circumvent the blockage," Cross Fox replied as she began to unpack a sleeping bag.

"We'll have to keep close tonight," Kestrel said, smirking.

Shrew laughed.

The camp began to settle in for the night. Kestrel unfurled a sleeping bag, and Shrew brought his close. The rest huddled as close as they could, pushed against the rocks of the mountain. Kestrel slipped into his sleeping bag as the light of the sky above faded into inky black.

In the darkness, he saw Lynx sitting nearby, staring up at the burgeoning stars.

He pulled the top of the sleeping bag over his head, closed his eyes, and tried to sleep.

Hours later, he turned over. His body felt stiff against the hard ground, his legs cold and sore from traveling. They would have to do it all over. He crawled out of his sleeping bag and saw Bowhead leaning against the mountainside, his eyes dangerously close to shutting. The last watch grew weary.

Everyone had huddled close through the night—bodies on bodies on bodies. Thinhorn and Gannet were sleeping next to their bag of bones. Kestrel couldn't help but wonder how many people were inside the canvas. Were they all once members of the group, or were they enemies picked off along the way? What were they for?

Kestrel jumped at a loud burst of sound.

The others stirred, and Bowhead's eyes shot wide open.

It came again—not from a hunter but from Gannet. He snored. Loudly.

Kestrel watched Cottontail climb out of her sleeping bag, nudge Gannet on the head, kiss her talisman, and curl back up next to him. Seeing the little girl made him more confident in his decision not to run yesterday. He had to save her, too. He turned over and tried to sleep.

FIVE

THE BURNT CABIN

The next morning, he woke to see Lynx, Cross Fox, and Hoatzin packing their bags. Stoat rose from beside Cross Fox and began to wake up everyone who was still asleep, giving each a little shake with her hand before calling out their names.

"Morning," Shrew said as he stretched, rubbing his hands together for warmth.

"Sleep well?" Kestrel asked as he took a sip of water.

"Too cold. We should've conserved heat," Shrew said, eyes sparkling with a hint of mischief—and something more.

"Get up, you two," Stoat said as she bent down in front of them. "There's no time to waste."

"Let's get moving," Lynx shouted.

Kestrel and the others hurried to pack up. Bowhead began searching for traces they left behind as they headed toward the burnt cabin. Lynx led the line of ten up the eastern side of the mountain, along the beginnings of a well-worn trail, until they were far from the lowland, the river Snake, and the now-obscured way back.

The trees reemerged and painted the landscape with evergreen. The cloudy sky above Kestrel obscured the sun, and every shadow seemed to creep beside him. He turned his head whenever a branch broke, hypervigilant. His legs burned as they walked for hours.

And hours.

And hours.

Kestrel thought of the night to come, unable to stomach the thought of eating anything. It was like there was a hole in his stomach. The ritual's inevitable approach loomed over him, and he knew he would have to go through with whatever they were planning. He still couldn't bring himself to say what—*who*—he would be eating even though the hunger was rattling his belly, begging for a morsel, pleading to be satiated. The fruit and nuts were long gone, turned to waste left in the shade of a small tree growing out of jagged boulders.

The others were silent. Though Lynx gave no commands, they followed her steps. It was easy. Kestrel felt like he was stuck on a circuit—no deviating from the path, no straying, no escaping. As if it had to be this way. Maybe he had to go further in, immerse himself in the group in order to survive.

Clouds eventually gave way to dusky night. He couldn't believe the day had vanished like morning vapor. All the walking, all the adrenaline, all the fear burned through time.

The hunger returned.

A branch reached over the path ahead of them. Stoat bent under it, grabbing the branch above her. Kestrel did the same as he ducked, but as he released the branch, he felt his hand sting. The red, scraped flesh from the boulder had come in contact with something. He sniffed his hand, smelling the sweet sap of the tree. Red mingled with it, and Kestrel licked his palm.

He was so, so hungry.

"We are almost there," Lynx reassured the group as she walked ahead of them.

The night drifted over them, making their steps uneasy on the shaded, uneven ground, the biting wintry breeze gusting along the walls of the surrounding mountains. The world turned icy as the sun set.

Up above him, a few hundred yards away, the outline of a dilapidated building revealed itself, hidden under the shelter of a snow-capped mountain. The remaining walk to the burnt cabin was quick, and the group arrived in minutes despite the weariness bearing down on them.

Kestrel tried to see the details in the dim light, but the shard of moon was too small to illuminate the land around him, much less a deliberately concealed cabin. The others disappeared into darkness as black as a raven's wing where a door once stood. He followed them up the few steps of the cabin, the old front porch creaking under his weight, and gazed inside.

The eerie depths gazed back.

Bowhead trailed behind him with a yawning Cottontail riding on his shoulders. She had barely stayed awake on the last half of their journey. The large man nodded toward the empty doorway, and Kestrel took a breath and stepped inside.

As he did, a flame as small as a flea materialized and jumped to a stone-laid hearth. The dried wood caught quickly, illuminating Hoatzin's wickedly proud smile in the thunderous blaze.

"Let's settle in," Lynx softly commanded the group. "Cottontail, can I please have the salt pack? Shrew, hand me the dried meat."

Relief seemed to settle on the others as they now moved without fear of being heard. Kestrel assumed the cabin was a safe place for them to rest.

"Thinhorn, help me get the supplies from the cellar," Cross Fox said. Thinhorn dipped his head in acknowledgment, and the two disappeared through what remained of a back door that was off one hinge. It shrieked as they pushed it open and creaked as it lazily swung back to its resting place.

The door was crisp, burned like the remnants of the back half of the cabin. Only the front porch seemed to have survived the blaze, its face preserved as in amber. Inside, the burnt cabin was exactly as described. In the firelight, the wooden beams were charred black; he was sure they were unfit to hold up the building. The cabin walls had tinges of carbonized logs, a testament to a former fire having reached too far, flaming hands grasping. At least the living room and kitchen remained largely intact. Beyond that was a mystery.

"We camped here for a week last fall on our way to the sacred mountain," Shrew told Kestrel as he set up his mat next to him. A shiver went across Kestrel's back. "Grouse and Gannet were supposed to be watching the fire outside, getting it ready for a meal while the others hunted, but the fire got out of control. The earth was too dry."

"They were playing around," Hoatzin said.

"Gannet," Lynx spoke as if to offer him kindness from the guilt of his mistake, "why don't you go out to the well and see if the water is still flowing?"

The others looked at him.

Gannet, who was rummaging in his possessions for more food, seemed caught off guard by the request, as if he wasn't usually tasked to do such things. Gannet's eyes darted between the rest of the group and Lynx and then to the back door.

"Can I use a torch?" Gannet asked.

Hoatzin rolled her eyes and scoffed, her body shifting like a bird of prey watching a wounded animal struggle to move. She flapped her arms and dismissed him, but Lynx allowed it. Gannet went to a bundle of sticks beside the fireplace, found one that could last all the way out to the well, set it ablaze, and left the cabin.

There was no furniture in the sparse room, just a few extra blankets in the corner, and the remnants of a basic kitchen—a sink, a cooktop that likely didn't function, and a yellowed fridge with the doors hanging open. Mounted animals watched from along the walls, stuffed and halted in time. Their eyes were as black as scars of the fire —ever watching in stilted death.

Hoatzin noticed Kestrel staring at the stuffed prizes on the wall and commanded Thinhorn to unpack and prepare for the ceremony.

"Stoat and—Shrew." Hoatzin had briefly hesitated before choosing who she wanted to perform her task. A knowing smile crept along her haggard face, heavy with age and mystery. "Take Kestrel outside and prepare him for the initiation."

"Follow us," Stoat commanded as she left her task and met the two others by the front entrance. The three wandered into the fluid night, the clouds like the crest of waves. The wind crashed down, warning of a coming storm.

"What's about to happen?" Kestrel asked as they all crossed their arms to ward against the frost that swept around them.

"You will be initiated into the thirteen," Shrew explained as if reciting from a script. "For this you were named and chosen. The Gambit Stones will be rolled, the gods will speak of your purpose, and then you will eat and drink their blessing."

"The gods?"

"The Eidolons. The ones who chose you," Shrew said.

"If you refuse, or if your body rejects their gift three times, you will be proven unfit for their service." Stoat raised an eyebrow and spoke precisely, every word dripping with warning to remind him of their earlier conversations.

"Unfit for service?" Kestrel asked.

"Those who are not called to serve with their lives will serve us in death. It is the demand of the gods. You will forfeit your spirit, your blood will flow, and the gods will claim what remains of you for their feast," Shrew said with drops of despair. As if he didn't believe.

"Is that what happened to Grouse?"

The sound of sloshing water came from the darkness like a trickle of melting mountain snow coming toward them. Slow, steady, uneasy.

"No. Not exactly," Stoat chimed in quietly. "There can only be thirteen of us. When we found you, Hoatzin had to seek the word of the gods by rolling the Gambit Stones since there were fourteen of us.

One of us had to go. The Eidolons proclaimed you were to be the next initiate, and Grouse would—"

She could not say what came next, but Kestrel knew.

"You saw what happened," Shrew said, wincing.

"What about the hunter? What if he is meant to be one of the thirteen?"

Kestrel recalled the story Hoatzin told earlier.

"Caiman had killed the hunter who could've taken the place of Wapiti," Stoat told him.

"Wapiti?" Kestrel asked.

"She was one of us," Stoat said. "Wapiti was slaughtered when the hunters ambushed us."

"We had to find another. Which was, ironically, the reason we were close to the human lands. We numbered eleven then, and there must be thirteen to go to the sacred mountain. As far as I know," Shrew admitted, "Stoat's initiation was the first time we completed the number. We were hunting—gathering food for the winter, preparing for our long journey to the mountain—when we found you."

"And you had to choose," Kestrel realized. *Hoatzin had to choose.* She was responsible for rolling the stones everyone kept mentioning. She was choosing who was in and who was out, as the voice of their gods, or pretending to be. Yet despite her and Cross Fox's derision for Gannet, he hadn't been chosen to be...removed.

"When you drink and eat, you'll see—" Shrew stopped to look.

The other two froze in place. All Kestrel could see was the little light of a bobbing firefly in the distance. Neither spoke a word as the distant flicker grew with every passing moment. Not a firefly—a burning branch. Someone was coming toward them.

Kestrel realized there hadn't been any fireflies, mosquitoes, or buzzing insects. When was the last time he heard birdsong or frogs croaking?

Gannet.

But not just Gannet—three others were with him. Caiman slithered out of the dark shadows, his scales shimmering green, gold, and blue in the flames, his eyes as yellow and violent as the center of the blaze. Pronghorn shadowed Caiman and pushed Gannet forward when he struggled with a bucket full of water.

"Leave him be," Muskox said as he stared down Pronghorn. The two looked like rivals, but Muskox was clearly not to be trifled with. One blow from the man would likely end Pronghorn's life. Pronghorn held back, clenching his fist around the torch that he had taken from Gannet. The group approached menacingly. Had Caiman heard what they were saying?

"What is this?" Caiman asked as he shifted his jaw from side to side.

"We are about to initiate Kestrel," Shrew answered.

"Just in time," Pronghorn laughed.

Kestrel hated that laugh. It was far too knowing and sinister to be funny.

"Where is the hunter?" Stoat asked Muskox, avoiding the lingering gaze of Caiman and Pronghorn.

"Dead," Muskox affirmed.

Another foolish murder at Caiman's hands. Kestrel supposed he was doing it on purpose—avoiding a roll of the stones, ensuring he would survive longer than the rest, skirting the wishes of the gods with his own hand—but maybe he was just too foolish, too quick in his primal urge to destroy. He certainly looked the part.

Wishes of the gods. Kestrel balked at the absurdity of his thoughts. It sounded like he believed in the wicked gods of the wild.

He was no acolyte.

"Lynx will be pleased," Shrew said with a nod.

"Hoatzin will not," Gannet said as he juggled the bucket of icy water in one hand and the torch in another.

"Do not question the outcome," Caiman barked. "We took care of the killer. Or would you rather the man put a bullet in your head, drink your blood, eat your flesh, then mount you to the wall so you can watch him feast and laugh at you for eternity?"

Caiman took his finger and began tracing a circle around Gannet's head until he found the center spot and poked it. Gannet stumbled with the metal pail, but Pronghorn caught him.

"Might be better if the hunter had his way with you," Pronghorn laughed again. "It would save us from you eating all our food, and then we could eat you."

Stoat scoffed, giving him a side eye. Kestrel tensed his jaw. There was no reason for them to be so cruel to Gannet, even if he had eaten more than his share; joking about eating him was downright horrible, even if it was not out of place.

"Your haughtiness will be your downfall," Muskox chastised Pronghorn. "If the hunter had killed any of us, then we would not have been able to go to the sacred mountain. Do you want to spend another cycle of seasons out here? The gods wait for us to feast with them, but you'd rather delay us with your squabbling."

No one answered. They didn't need to.

Kestrel realized it was the most he'd heard the man talk. His features looked stronger in the dim firelight, a brooding beast with horns and fur. A frosted draft sang through the alpine slopes and worsened the chill among the seven of them. The torch flickered violently.

"Caiman," Lynx spoke his name like a command from where she stood on the cabin's front porch. Caiman turned to her and led the scouting party and Gannet back into the house. Lynx looked to the three who remained outside. Even in the blackness of night, the amber in her bolo tie shone.

"One more minute?" Shrew proposed. Lynx agreed and returned to the shining cabin.

Rays of canary- and fox-colored light leaked through the boarded-up windows from the hearth, dissipating before they reached Kestrel. He turned to Stoat, who looked at him with pity—or maybe it was kindness.

"It won't be easy, but you must do it to stay alive," Stout assured him. "If we want to get out of here, you have to survive both this and the winter."

Kestrel couldn't help but be surprised at her candor in front of another member of the tribe. He hadn't known Shrew long, but he certainly couldn't trust him. While he wasn't entirely confident that Stoat was trustworthy, he found no reason for her to lie and keep him from escaping. She certainly wasn't as devoted as the others.

"If you want to make it out alive—" Shrew couldn't finish his sentence. Lynx and Caiman appeared at the threshold of the glowing cabin, the light now shimmering as if it possessed refracted and manifold fire within. "We must make it to the sacred mountain."

Kestrel was sure he was about to say something else. The presence of the others meant that words must be left unspoken; the charade carried on, so as not to threaten their very lives. Kestrel supposed that Shrew might be on their side, but unless he got them alone, there would be no way of confirming the assumption. He might as well extend the same faulty trust to Shrew, at least until it was proven otherwise.

There was something comforting about him, but Kestrel couldn't pin it down.

Alone. That's what he had to figure out. How could he possibly get the three of them separated from the rest? There were twenty eyes upon them at all times.

Had he thought of it earlier, Kestrel believed he could've slipped away with Stoat when the group was down to ten. Some had been carrying extra weight, tired and distracted from avoiding the hunter, missing the strongest of the pack—save for Bowhead, but he was occupied with erasing their tracks and caring for Cottontail.

Lynx interrupted Kestrel's plotting and called them forward. Stoat and Shrew pushed him forward, offering him up to the foreign and false gods. He would have to comply with their ritual *now* in order to escape *later*.

The future was unclear, but his choice tonight was clear.

Flesh awaited him.

Against his will, but for the sake of his life, he would become one of them. Kestrel walked to the front of the cabin as if heading to a predator's den. Lynx and Caiman stood at the door with Shrew and Stoat just behind him, and they welcomed him like the carnassial teeth of a lion.

The burnt cabin was the unhinged jaw of the predator—hungry, salivating.

SIX
STRANGE RITUALS

The fireplace in the cabin boiled the thin atmosphere, replacing the chill with a burning temperature that made Kestrel see the heat shimmer. The haze hit him upon entry, and he saw the others gathered in a circle, draped in sheets. He took a step back. They weren't all white like a costume. One had little blue flowers and green vines, another was striped with thin gray lines, and one was thick and pilling flannel. Slits were cut out for their eyes, and all the eyes were on him.

Someone shifted under their sheet. It was Cottontail. She was shorter than the rest, though her rabbit ears made her look taller than she was, and half of her sheet pooled on the floor. Kestrel could see the vague outline of the foot around her neck.

"It's hot in here," Cottontail whispered.

Someone next to her, maybe Gannet, shook his head and hushed her. Bowhead's size distinguished him from the others, and Kestrel could make out Muskox's horned mask.

Ghosts. He felt like he was surrounded by the specters of these people.

Aloft in the cabin, hanging from the rafters, were the bones of the others that had been sacrificed. Strung up by red rope, broken bodies dangled above him, a crimson web he didn't want to be caught in. There was no wind in the cabin to make them chime their music of death. For that, at least, he was grateful.

Hoatzin and Lynx were the only ones without sheets over their heads. Hoatzin donned her mask, which had orange and blue spikes protruding from the eye holes and a beak where her mouth should be. Her arms extended like the breadth of wide wings. She looked angelic in her white sheet, but her stature was demonic.

As she approached Kestrel, a violent scent ripped through his nose, burning the hairs inside, poisoning his very breath.

"Welcome, Kestrel." Lynx strode across the room, following the path of the ring around him, ready to pounce. She was the only one to have her face fully exposed. Her garment was different from the rest. Ornate embroidery covered every inch of the sheet and made her look like a high priestess. Lynx paraded around as if she were the representative of the divine.

Kestrel followed her with his eyes as she moved. He hadn't noticed that Stoat and Shrew fell into the circle around him, each bearing their own set of sheets, one sage green and the other a deep burgundy. Their eyes stared back at him blankly as if this were rote.

"Kestrel, you have been chosen by the Eidolons to join their cause," Lynx pontificated. "You survived the journey to the burnt cabin and will be initiated as one of the thirteen who will ascend to the sacred mountain and fulfill the desires of the gods of the Hinterlands. Tonight, you will dine as a foreshadowing of the feast to come! Kneel before the Eidolons."

Kestrel couldn't move. He couldn't think, and he certainly couldn't stomach the feast to come. It was too much, too soon, too grotesque. The room felt like an inferno, and he was surrounded by whitewashed bones of cannibals. He closed his eyes as his heart pounded in his ears.

"Kneel before the gods," Caiman hissed from beside him.

"Our blessed ritual must begin," Hoatzin said as she moved to the mantle above the heart. In a flash, she took something in her hand. She approached Kestrel and peered down at him. He bent his knees and felt his legs tremble as he stared back up at her.

"The path is set before us," Hoatzin began. "The Gambit Stones will roll, and the gods will speak of Kestrel's purpose, confirm his position among our ranks, feed him by their hands, and bless him with their sight as they have done for all of us."

Kestrel pressed his shaky hand against his thigh. *Stones* were going to determine his fate. He wanted to laugh at the insanity, but fear extinguished the absurdity of it all. Stones couldn't determine direction or purpose. He knew that, but did the others? Did they all believe in these so-called gods?

Hoatzin took the container and opened it, emptying the contents into her concealed palm. She passed the container to Caiman. He held it tightly while she cupped her hands together, shaking them as if she were about to roll dice. The birdlike woman bent low to the ground, let out a shrieking cry, blew into her hands, and then released.

Little items jittered and tumbled across the old wooden floor, each slowing to a stop before Kestrel. The Gambit Stones were a constellation of variable outcomes, the whispers of the stars that guided them, misshapen. Hoatzin bent her head as if to listen. Kestrel's eyes flitted to each one, a nonsensical pattern scattered before him.

Not stones. Trinkets, Kestrel realized as he examined each item quickly. There was one black die which had five white dots on the top, a single murky green gemstone that could barely capture light within its facets, a silver house key that pointed directly at him, a compass that couldn't seem to find its bearings, a broken wishbone, and a glass orb that rolled right in front of him.

Not an orb—an eye—glassy and fixed on him, preserved as if it were a marble. The eye appeared to watch him, unblinking in the firelight. Kestrel stared into it, watching the inky purple and silvery blue iris ripple within, a constantly shifting illusion like starlight.

Kestrel felt something ancient and dark staring back at him.

"Liberator," Hoatzin said as she tilted her hand to the right, suddenly upwards, and then back to Kestrel's direction as if she could see through him. "The gods have declared that you are the one, the final one, and we will want for nothing. The thirteen here will not die; we will all go to the sacred mountain, and the gods will us to fulfill their purpose. They welcome us to their feast and will bring us into their country."

"Kestrel, do you accept the will of the gods?" Lynx asked pointedly.

He knew there was no choice. Denying the will of the false gods and rejecting their so-called blessing would certainly mean his death. He would be welcomed into the afterlife with bite marks and marred flesh. There was no way around it. What Hoatzin promised was impossible. There were no gods on the sacred mountain or feasts readied for them in preparation for a new world. Being eaten, on the other hand, was a guarantee.

"I do."

"Then you will eat and drink of us," Lynx said.

The moment had arrived—the one he'd been warned about for the last few days. Kestrel was about to eat human flesh and drink whatever concoction Hoatzin had been brewing for him. The circle around him tightened, the others closing in on him—monuments of the strange rituals, haunted survivors. If they had done it, then he could too. If only for his survival.

Hoatzin pushed back the cloth draped over her arms, showing her skin, rough with age and scars. Her arms were crisscrossed, pink and white. She extended them wide and opened her hand. A shrouded Caiman handed her an object that glinted in the crooked light of the hearth.

A chill crept down Kestrel's spine.

In her right hand was the silver tool, but her left arm moved in front of her. Hoatzin turned it over revealing an unscarred area on her upper arm. The stench of her body made it hard for Kestrel to focus, but the metal now touched her bare skin.

Vegetable peeler. Kestrel realized what it was. The scars, the object, the ritual. He had to eat flesh. *Her flesh.* Sourness flooded his mouth.

Hoatzin took the peeler and, without flinching, dug the blade into her skin. Even from his spot, Kestrel could tell it was too dull. The woman had to press harder and longer in order to slice off enough of her body to satisfy the god's demands, but she didn't wince. How many times had she used it? Blood began to run from her arm, dotting the floor and fouling the stuffy air.

Kestrel had to steel himself, to pretend that he wasn't dying inside, begging for the food portion of the ritual to be the dried meat—at least he could pretend that it was a cured delicacy from a butcher shop. This was so blunt, so brutal, so apparent that he wasn't sure he could stomach it.

But he had to. His only other option was to burn and be consumed. There was really no choice at all.

A hush fell over the others in the cabin like ghosts watching from a netherworld, knowing what was to come, pillars upholding what remained of an ancient, foreign, and dark religion. The saddest part was that they were victims too. Each had to endure the same rite. They would never be free if he didn't go through with this.

Kestrel was their thirteenth. Their Liberator. He vowed to do everything in his power to see that no one would have to endure such monstrous cruelties again. He would take them at their word and liberate himself from their hand.

Hoatzin peeled off the last bit of flesh from her body. A shrouded one appeared with a stained towel and dabbed at Hoatzin's bloodied arm. Once clean, the figure wrapped a bandage over the open wound and returned to her spot in the circle.

"Thank you, Cross Fox," Hoatzin said as she concealed her arm once again and moved forward. She held the sliver of flesh high in the air like a priest giving communion and began to whisper. Kestrel couldn't look away from the thin peel. The firelight seemed to make it glow. Little blood-soaked hairs shaded the strip.

The others began to whisper as well. If they were prayers, Kestrel did not know them. He wasn't even sure it was in his native tongue. A wall of whispers pushed in on him. The sounds of the creaking floorboards, the roaring fireplace, and even the night seemed to be drowned out.

"Eat," was all Hoatzin said. She swung her hand down slowly, a torturous hammer of judgment, the peeled chunk of her body stopping in front of his lips.

Kestrel moved back instinctively, shuffling on his knees, but he couldn't go any farther. This was his only way through this grim wilderness. Inches away was the only choice he could make.

"The old gods are watching," Caiman hissed.

Not much of a choice, he thought as he swallowed apprehensively. There was a hunger in his belly, and his mouth had watered all day for food, but he didn't want what was being offered to him. He considered the alternative once more. He had to think of it as nothing more than eating his least favorite food—a brief moment of disgust—and then he could eat something more appealing than fresh flesh, though less appealing than anything else.

It took all the strength within him, but Kestrel parted his lips and bared his teeth. It felt like he was prying his own jaw open like a dog about to swallow a pill. He thought of cheese and almost cried. His mouth open, his body hungry, his mind reeling, Hoatzin placed her peeled flesh on his tongue as if it were a gift, a blessing, a delicate grace.

In a way, he supposed, this was a devious salvation. The symbolism was not lost on him.

Kestrel partook.

The bite was sharp and bloody, the flesh squelching between his teeth. The taste was bad enough. It tasted like Hoatzin's body smelled—rotten, fermented, sour—but the skin was hard and chewy, the hair coarse and gag-inducing, and the whole piece was foul.

Chewing as fast as he could was his top priority. Then he would have to hold it down. He could already feel his stomach churning, roaring like azure and violet-dark ocean waves tossed in a maelstrom. The wrath of the crashing acid made his throat shudder, his body urging him to spit the morsel out.

Every eye was on him. At least the ones he could see, but he knew that Stoat and Shrew were staring at him, begging for him to eat and drink and pretend. *Dream.* That was the hardest part—pretending that any of this was normal, playing along with their delusions. Kestrel took another bite and wanted to cry and laugh. Sanity fleeing with every taste.

Pretending was *not* the hardest part. Chewing was.

Finally, with eyes watering, jaw clenched, and stomach revolting, Kestrel swallowed.

Hoatzin leaned in. Her burning eyes watched his every move, her hand moving as a bird of prey, her claw-like hands reaching for his chin. Before she demanded it, Kestrel opened his mouth and showed her the proof that it was gone. He had eaten of her flesh. The worst part was over. Now all he had to do was drink and wash the taste out of his mouth.

A gurgle in protest arose from his belly, but Kestrel commanded it to cease. It obeyed.

"Kestrel has accepted the first gift," Lynx praised. "Now to the second."

The second gift, if one could call it that, was to drink. Stoat and Shrew hadn't warned him of what that would entail, but he assumed it would be less distasteful than Hoatzin's flesh. The smell still lingered on his breath, a constant reminder of what was now inside of him, digesting within his body, becoming him.

Cross Fox moved to the fridge, which acted as a storage box without power, opened the old door, and pulled out a small silver pot with a copper bottom and black handle, though all of it was dirtied and dulled with age and use. She brought the pot to the kitchen counter, took a glass from the cupboard, and filled it.

Kestrel was surprised that the elaborate ritual didn't require its own special chalice.

Once the glass was filled, it was presented to Hoatzin. Instead of taking it in her hand, she reached under her wide robe and took off the canister that was strapped to her body. She unscrewed the lid and tipped the container forward, a thick liquid pouring into the glass.

Hoatzin held it high once again. She commanded Kestrel to drink and brought it to his lips as she did with her own flesh. This was, at least, less gruesome, but Kestrel now realized the rotting smell of the bird-like woman was coming from the canister.

Whatever she had concocted was like a witch's brew—a blend of fermented fruit, possibly the other eye of the Gambit Stone, and likely bits of flesh and blood. It was disgusting—foul. It burnt his nose hairs, poisoning the air around him and consuming every other smell in the room.

Kestrel looked at the cup. Passing the etched images of a cartoon dog surfing on the glass, he could see chunks of what he hoped were fruit and not flesh. The swirling maroon liquid taunted him, and he wanted to plug his nose, but he couldn't.

The edge of the glass touched his lips, and he accepted the drink.

At least he didn't have to chew.

The sour, sharp drink flooded his palate—a mix of vinegar, fermented food, and the metallic taste of iron. In an instant, Kestrel felt it reemerge from his stomach, shoot up his throat, and burn within his esophagus. His cheeks filled with putrid breath as he tried to contain it, to keep it down. His eyes watered as the food and drink mingled together, a rank blend of sacraments. There was a certain cruelty to make him believe the drink would wash away the unsavory flesh.

Kestrel swallowed and opened his mouth as evidence, as a taunt in return. They would not sacrifice him for this.

"Kestrel has accepted the second gift." Lynx proclaimed with a smile on her face. "Now for the third and final gift."

The third. Kestrel thought. They hadn't warned him of a *third* gift. His eyes rolled up to stare at Hoatzin and Lynx, waiting for whatever horror awaited him now. A volley of thoughts hit his mind, yet he couldn't foresee what was to come. He watched, but no one moved—no one did anything, no one spoke.

"What—" the words barely left his tongue when his head was thrown back. Not by his own volition, but by something arising in his frame, an unseen claw pulling on his skull.

The tears in Kestrel's eyes had gone, and he saw what was above him. The bones suspended from the rafters were beginning to shift. He would not join them tonight, would not be wrapped in crimson rope, would not become a skeleton on high, and would never be the digested flesh in the bowels of those other twelve.

The whispers grew louder; the ghosts around him were speaking in a language he didn't understand, and the bones above him began to clatter together, chiming from an unseen wind. Rattling, *singing*. The fire was extinguished, frosty tendrils wrapped around his body, and the night shrouded him.

He could not look away from the ceiling, but soon his eyes began to blur, darkness bleeding into his sight, and the sounds of fury and the whispers of the forest overcame him.

SEVEN
A VISION OF THE GODS

The flies encircled Kestrel—a million buzzing little beasts hitting his body. They crawled on his face, trying to infiltrate his ears and nostrils. He couldn't breathe. They were suffocating him, biting at his flesh, hungry for his rotten essence. Their noise drowned out everything else.

In the humming darkness, a speck of sunlight, bright and burning, called him forward. Kestrel stepped, and the flies followed, tormenting him. They were everywhere. He brushed away all that he could and covered his mouth with his hand, trying to defend himself.

As he approached the light, it glinted against slick stone walls. Stalactites hung above him like teeth. He was in a cave, but it wasn't Salt Hill. The opening was larger, the scenery outside unclear, and the salt gone.

Kestrel sprinted to be free of the infested cavern. The amber sun burned harshly; he felt the flaming heat on his skin as he stepped into the light. When he opened his eyes, the flies gathered tighter, their glinting green and black bodies like shifting dark clouds.

A pinprick of light hit Kestrel like a spotlight, drawing him forward. He shielded his eyes from the blinding brightness and pressed on.

Someone stood before him.

Lynx.

The catlike woman smiled. She wore only her bolo tie with its gleaming amber stone in the center—the source of the light. Out of the corner of his eye, he saw the others. Caiman, Hoatzin, Muskox, Pronghorn, Thinhorn, Cross Fox, Gannet, Shrew, Stoat, Cottontail, Bowhead. They were all naked. He looked down at his body—he was too.

The twelve reached up, and the starlight descended to them. The sky was now as dark as the infinite abyss. The flies whirled around the twelve others. Kestrel alone was spared, but the others didn't seem to mind the annoyance.

The flies swirled, their tiny bodies turning into flakes of snow. Gradual at first—gentle little flurries—then the entirety of the swarm turned to heavy drifts of ice. The torrent of frost pummeled the group and hoarfrost blanketed their faces, but they remained unmoved. But Kestrel didn't feel the biting cold—not the way he expected, as if it wasn't real.

It became impossible to see, and the others disappeared in the blizzard. The world around him was now white as a crane.

He didn't understand what was happening.

The amber light appeared once more. Kestrel trudged forward, shielding his face. He knew Lynx was waiting for him. Time seemed to stand still until he finally reached her. The stone still beamed from her bolo tie, but her body resembled the hushed, icy blue of a frozen corpse.

The blizzard began to dissipate. Kestrel blinked, and Lynx was gone, as were the others. He looked up as the snow shifted back into the swarm of flies. Pain shot through his skull. None of it made sense.

Kestrel looked around him, finding their bodies in a circle half-buried in the snow. He counted their faces, still wearing their masks.

Nine. Cottontail, Gannet, and Stoat were missing. Kestrel hoped they were alive somewhere far from the wilderness.

Had the flies carried them away to a safer place?

A static hum flooded his ears, sounding like the whispers of the twelve Kestrel heard moments ago in the cabin. The words were unclear. He could've sworn he heard his name within the static. As he looked, snowflakes landed in his eyes, stinging pain searing his pupils. Kestrel rubbed his eyes with fury, but the burning only grew. Snowblind and confused, he wanted nothing more than to be back in the cabin.

His eyes still burned, but he walked on with them closed tight, hands held out to feel for anything that might guide him. He stuck his tongue out and tasted the flakes that flurried around him. Not snow. Salt. No wonder it burned.

Pushing forward, Kestrel blinked furiously, tears carving trails down his cheeks. Kestrel shielded his face with one hand and continued to search with the other. His steps dragged, slogged down by the weight of the salt-laden landscape, though time rushed by as fast as the storm, whipping through the mountains and valleys.

The blinding pain in his eyes began to ease. He looked up to see a mountain. Not just any mountain—a peak that reached up to the stars. The salt-snow still swirled around him, but he could see the path forward. He headed toward the mountain. The amber sun crested above its peak as if peering over a balcony. He wondered if it was the sacred mountain the others had mentioned.

Kestrel blinked again, and in an instant, he was climbing, moving up the craggy cliffside, scaling the face of the mountain. The salty snow was gone. The mountain shifted into spring, awash with fresh blooms and swaying grass. Kestrel inhaled, but the flowers of the mountain were foul. They smelled of blood, bile, and the fermented drink. Beauty corrupted by twisted nature.

Kestrel climbed as fast as he could and found himself near the precipice. As he scaled toward the top, he heard the caw of a bird.

Turning his head, he saw a large raptor circling him, its wings made of salt, snow, and flies.

Panic flooded him. He climbed faster to get away from the creature and reach the top of the mountain, knowing he would find safety there. The giant bird hovered nearby, the large flapping wings conjuring chaos. Its taloned feet extended forward, grabbing at him.

Claws scratched his skin. Kestrel clung to the rock, but the raptor latched onto him. Its talons pierced his flesh, and he screamed as the bird peeled Kestrel away from the rock face. Out and upward they flew, the creature of bone and salt carrying him to the top of the mountain. The trees gave way to stone, and the talons wrapped around him loosened, releasing him. As the ground sped toward him, his heart felt like it was about to be torn out of his chest.

He slammed into the earth.

Blood spilled from his head, and his vision blurred as the winged beast dissolved on the whispering wind as if it were a dandelion seed. He was alone at the precipice. The top of the mountain was covered in white save for where his blood speckled the ground. Kestrel bent down and ran his finger through the drifts. It was wet and cold, but when he touched his finger to his tongue, he tasted salt and iron. Somehow, the taste satisfied him. A new hunger arose within him—a stinging desire to devour.

Kestrel surveyed the area, noting the altar sitting empty before him. Something glinted in the light—Hoatzin's Gambit Stones, the single die, the broken wishbone, the murky stone, the dulled silver house key, the wandering compass, and the dried-up eye.

Fate.

Yet the sacred mountain was deserted—abandoned—and certainly not home to gods. There would be no feast here, no grand revelation of divine will—nothing but thin air and a view of the Hinterlands around him. Kestrel hurried over to the edge of the cliff and searched for any sign of life.

Past the salty snow, beyond the evergreen trees, and shrouded by the dense wilderness, was the outline of a small town. His mouth hung open as he tried to trace a way down. Then he saw it—a path to civilization, the exit to this horrible nightmare.

Kestrel scaled down the right side of the sacred mountain, and as he searched for a place to put his feet, he saw smoke rising from the village. He ran down as fast as he could, dodging crooked tree limbs and rebounding off boulders, but the closer he got, the further away it felt. He could never reach it.

He looked around, but he couldn't see the town anymore. Kestrel's eyes strained, his head pounding as he tried to escape. The pain resounded until he closed his eyes and pressed his hand to his head.

When he opened his eyes, he was somewhere else.

Somewhere far away.

Kestrel was in a car—an old car from the stained floorboards and wood paneling—and he wasn't driving. Stoat was at the wheel, her head bobbing to the blaring radio. She looked at Kestrel and smiled.

"Stoat?" Kestrel said, but she raised an eyebrow like she didn't understand her own name.

Kestrel turned his head to avoid the sun's glare reflecting off the hood. His view from the passenger window showed a bright summer sky and trees swaying in the warm breeze. His reflection in the side mirror caught his attention–his sharp jaw, dark hair, and narrow eyes. Familiar, but it had more life in it now than the last time he saw it.

"Hey, are you okay?" Stoat asked as she turned down the radio.

Kestrel tried to look at her again, but she was fuzzy like static, as if she didn't belong there. Her real name was on the tip of his tongue, but he couldn't recall it. His mouth tasted of the flesh he'd eaten. As he opened his mouth, flies poured out, covering every surface until the car was a swarm of bodies, and he was covered from head to toe. The sound made him want to scream, but when he tried to shout Stoat's real name, the buzzing darkness drowned him out.

The moment faded like a memory.

It must have been a glimpse into his past—a moment from his life when he and Stoat were friends. When the flies dispersed, Kestrel was mere steps from the village.

There were no signs of life. Withered ivy grew thick over the nearby buildings, doors hung off their hinges, and no light came from any of the windows. He walked down the lonely road and found no one—only emptiness. "Help!"

No one answered.

He moved through the village quickly. Like the mountain, it was long abandoned. A low rumble came from the woods; the hair on the back of his neck stood up. The sound of rushing water filled his ears.

The river was ahead of him, its dark current coursing through the land like a snake coiled around a precious treasure—the guardian of the sacred mountain. Kestrel went to the river's bank, dropping to his knees to run his hands through the frigid water. He leaned back on his heels, the mud shifting beneath his weight. His palm touched the wet earth in front of him, and he recoiled. Something stuck out of the ground.

Muddied faces. Cold and buried near the edge of the river. Kestrel wiped the mud from their eyes to see who they were.

The first was Shrew, his red-toothed smile beaming. The second was Cottontail with her soft cheeks and little button nose. The third face was buried deep. Kestrel tried to wipe it clean of the muck, but as he did, flies reemerged from the ground, bringing the smell of shit and rot with them, turning the world black once more.

Kestrel scrambled to get to the river, to hide beneath the water, but as he reached the edge, he tripped. On all fours by the bank, he stared into the churning surface of the Snake and saw his own reflection.

He instantly froze.

His eyes were glowing amber, a perfect reflection of the stone from Lynx's bolo tie. Kestrel stood and brushed off his body, realizing he was clothed in animal skin, feathers, and hunting gear. His eyes burned, but he wasn't sure if it was from the salt, the tears, or the shimmer in his eyes.

Kestrel found what he had tripped over. It wasn't a body or a swarm of flies or some creature conjured from the recesses of his imagination. It was a milk jug and an old cell phone, half-buried in the mud. He grabbed the phone and touched the buttons. Dead. He picked up the jug—filled with water, not milk. It sloshed as he cleaned off the label.

A clunking sound came from above him before he could read it. Kestrel looked up to the sky, but all he saw were the slow swinging bones hanging from the scarlet rope. They stopped moving. He tried to read the label on the milk jug and grab the phone, but they were gone—replaced by the wood floor of the cabin.

The whispering stopped, and he looked around him. Hoatzin and Lynx peered at him, examining his hazy eyes, the fireplace blazing at his back. The world returned to normal.

Not normal, he thought—just where he was before. The dream was over.

"He has seen a vision of the gods," Hoatzin announced. "They have given you their sight and your purpose."

"Kestrel has accepted the third gift." Lynx grinned widely.

The others cheered and removed the sheets from their heads; the cloths thrown on the floor reminded Kestrel of the salty snow. It took him a moment to readjust, to remove himself from the dreamlike state and recall that he was in the burnt cabin. The ritual was complete.

He survived. Kestrel ate the flesh, drank the brew, and saw the vision of their so-called gods. *It was so real.*

Now he had a mission. It was clear he'd known Stoat in his former life, had been friends with her, like she said. He was more certain than ever that he had to escape with her. Kestrel resolved to save Cottontail and Shrew and anyone else who would come with him, but he knew he had to play along until the time came.

The path to the sacred mountain would lead him to an abandoned human village, and beyond that would be the way out. He wasn't sure why he trusted what he had seen, but it felt more concrete than any other plan he could create. It was the only path he could take. The assurance was as curious as the vision.

Dried meat and water were passed around, and Kestrel partook to get the acrid taste out of his mouth. His tongue was pleased with the change in flavor, but his stomach still roiled. The rest ate, drank, and joyfully talked among themselves.

Stoat looked at Kestrel with a knowing smile and nodded, but didn't engage with him in any sort of discussion. He knew that he would have to tell her in time, but they needed to be away from the others. Shrew moved his mat close to Kestrel, closer than expected, and he shared his bottle of water as he got ready for bed.

Kestrel noticed the kindness in Shrew's eyes, and a salty tear trailed down his cheek. Shrew wiped it away with his thumb before gently kissing his hand. Kestrel curled up in his tattered sleeping bag, rolled over on his back, and looked at the ceiling.

Everything around him felt wrong, but Shrew felt right.

Kestrel stared at the bones above him and drifted off.

EIGHT

THE WELL

A thin layer of frost coated the grass, and leaves crackled under his feet. Kestrel moved quietly to find a place to relieve himself. The morning was quiet—too quiet—without even the sound of a mourning dove or cawing crow. In fact, he realized he hadn't seen any sign of animal life. He shivered despite the rays of sun cutting through the trees surrounding the cabin. From here, he saw the scars of the fire, a burnt blemish running up the wooden frame—damaged but still standing.

He felt the same.

As he walked back to the cabin, he saw Bowhead watching him from the window. The man's commitment to disappearing was admirable, though Kestrel realized removing any trace of them kept their pack a secret. They could move mostly undetected, almost invisible. If he was ever to get out of this forest and find his way home—wherever that was—he would need to find a way to make a mark.

To save Bowhead the trouble, Kestrel walked back to the spot where he had relieved himself and covered it with snow before dragging his feet across the ground. Bowhead nodded and left the window as if he was satisfied. Maybe he was too tired.

Kestrel took a breath and felt the chill in his throat. The burning taste of Hoatzin's flesh and the strange elixir he drank were gone, though he feared it would never really leave him. At least he wasn't hungry anymore. He wanted to figure out the abrupt interruption in his vision. The glimpse of a memory wasn't enough—he was desperate to know who Stoat really was, how long they had been friends, when that drive took place, and what their real names were.

Kestrel, Kestrel, Kestrel.

The name tasted wrong even now. He supposed it always would.

A shuffle of feet rang through the early morning silence. Someone stepped onto the porch of the burnt cabin and walked down the stairs. Kestrel froze.

"Hey, hey," Shrew greeted him with a smile.

"Morning," Kestrel responded.

They walked to meet each other; something comforting was brewing between the two of them, something he couldn't quite name. He looked to the window to see if anyone was watching, but the frame was empty.

"How'd you sleep?" Kestrel asked, tucking his hands in his armpits to keep them warm. He needed gloves and maybe another coat. The one he wore was light fur, but the stench of the dead animal still clung to the hairs, and it was a little too small for him.

"Fine. It's funny—I haven't been asked that in a while," Shrew said with a grin. His breath was hot, the steam from it grazing Kestrel's face. "How about you?"

"Not well," he admitted, rubbing the back of his neck.

"What did you see?"

"It was a lot."

"My vision was confusing, to say the least." Shrew stepped closer to Kestrel and took his arm. He led him away from the cabin, as if they were on a stroll through the park. "I'm sure yours was the same."

"What the hell is in that drink?"

Shrew laughed. The mountains reverberated with his joy. If there had been any birds, they would've fled their perches. Everything about Shrew was beautiful: the crow's feet his smile revealed, the way his Adam's apple moved, the cleft of his neck, the softness of his skin despite all his time in the wilderness.

"Hoatzin won't tell anyone," Shrew said. "We think it's mostly fermented fruit, water, and nettle. Maybe some thistle or pine needles if she finds some. She claims it comes from the gods themselves."

"Damn the gods," Kestrel said with a laugh.

Shrew shot him a warning look. "The wilderness has ears. Be careful what you say, even in private."

Shrew led Kestrel through the soft snow away from the burnt cabin and anyone who could eavesdrop. After a few minutes, they arrived in a bit of clearing where the trees didn't crowd out the morning sun, the sky above a baby blue.

The sun hit a polished surface, blinding Kestrel, and he covered his eyes. Shrew moved him out of the path of the beam. There was a metal structure low to the ground. Bits of rust invaded the dull silver. Blue sheets of glass were affixed to the frame.

"Solar panels?" Kestrel asked.

"Someone lived here once." Shrew looked across the four panels. "Lots of people have cabins across the mountains. Most of them are abandoned. I don't know how long they've known about the burnt cabin, but whoever lived here is long gone. It seems like the owners fled overnight."

"There are others?"

"We don't go to the other cabins," Shrew said and looked down. "The hunters use the ones on the other side of the mountains and would kill us if they got close enough."

"Do you know anything about an abandoned village?"

Shrew scrunched his face. He looked at Kestrel, then back to the empty clearing. He knew more than he was saying.

"There are human lands somewhere along the mountain range. I think they're past the river, but I can't quite remember. I know that we're far from their territory, and the last time we went near, it was teeming with people, but we are not headed in that direction. We're going to the sacred mountain to commune with the Eidolons now that you're here."

"Do you really believe that?" Kestrel asked. "In the—gods?"

"There's something out here." Shrew looked to the sky. "The Hinterlands are ancient and untouched. I don't know if there are gods on the sacred mountain, or if they are calling us to follow their will and have a feast. For all I know, that part is made up, but there *are* strange things in the woods. The visions, the whispers. I don't know where we come from, but I am *sure* we have to believe what they tell us in order to survive. At least for now."

"So we play along until the time is right?"

"Until we're free, *Liberator*." Shrew smirked and nudged Kestrel.

"We will be." Kestrel touched Shrew's back and rubbed it gently, and Shrew leaned in. They were closer than before, almost in each other's arms—a glimpse of warmth in the frost.

"We need to be careful," Shrew warned. "Even now, I'm not confident that we're alone. The old gods are watching, as they say."

Kestrel looked around. He assumed Bowhead followed behind them, observing, ready to brush away their footprints.

"Do they work?" Kestrel nodded toward the solar panels. The slabs looked worn, but weren't cracked or severely damaged from the weather. There was likely a converter or battery storage nearby. Maybe the batteries were in the cellar along with the other supplies.

"Not sure," he shrugged. "We haven't tried. There's never been a need for electricity."

Out of the corner of his eye, Kestrel saw Bowhead lurking behind a tree. He was far enough away that he wouldn't be able to hear them, but they stopped speaking entirely and looked off toward the mountains.

Bowhead was already examining the ground where they were standing.

"Let's go back," Shrew said, grabbing Kestrel's hand. Their

fingers interlaced, and Shrew pulled him back toward the cabin. They walked hand in hand as they passed Bowhead, already sweeping to disrupt the forest floor.

Back in the burnt cabin, the others scurried to pack up their belongings. Cross Fox opened the refrigerator and took out a cache of supplies.

Shrew whispered, "There are stashes of weapons, dried meat, and water across the mountains in case of emergency."

Pronghorn and Thinhorn had already taken the bones down from the rafters and were carefully wrapping them up. Kestrel wondered how, since he hadn't noticed a ladder. Cottontail helped Gannet lace up his boots, while Caiman, Hoatzin, and Lynx discussed strategy for going to the sacred mountain.

"No one knows where the path is," Stoat whispered to Kestrel as she rolled her mat. He furrowed his brow, and she read the question on his face. "They'll have to ask the gods to lead them to the peak."

Muskox swung open the back door with such force that it rattled the windows and almost fell off the hinges. He shrugged a half-apology, but his arms were full of supplies. Cross Fox grabbed a few heavier coats from the closet and distributed them. She tossed one to Kestrel to replace the one he had, asking him to pass his coat to Cottontail. The rabbit girl was happy to get a new coat, even if it almost dragged on the ground. She twirled around in her droopy sleeves.

Kestrel touched his coat gently, finding it surprisingly heavy. The outside was deep brown with streaks of steel blue and orange. The inside was made of fur or wool, but the outside had hundreds upon hundreds of feathers sewn onto it.

"Gannet!" Cross Fox yelled. "Did you get the extra canisters from the cellar like I asked?"

"Sorry," Gannet said as he scurried up from the floor, ran to the back door, and tripped on his untied shoelaces. He recovered quickly, ran to the open doors in the earth, and descended.

"Kestrel." Cross Fox appeared before him in a flash, and he

jumped at the surprise. "Now that you're a part of our group, you will help with the load. You'll carry the extra supplies—the rest of us are strapped down as it is. You'll be responsible for the extra containers of water. Winter is coming, and the rivers will freeze over. We *have* to carry extra water."

Kestrel nodded.

"Gannet is bringing them up now. Fill them at the well outside. You'll take food rations and a few other supplies." Cross Fox left as quickly as she appeared, her hurried temperament in full force. He overheard Lynx ask about a certain cache in the north, and Cross Fox's eyes flicked back and forth until she could pinpoint exactly where it was.

She knows the mountains, Kestrel thought. At least well enough to have stored supplies across them. Kestrel saw Stoat watching him, but she returned to her pack before he could acknowledge her.

Once Gannet returned with the bottles and canisters, Kestrel placed them in the bag—an old, scratched military green pack that had been patched after years of use. He left for the well. On his way out, he ran into Bowhead, who, upon realizing he was going to the well, sighed.

"Tread lightly," Bowhead said and sat down on the steps.

"Will do," Kestrel said as he walked to the stone circle. He took more steps than he should have, so Bowhead would have to work harder. He saw how exhausted Bowhead looked and thought he could break him down further to ensure evidence was left behind.

Kestrel arrived at the well. A large wooden lid covered it to keep animals and debris out, so he pushed it off and picked up a bucket attached to a rope. He dropped the pail down into the well, watching as the ripples splashed against the stone walls. Once the bucket sank beneath the water, he began to pull it up slowly.

Kestrel was so focused on lifting the pail that he didn't hear the footfalls behind him until it was too late. A hand gripped his shoulder. He screamed and dropped the bucket back into the water, the rope snaking quickly behind it.

"Don't drop it," Stoat sneered as she grabbed the rope. There was just enough left to save it from fully disappearing down the shaft. She let the bucket sink beneath the surface to refill.

"You scared me!"

"I had to talk to you away from the others," Stoat said quietly. "Are you okay?"

"Last night was…" Kestrel couldn't finish the sentence. He went through the ritual without a hitch, but all he wanted was to bury the experience deep in the earth where it could never rise again. Her question was an auger, burrowing deep and pulling up the depths of his soul.

Kestrel had eaten flesh, had drunk a hallucinogenic, and had seen this place for what it was.

"What did you see?" Stoat asked as the two of them pulled the bucket back up and set it on the edge of the well. Their hands growing colder against the metal pail, they began to fill the canteens and bottles in Kestrel's backpack.

He recounted his vision with as much detail as he could remember.

"That's something," Stoat said as she filled a bright orange plastic water bottle. She sealed it tightly and checked for leaks before placing it back in the bag.

Kestrel wasn't sure if he wanted to tell her what else he'd seen. Maybe she would remember something from before or help him understand.

"I saw us. Maybe from before? We were in a car, driving some-where, the radio was playing, and we were having a good time," Kestrel said as he emptied the bucket into a wide-mouthed thermos.

"Back when we were friends." Stoat clenched her jaw. "I don't have many memories from the past. From what I've gathered, most can't recall anything from their time before, except when we drink the spirits Hoatzin makes. The others dismiss them or lump them together with the confusing visions they received."

"What have you seen?" Kestrel noticed the *"back when we were friends*" and wondered if they had had a falling out. He tossed the pail back into the well, making sure to hold onto the rope so he wouldn't have to climb down to retrieve it. They repeated the process once more.

"The visions don't matter," Stoat admitted. "The few memories are what I held onto all this time. There was one from my time before. You were there—I'm sorry, but I don't remember your real name—and we had an argument. It was bad, whatever it was about, and you left."

Kestrel started to apologize, but Stoat stopped him. She brushed the hair from her face and pulled her hood over her braids. Little ears stuck up on her head. Once the bottles were filled and packed away, she helped Kestrel replace the wooden lid.

"There's no need to apologize," Stoat told him. "I don't even remember what we were fighting about. It was so long ago, and none of it matters now. I didn't even know who you were until I saw your face the day you woke up. It was like something clicked into place."

"Do you know where they found me? I need to know something, anything that would figure out where I was or what I was doing out here."

"I don't. I was back at the basecamp. Muskox and Grouse had gone out to survey the area and make sure it was safe. They were gone for hours. Too long. You were with them when they found their way back. Grouse was wounded, and—"

"Bowhead didn't go?" Kestrel interrupted in surprise.

"Bow doesn't follow everyone. It would be too much for one person. Anyone who goes scouting or hunting is trained to leave as little a trace as possible. When they get close to camp, he'll make sure their tracks are gone. We move mostly untraceable, but we are not invisible."

Kestrel tucked that information in his pocket for safekeeping. He would need it one day.

"We'll get through this together," Stoat said. Kestrel expected her to pat him on the back or at least smile at him, but her demeanor remained distant.

The pair walked back to the burnt cabin to rejoin the others. All the supplies were packed and ready—Cross Fox had made sure of it. The others were already lining up in their order behind Lynx as she conferred with Caiman and Hoatzin.

A gunshot rang through the mountains.

NINE
TREAD LIGHTLY

Kestrel shuddered. Every time he heard the gunshots, he felt his life was but a moment away from ending. This shot was closer than the last. If there were no animals in the Hinterlands, what were the hunters shooting at?

"Not again," Gannet cried, covering his ears. Kestrel watched as Cottontail patted his leg with her little hand. She held the small foot around her neck, said a prayer, and kissed her charm. Gannet picked her up and set her on his shoulders.

Caiman searched the horizon of the jagged mountains while Hoatzin took out the Gambit Stones and rolled them before going into a meditative state. Lynx tilted her head and listened carefully, pushing her hair back as if to sense the direction better. Her eyes seemed unsure. Cross Fox and Pronghorn reached for the guns strapped to their legs. Everyone was on edge.

Shrew moved closer to Kestrel. Stoat stood by herself, her eyes locked on Cross Fox and the gun in her hand. Kestrel watched all of them, studying their every move, trying to memorize their reactions.

"You took care of the last hunter, correct?" Lynx asked and shot a glance at her third in command.

"Yes," Caiman assured her. "There must be another."

More gunshots rang out. *Two, three, four.* Too fast for a single shotgun. The burst of gunfire made Kestrel coil in on himself. He thought about running to hide in the cabin, but no one else moved. He looked to their leader. Lynx scrunched her face, brow furrowed, mouth frowning. She listened for more. Several more shots echoed and broke the midmorning quiet.

How many hunters could there be? Kestrel thought. Shrew, who was just a bit shorter than him, slid next to him. As if it were second nature, he put an arm around him, pulling Stoat's attention to them. Her gaze was curious, but her face was unmoving.

"We have to get to the mountain before they come," Hoatzin demanded. She flapped her arms as she gathered the Stones and secured them away. Her high-pitched voice accelerated with urgency.

"How many are there?" Muskox asked calmly.

"Hard to say," Caiman answered. "At least three based on the rate of fire, but that's assuming they're using a shotgun."

"It's a hunting party," Lynx said, her face blanching with fear.

"They're after us," Hoatzin warned. "They know we are heading toward the mountain of the gods, and they want to stop us. Remember how they killed the others?"

The rest exchanged horrified glances. Cross Fox scowled, and Bowhead's head hung heavy with shame. Each wore their emotions on their face like baggage. Cottontail curled into Gannet, and he pressed his forehead to hers. Stoat stared off into the distance. Kestrel felt Shrew reach for him and gave him his hand to hold.

"Who are the hunters?" Kestrel asked.

"They're invaders from the other lands," Stoat said, biting her lip.

"Hunters serve false gods, right?" Gannet asked Hoatzin.

"Why are they after us?"

"They'll slaughter all of us," Pronghorn grunted. "Just like last time."

"Everyone, calm down," Lynx commanded.

No one listened.

"I'm scared," Cottontail cried.

"Don't worry," Muskox told the girl. "We'll protect you."

"Evil, evil, people!"

"They want to stop our mission."

"False prophets!"

"They'll do anything to make sure we never reach the mountain."

"Murderers!"

"We can't let them get us."

"Gods help us!"

The flurry of voices made Kestrel's head spin. He couldn't keep track of who was saying what as the volley of accusations and fears flew around the group. The conversation descended into chaos.

Bowhead cleared his throat, and one by one they quieted.

"The hunters won't be able to find us if we follow the rules," Bowhead reassured them. "Leave no trace. Travel quietly. Stay together. Tread lightly."

Everyone nodded.

He made them repeat it.

Even Kestrel found himself mouthing the words. Lynx left her conference with Caiman and Hoatzin to stand in front of the group, her face serious. Kestrel could see she was unafraid, but couldn't tell if it was just another mask she wore. The other two—the prophet and the protector—flanked her.

"Caiman and Pronghorn will go toward the ridge." Lynx pointed up to the left. "They will ensure the hunters do not come near us. If necessary, they will lead them in the opposite direction. We must not let them take us off course. All of us must go to the mountain. Our mission is as serious as the grave."

Pronghorn gave his bag of bones to Gannet, who passed Cottontail to Muskox. Pronghorn pulled a black hood over his white hair and kissed the silver tag hidden beneath his shirt. Cross Fox handed him a rifle with a scope, and he strapped it to his side while Lynx handed rations to Caiman and Pronghorn. They said their goodbyes, Thinhorn running to Pronghorn to give him a quick hug, whispering something in his ear.

"We move!" Lynx commanded with a controlled, fierce voice. She touched the small gem on her bolo tie and nodded to Hoatzin. The others fell into line and started their march as Caiman and Pronghorn went up the ridge.

The speed of their action caught Kestrel off guard, but he quickly stepped in line with the others as they hurried to put distance between themselves and the gunshots.

The line of ten went up the right side of the range, past the well and the solar panel array, far from the clearing. Kestrel wished they could've stayed longer. It wasn't much of a home, but it was a shelter from the creeping winter—a place with a warm fire, cozy for what it was. If the hunters were really a threat to his life and not an exit strategy, he worried that leaving would put him in danger. He didn't want to die.

Even the sun couldn't warm the earth. The frost that lingered on the ground shattered under their boots. The wind carried warnings of winter.

"It will be a harsh season," Hoatzin claimed as they climbed through a crag in the rock leading to a higher path. "The snow will come heavily."

Kestrel remembered his vision and the blizzard of salt. As he squeezed between the rocks, he tried to guess how long the journey to the sacred mountain would take. How far had the group traveled away from the mountain to be unsure of how to get back? Lynx and Hoatzin were relying on the unclear directions of their unseen deities, and the rest of them blindly did the same. Unless Lynx, Hoatzin, and Caiman had lied to them.

Kestrel wondered why no one questioned their leadership. Had they been convinced there was something out in the woods? Was it simply that everyone was playing along—like he, Stoat, and Shrew were—but that they were too afraid to band together to escape?

The trek would be long, so Kestrel decided to mentally list which way everyone fell. Lynx, Hoatzin, Caiman, and Cross Fox were clearly loyal to their beliefs. Cottontail was too young to know any different. Bowhead and Muskox didn't say much, but they fulfilled any duties asked of them. Pronghorn worked with Caiman often, but Thinhorn was a bit of a mystery. He carried the second set of remains, but was not relied upon like the others.

Who's left? Kestrel wondered. Gannet was young and not very bright. His allegiance could fall either way, but the others didn't treat him well. He might be willing to forgo their false gods and rituals. Stoat and Shrew were on his side. They were in his vision, along with Cottontail, and would be with him when he escaped.

Yet, he had seen their faces in the mud. He shook his head slightly, dismissing the thought.

Kestrel knew he must lead the charge. With Shrew and Stoat by his side, they could get anyone who would come with them down to the human lands. His lips trembled.

During Kestrel's initiation ritual, Hoatzin had rolled the Gambit Stones and determined he would be a liberator. Those were her words. Better yet, those were the oracles, the very divinations of the gods she trusted in. Kestrel would do everything in his power to ensure it came to pass.

Liberator.

If that meant the downfall of Lynx and her band of zealots, then so be it.

Kestrel revisited the vision, trying to analyze every aspect and recall the way up to the sacred mountain. If he could sway them one way or the other, it might shorten their trip. But there was no map, and his vision was a tapestry of incoherent pieces. He wasn't even sure where he was now.

"Hey!" Cottontail's rabbit ears bounced up and down as she held on tightly to Muskox's head. Muskox apologized, gripping her legs firmer so she wouldn't slip off. Cottontail was designated as their lookout, though she was often distracted by the sounds of the wilderness; Stoat and Bowhead were her backups.

Luckily, there had been no more gunshots. Kestrel was grateful for that, even if they were going further away from others.

Lynx informed them that Caiman and Pronghorn would return the next night, or at the latest, the morning after. They had set up a meeting place in the northern pass. "Once we are reunited, it will only be two days until we arrive at the Sacred Mountain," Lynx said as she looked to the blue sky like she could see the stars despite the midday sun.

"What's there?" Gannet asked.

It was one of the few times he spoke up. Kestrel knew he kept to himself, since every time he opened his mouth, he was ridiculed by the others. It wasn't his fault; Gannet wasn't able to survive out here alone.

Kestrel knew he was only with them because the Stones commanded it. How lucky.

Nobody answered Gannet's question. It had already been given, in part, many other times in vague, passing words. It took Lynx time to conjure up the right phrase. She turned around to face the line.

"The abode of the gods. We have been sent to gather the bones and bring them up the mountain. Then we will be granted all we desire," Lynx fingered the amber stone and ran her hand along the faded black leather of her bolo tie.

"It will be joyous," Hoatzin squawked.

Joyous. Kestrel wanted more, wanted to rip away the veil of unanswered questions and strip their response bare, to make them reveal their true intentions and what really waited at the top of that mountain.

Kestrel checked behind him. Bowhead was further back than usual, making sure to erase every trace. He tapped Stoat on her back, and she looked over her shoulder. He pushed his hands down to signal her to slow.

"What's with Hoatzin?" Kestrel whispered as she fell into step alongside him.

"She's the oracle for the Eidolons. Hoatzin became the prophet when she began to have visions in the night. She brewed her drink and saw what the gods wanted her to see. The Gambit Stones—a die from a game set in a bunker, the gemstone from the Snake, a house key from the burnt cabin, the compass that never ceases, the wishbone from Salt Hill, and the eye...the eye was from Jackal, the former prophet. Every prophet gives their eye to the next when they pass on their position."

"Jackal?"

"Hoatzin predicted her death. It came to her in a dream. A week later, she was dead in some kind of accident, but not from hunters," Stoat whispered. Then she stood at attention, eyes wide, and returned to her normal walking pace. Her whole demeanor shifted. She added, "Hoatzin is the voice of the gods. Listen to what she says."

The hairs on the back of Kestrel's neck stood up. Bowhead towered over him, casting a shadow. Kestrel continued on and fell back in line. There was no way he was listening to Hoatzin. Not after that made-up tale.

Kestrel could see things as they truly were—naked nothingness.

Just like his vision.

TEN

FIRST SNOW

Night swayed above them as the sun sank. A raging wind cut through the rocky path, forcing Kestrel to cup his hands together to stay warm. Lynx led them to a large stone outcropping where the others dropped their stuff and unpacked. Kestrel followed suit and saw that the mountain peaks were closer than they had been before.

"We need a fire," Lynx shouted.

Thinhorn, Muskox, and Bowhead walked the perimeter and gathered fallen branches. Cross Fox and Stoat passed out provisions of dried meat as everyone set up their spots for the night. Kestrel distributed extra water to those who needed it.

"Conserve as much as possible," Cross Fox said, with a pointed look to Gannet. "If we run out, we'll have to find a mountain stream, melt snow, or walk further out of the way to one of my stashes. Be mindful of how much you take."

Kestrel wondered if going out of the way would be a benefit or a hindrance, but he had to stick to his plan and make it to the top of the mountain. At the very least, it would provide a vantage point to find the way out.

They'd heard gunshots throughout the day—distant, but still close enough to hear each one, and Kestrel's heart jumped at every shot. The gunshots disturbed the tranquility of the gentle rustling leaves and branches, falling snow, and rolling rocks.

Hoatzin said a prayer for Caiman and Pronghorn to ensure their safety, but Kestrel kept his eyes open to study the others while their eyes were closed. Lynx, for the short length of the prayer, seemed concerned. If the group lost those two, the process would begin again, and two more people would need to join their ranks.

Cottontail had passed out hours ago. The others seemed thankful for that. She had become bored halfway through the journey and started asking every question that came to her mind. Gannet bore the brunt of her curiosity, but he didn't seem to mind. He happily answered as best he could, and when they set up camp, he told her a bedtime story that lulled her to sleep.

Kestrel wondered if the story was something Gannet's parents told him long ago, a memory from his childhood, or if Gannet made it up on the spot.

As he bit down on his portion of meat, Kestrel thought about who the meat once was and wondered which of the many bones they carried belonged to them. It didn't taste as awful as he imagined. It was mostly salt and smoke, but the thought of eating human flesh made it difficult to chew. But his hunger was stronger than his disgust.

"I have just the thing." Shrew got up from their spot, taking Kestrel's portion and trotting off to the nearest trees. He pulled out a knife and stabbed the tree, twisting until something thick bled from it. He dipped his blade in the sap and smeared some on the dried flesh. Shrew returned and gave it back to Kestrel, tossing him an encouraging smile.

Kestrel took a bite. It tasted sweet like syrup. He ate another bite, the smoke and salt and sweetness delighting him. It was better than the last time. The sap made his mouth sticky, but it covered up the gamey flavor and almost made him forget what he was eating.

Almost.

"Can we have spirits?" Gannet asked with his mouth full. He was always the first one to finish his meal and often asked for more, which Cross Fox always denied. Usually, Cottontail offered him her left-overs, but she was asleep.

"You know that's only for special occasions," Hoatzin said as she leaned against the wall of the outcropping and ripped at her meat.

"Rituals, initiations, deaths, and when the gods deem it necessary," Stoat said.

"What about the hunters?" Kestrel asked.

"We'll be safe tonight," Lynx said as she stared toward the sky. "The Eidolons will tell us if they are near. The others will handle them. Don't be afraid."

"I'm not." Stoat shrugged.

Kestrel looked at her. She was sitting up with Cross Fox leaning on her, resting her head on Stoat's shoulder. They looked comfortable with each other, like how Kestrel felt with Shrew. Gannet sighed and struggled to take off his tightly laced boots.

"They're back." Shrew nodded toward the darkening woods.

Thinhorn, Muskox, and Bowhead appeared quietly, their arms and backs laden with logs and bundles of sticks. They set up the wood in a pyramid shape for a fire. Cross Fox opened her tactical bag and pulled out a box of matches. She counted them carefully.

Darkness bled down the mountains until they were drenched in shade. The night was silent—no cricket chirps, wolf howls, or hooting owls. The crackle of the wood and simmering flame were all that serenaded them. Kestrel had hoped the fire would send up a signal and that someone—the hunters or anyone else—might find them, but the ashen gray smoke collided with the rock outcropping above them and stained the stone black.

But still, the fire was a blessing on the cold night.

Everyone circled its warmth, moving their sleeping spots closer and gathering as close as they could without being on top of each other. Kestrel hated being so near to the others. He couldn't speak freely, and he felt their eyes always on him.

"Why is everyone awake?" Cottontail stirred and wiped her eyes.

"You're the only one who fell asleep," Gannet said as he petted her hair.

Cottontail yawned.

"Would you like to sing the song?" Lynx asked with a smile.

The question took Kestrel back. Her words seemed almost motherly, and he couldn't picture her singing. Cottontail nodded, and Lynx began to sing a low tune. It started as a hum but grew into an unexpected melodic flow. There were no words, but that was enough.

Lynx closed her eyes, seeming to channel the music of the milky darkness above them, the ancient, pulsing chants of the starlight joining a chorus that began upon the pillars of creation. Magnificent and still unfolding, ever expanding, lovely.

The others joined in, as if they were familiar with the song. Kestrel wasn't sure how they would've known it. He'd never heard of it, and yet, he found himself singing too, hushed at first, but growing louder. It was easy to join in—almost uncontrollable. It was a melody ingrained within him, a primal tune that could only be sung out here with the others, away from it all.

When the song ended, Kestrel was left with a sense of belonging. The song had chained them together. He couldn't explain how it worked or where it originated; it simply was.

"Look!" Cottontail raised her finger.

Little iridescent shimmers fell around them, drifting across the land, swirling in silvery white—the first snow of the season.

"It's beautiful." Shrew smiled.

You're beautiful.

Kestrel beamed after looking at Shrew's face. The truth couldn't be hidden. His face warmed—a natural attraction. It was the first time he'd seen someone seem truly happy in the wilderness. It was so simple, yet it meant everything to him.

If Shrew could find something to smile at in this chaos, then so could he.

"Don't you think it's beautiful?" Shrew asked as he pushed closer to Kestrel.

"It's lovely."

His relationship with Shrew was...new. If Kestrel was honest with himself, he didn't understand what was growing between them. Their chemistry was unexpected. To see Shrew smile was like waking up for the first time.

Kestrel put his arm around Shrew and held him. Shrew nuzzled in, and they watched the snow swirl. The world was like a little snow globe. He looked around, expecting eyes would be upon them, but no one seemed to care. Either that, or they knew his fondness for Shrew meant he was more enmeshed than before.

Cross Fox and Stoat stood and walked away from the camp to stand in the flutter of snow together. They held each other and watched the snow flurries as others joined them. Gannet hoisted Cottontail onto his shoulders as the little girl laughed at the tiny snowflakes.

"Can we build a snowman?" she asked.

Gannet tried, but there wasn't enough snow yet. The little half-formed ball was mostly leaves and mud held together by frost, and melted in his hand as he formed it. Cottontail collected twigs for arms and rocks for eyes and a smile.

Kestrel was captivated by the makeshift man, how human it looked for a brief moment before slipping back into the mud.

Muskox rolled a snowy mud ball and threw the mass at Thin-horn, who was still licking the salt of his portion of meat, and whined that his food was now dirty. Bowhead threw a rock at Muskox, and the two scuttled in a pretend wrestling match.

The night was a welcome respite from the days of despair.

"Maybe this does call for the spirits," Lynx suggested, raising her eyebrows. She smirked at Hoatzin.

Hoatzin seemed caught off guard, but took the Gambit Stones from their container. She threw them on her blanket, watching as they scattered. The nine of them waited with bated breath.

"The first snow is a warning sign," Hoatzin said as she examined the objects. "Winter will wrap its claws around us. The gods say to enjoy the snowfall tonight. It will make this difficult for us. I'll prepare the spirits."

"The gods have deemed it so." Lynx cheered, and the others joined in the revelry. Cottontail and Gannet danced in the snow, Cross Fox and Stoat came back to their sleeping spot, and Muskox took a swig of water from his jug.

The milk jug. Kestrel's eyes went wide as he realized Muskox was drinking out of an old milk jug, just like the one in his vision. He tried to examine it in the firelight, but it was hard to see. The label was covered in a dried layer of mud, just as he'd seen in his vision. Muskox lifted it, and a thin trail of water ran down his beard.

How many milk jugs could be out here in the woods? Kestrel would have to get a hold of it somehow. Maybe when Muskox was asleep or distracted. Either way, he would need to come up with a plan to get it, wipe off the dirt, and see if there was any information he could glean.

"Drink of the spirits," Hoatzin said as she poured out her special brew from her secret container into an empty bottle.

The smell was the same as it was when Kestrel drank the day before. He didn't want to drink any more and was annoyed at Gannet for the suggestion. They passed the bottle around until it reached Shrew, who took a swig and passed it to Kestrel.

He hesitated. What would it do to him this time?

Stoat nodded and mouthed, "Drink up."

Kestrel nodded and sipped the sour liquid. Not quite as bad as the night of his initiation, but still not his choice of drink. He quickly washed it down with water to get the taste out of his mouth.

He passed the bottle of sloshing brown spirits to Gannet, who took the rest of Kestrel's portion and then his own. His cheeks were red within moments of drinking. Even Cottontail took a sip. Casual conversations started, and soon they were all relaxed. Some watched the snow fall, and others the crackling fire, but Kestrel couldn't take his eyes off the milk jug.

"Hey, are you okay?" Shrew asked. He lay his head on Kestrel's leg and looked up at him, his legs stretched out on the old sleeping bag. Without hesitation, Kestrel ran his fingers through Shrew's shaggy hair. He feared the gesture was too much too soon, but Shrew didn't seem to mind.

"Are we all going to have visions tonight?" Kestrel asked quietly.

"Depends," Shrew shrugged. "The gods are the ones who grant us their sight. Everyone has a vision when they are ritualized into the thirteen. Some are given more when they drink the spirits, but it doesn't happen every time we partake."

"What did you see when you were initiated?"

"It was one of the most intense dreams I've ever had," Shrew chuckled and adjusted his bent glasses. "I was running into a cavern, going deeper into the ground, and turning down tunnels like I knew the way through them. I came upon an overturned bus and heard screaming, but no one was trapped underneath it. A bright light hit me from above and lifted me out of the cave. I awoke, and everything around me was white. It was as if I were in a sacred place. There were voices around me, but I couldn't make out what they were saying."

"Were there any parts that seemed out of place? Like they didn't fit with the rest of the vision?" Kestrel ran his fingers through Shrew's hair again.

"There was one little moment when I was walking through the tunnel. I turned down a corridor, and someone was standing before me. He turned around, but I didn't know who he was. I was in this kitchen, one so similar to the burnt cabin, and we were arguing about something. I yelled at him, and he vanished. Then I was back in the tunnel, and I went on."

Kestrel didn't say anything. His memory seemed more real, a precise time carved from his past. He looked down at Shrew and brought his hand to his cheek. Shrew looked up and grinned.

"How'd you get that red tooth?" Kestrel asked.

"I'll tell you, but first you have to tell me what you saw."

Fair enough.

But Kestrel couldn't tell him the details. There was too much horror bound to the dreamlike trance. The dead and frozen bodies of those who now sat merrily around him, the empty mountain ahead of them, the abandoned village beyond, and that he was the only one to make it out alive. Or so it seemed.

Even the part about Stoat couldn't be said aloud. He didn't want the others to know one of his memories had been recovered or of his friendship with Stoat. That could jeopardize their chances to make it out alive.

Kestrel had to play it off. He began to open his mouth, but stopped. The spirits were hitting him, and from the looks of it, he wasn't the only one. Some were drowsy, others already asleep, but the rest were laughing or staring off at the moon.

Maybe drinking the spirits, even the little bit they had, was a mistake. He wondered if their inhibitions would allow the hunters to slaughter them all.

"It's getting late," Stoat said from across the fire, as if she could sense what was about to unfold. Kestrel tossed her a quick nod of thanks.

"Stoat is right," Lynx agreed. "We have a long journey to the rendezvous point. It's best to get some sleep. We leave at dawn."

Time didn't matter anymore. Just sunrise, midday, and sunset, which were ever changing with the seasons and the position of the mountains. The group settled into their sleeping bags or under their blankets. Shrew and Kestrel decided to share theirs to conserve body heat—a likely excuse. They nestled into each other and drifted—drifted off into sleep like the snowfall. Drifted off into an unreality.

As Kestrel's eyes flittered, he remembered the milk jug. He thought to get up, to find it among Muskox's things, but the spirits were tugging on him to slumber, to dream. His eyes closed.

Upon the backs of his eyelids, the spirits began to paint.

ELEVEN
RENDEZVOUS

"Wake up!"

Cross Fox clanked a knife against a metal canteen, but Kestrel was already awake. The cold night hadn't been kind to him, and the sounds of the wilderness had kept him up after his dream woke him.

Kestrel and Shrew untangled their intertwined limbs; Kestrel stood and stretched his sore legs. His body was heavy from the spirits that descended upon him last night. Cottontail yawned and wiped sleep from her eyes. Kestrel swept his gaze over Shrew and grinned. This was, strangely, the one thing that felt right in the woods.

Gannet rolled over and kept snoring.

The sun was barely over the edge of the peaks. The snow had picked up overnight and blanketed the ground in white, but the outcropping saved them from being covered.

He got up to relieve himself. The frosty air made him thankful for his thicker coat, its feathers brushing against him when he pulled it over his shoulders. Kestrel noticed the muddled snowman had returned to the mire, hidden beneath the tiny avalanche that had occurred overnight. The flesh dissolved, the bones of stone and sticks lost.

"Take care of your business and get back to base," Cross Fox shouted.

"Cover your mess and obscure your tracks. Otherwise, I'll have to follow and keep an eye on you," Bowhead commanded with a groan. His eyes were red as if he hadn't slept a wink.

It seemed that Bowhead was growing tired of his purpose. Did the higher altitude make the hunters less likely to follow them, or were they more of a threat the closer they got to the mountain top? Maybe they would be easily spotted once the trees grew sparse. If that were the case, the ascent would be to his benefit. Maybe Bowhead's weariness would be the chink in the armor that would help him escape.

"We leave when the sun moves over that peak," Lynx informed the others as she packed her things.

A deep growl rose in Kestrel's belly—unearthed hunger crawling out from the ground. He had to eat a bit of his ration to quiet it down. His stomach didn't recoil, his hunger overriding his disgust.

The whole camp stirred with energy. Cross Fox and Stoat rolled up their gear. Muskox softly kicked Gannet until he woke up, and Kestrel watched as he scurried to shove his stuff in his backpack with Cottontail's help.

"I have to pee," Gannet said. Hoatzin groaned.

"Hurry!" Cross Fox said, waving him off.

Bowhead followed Gannet into the woods. Kestrel got in a rough line with the others as they waited for the last two to return. He looked at the spot where the fire was last night, but all he saw was a heap of snow. Inconspicuous. He traced the memory of the rising embers and saw that the top of the outcropping was still soot-stained. The black ash reminded him of the flies from his vision.

Gannet stumbled back to camp, Bowhead wearily dragging his broom across the ground to cover their tracks. With the two of them back in position, they left.

Kestrel didn't have time to process the vision from the night before, let alone talk to Shrew about it. But with his position in line, he might be able to talk to Stoat if Bowhead was distracted. The odds of that happening increased as he slowed down. With nothing else to think of but the footsteps of those in front of him, Kestrel decided to ponder the vision and try to make sense of it.

In his vision, Lynx stood in an open field. The world around them was littered with snow as far as the eye could see. The stars had fled and the sun had died, but Lynx was still searching, staring at the black void above them. Kestrel stepped forward, holding a red cord.

Kestrel tugged on it, realizing it was tied to his ring finger. He stared at his hand, which no longer had flesh. Every inch of him was bone laced together with the crimson rope. If he pulled any harder, he would come undone.

Lynx turned around. Her eyes and mouth were filled with the stars, shining little bites of heaven. She was greedy, not saving any for the rest of them. Her bolo was untied, the amber stone missing, and her hair frozen stiff.

"Liberator," Lynx said, stars falling from her lips. It was like an accusation. She hurled herself at him, and they became entangled in bloodied strings and streaks of stolen starlight in the black and white oblivion.

The horizon slipped as they fell through the sky to the world below them, crashing on the highest peak. The impact knocked the breath out of him, and he waited in the abyss of unconsciousness. Kestrel found himself transported to another time and place—a vision of his former life, a dream within a nightmare.

"What do you say we go to the cabin for the weekend?" Stoat asked him. She was dressed in normal clothes—almost too average. She stood out from the surroundings as if she wasn't supposed to be there, not like that—the Stoat he knew was incongruent with the wisps of his past he was grasping onto.

He woke from his dream. He was back on the mountain, the interruption gone. Kestrel saw the dark gray oblivion around him, blotting out the memory. Sitting up, he saw shrouded figures standing around him. They were not the twelve draped in cheap sheets during his initiation, but a phantom he'd seen before.

Ancient umber emanated from the six of them. Each had a hand extended, and in their palms they held one of the Gambit Stones. The shrouded beings crushed the objects in their claws. When they opened their skeletal hands, only dust remained.

The first took their hand and blew a foul breath, sending the black dust of the die into the air. The second followed with the white bone powder. A gust of green spilled into the air and began to swirl around him, and the fourth unleashed a silvery breath from the crushed key. The fifth shrouded figure puffed a reddish powder out while the sixth expelled light blue dust into the air. The fragments of the Gambit Stones shifted around Kestrel.

But it wasn't complete. One stone was missing. Kestrel felt something in his own hand. Lynx's amber gem. He pressed it in his palm until it felt like coarse sand, shifting and gritty. Then he unclenched his fist. He considered covering his mouth, but didn't. Instead, he inhaled.

Deeply.

The wind carried the crushed Gambit Stones, wrapping their dust around him like a maelstrom. The colors sparkled as Kestrel inhaled them. The Gambit Stones and Lynx's amber smelled of humanity and primordial beings.

Kestrel tasted the gods.

The shrouded ones closed in on him, gesturing to the rocky ground. Kestrel looked and saw Lynx under his feet. She was awake, barely, but alive. He stepped off her. She opened her mouth, releasing the sharp, tinny ring of a cell phone.

Then he awoke to the sound of Gannet snoring and Shrew nuzzled into him, sweat beading on his forehead and chest. The spirits had given him that dream, and now, as he was following in line, he pondered what it meant.

Hours passed in silence except for Lynx's simple commands.

Eventually, Kestrel would have to break his obedience, crush it like the stones in his vision, and free himself from under her thumb.

So many thoughts ran through his head that the journey seemed to pass more quickly than he expected. Soon, the eleven of them stopped for a midday break, sitting under trees to drink water, a few of them eating rations of dried berries and nuts for a snack. Kestrel noticed that Muskox had almost emptied his milk jug. By tonight, it would be completely dry. Maybe he could offer to fill it and, in doing so, find an answer.

Rest was only allowed at night. The break lasted a few minutes, but without a watch, Kestrel couldn't be sure. They moved out, and Lynx consulted Hoatzin and Cross Fox on the secretive location where Caiman and Pronghorn would meet them.

Kestrel examined the trio as they talked. He couldn't hear everything, but one after the other mentioned different pieces of the landscape. It was like each of them had committed portions of the Hinterlands to memory and had to piece it together. Lynx was supposed to be the one in charge, but he began to notice the elaborate scaffolding that kept her in power.

Caiman the enforcer, Hoatzin the decider, Cross Fox the supplier. Muskox, Pronghorn, and Bowhead were brutes that could easily overpower the rest. Gannet, Cottontail, and Thinhorn were useless in their own ways—not that it was their fault.

Kestrel would have to take the pillars down one by one.

The vague idea of a plan to overthrow Lynx and the others ticked on in his head. He would have to confer with Stoat and Shrew. If they got possession of the guns, Kestrel thought, they might be able to tie the others up and get away. Sneaking off in the night might work, but Bowhead was unusually alert, and there was always a loyalist keeping watch.

Cross Fox might be the first target. Without her, Lynx and the others wouldn't have supplies. It would be a risk since she knew the stashes of food and extra water, but Kestrel thought he might be able to use that to his benefit. He could use Stoat's relationship with Cross

Fox to infiltrate—maybe convince her to switch sides. A house of cards blown by winter's bitter wind.

Kestrel laughed at how silly it sounded. He didn't know his name, but here he was, trying to stage a coup against a cannibalistic group of people who resembled the animals they were named for.

The sun began to set over the surrounding peaks, hemorrhaging blood orange and dusky violet hues. Kestrel examined Lynx as she stared up at the emerging stars, their light catching her eye.

"Just ahead," Lynx called out to the party.

Everyone breathed a sigh of relief. Kestrel's legs were tired from the incline that only grew steeper as they trudged through the thick snow, and the bottoms of his pants were soaked through. He wished he had snow boots. The ones he wore were covered in ice.

The line stopped abruptly, and Gannet bumped into Thinhorn. Stoat held out her arm to prevent Kestrel from doing the same. Lynx and Hoatzin stared at the snow in front of them, then raised their eyes to a small, craggy valley that led down from their current path.

"Quickly!" Lynx called and sprinted off into the valley.

No one said a word, but the whole line tried to catch up with her, looking very much like a spring being pulled forward. The end eventually caught up, and by the time Kestrel passed the original intersection, he noticed the bright red snow.

Crimson footprints led from the valley. Kestrel wondered if this was the path to the point where they were supposed to meet Caiman and Pronghorn. One of them must be injured or dead. Maybe both of them.

"Go on ahead," Bowman told Kestrel. "Tell the others I'll meet up with them. I have to take care of this."

"Be safe," Kestrel said, nodding to him. He wasn't sure if he really meant it or not.

He caught up to Stoat just as they crested the hill. At the bottom was a large metal wall in the rock face. The bloody footprints went all the way to the wall and disappeared. Kestrel stared at it as Lynx touched a spot on the surrounding stone.

Someone was yelling from a small black box.

The metal wall began to rattle. With a squealing and grinding noise, it started to split in two like the parting of the sea. From his vantage point, Kestrel could see the wall curve upward. An old tan vehicle peeked out from the parting wall.

A bunker. He couldn't believe his eyes.

"Looks like an old military outpost," Stoat suggested. "How did they know about it?"

"Why is there a military bunker this far up?" Kestrel countered.

"Hurry!" Cross Fox shouted.

They ran to catch up. The large metallic doors opened just enough for one person to fit through at a time. Kestrel followed Stoat inside, and they joined the others.

Only emergency lights were lit along the curved walls of the otherwise dark bunker, their amber glow bending along the edge and arching across the all-metal interior. Boxes lined the corridor, marked by military labels and stacked at various heights.

"Kestrel!" Worry dripped through Shrew's voice.

"I'm here," Kestrel said as he and Stoat made their way to the others.

"What's going on?" Stoat asked, but Cross Fox said nothing, only gestured off to the side.

In a well-lit room, Pronghorn lay on a medical table. Blood spouted from his wound, pooling on the table before dripping to the floor. Caiman pressed blood-soaked bandages against Pronghorn's side.

"Someone get me more bandages!" Caiman demanded.

Lynx knelt at the head of the table by Pronghorn's ear, talking to him and gently rubbing his hair, while Caiman gave Hoatzin a brief rundown of the events that caused the injury. She called for Cross Fox.

Thinhorn sat in a chair next to the table, weeping.

Cross Fox grabbed Stoat, and they hurried to a nearby closet. They rummaged through the supplies, filling their arms with bandages, sterile water, alcohol, and a few tools. The two quickly returned to the makeshift medical wing and delivered the necessities.

Kestrel felt overwhelmed as they scurried around, gathering supplies and attempting to save Pronghorn. Being in the bunker was somehow more human than being in the burnt cabin. There were more artifacts of humanity, more evidence of a life here. It reminded him of the village he had seen and what was on the other side of the mountain—if his vision was true.

He reeled, and Shrew caught him. It was too much to take in all at once. Everything about the group was still a mystery, and now it seemed they were familiar with this place. How could that be?

Kestrel put a hand on his throbbing head, and Gannet offered him a canteen of water.

Without warning, a clamor came from outside the bunker—someone desperately, furiously pounding on the doors.

"Fuck!" Cross Fox screamed.

"It's Bowhead!" Kestrel shouted.

"Switch me!" Caiman demanded.

Muskox took his place and quickly re-applied pressure on Pronghorn's wound. He cried out, but Hoatzin poured some of the spirits into his mouth to ease him and called on Thinhorn to help fix the wound.

Caiman ran to a speaker box on the wall and pressed a button.

"Open the door!" Bowhead bellowed in his deep voice. "Hurry! They're out here."

Caiman pressed a switch, and the bulkhead doors sprang to life. The dying light sliced through the bunker, and Bowhead's large figure appeared and stumbled inside. Gannet and Kestrel ran to his side as Caiman began to close the doors. The sound of ringing metal barreled through the outpost.

Shots. He thought the hunters might be a way of escape, but it seemed they were poised to kill anyone from the group. Could he meet them and plead his case, or would he be gunned down the moment he stepped outside?

Kestrel put his body under the left arm of a limping Bowhead, Gannet did the same on the right side, and the three hobbled toward the medical room.

They only had moments.

TWELVE
THE BUNKER

A bullet shot through the sliver of the closing doors, and air hissed to their left. Kestrel looked back and saw the glass of the military vehicle crack. Screeching metal doors closed together, but someone was there.

Banging on the door.

"Hunters," Cottontail whimpered.

Stoat picked her up and held her close. "It'll be safe now that we're inside. See? The doors are closed, and they can't get in. The monsters are only sounds on the outside. It's getting dark, and they'll leave soon. Don't you worry, little girl. We're safe."

Monsters, Kestrel thought. If the hunters were monsters, what did that make them?

Bowhead groaned in pain. His leg was caked with snow and blood, and was bent the wrong way. Gannet and Kestrel set him on a chair, and Hoatzin came to take a look.

"It will need setting. Have some of this first." Hoatzin gave him a shot of the spirits.

Thinhorn called out to Cross Fox for more gauze, and she dug out an extra bundle. Kestrel could see him wiping tears and sweat away with his forearm as he sewed up his brother's wounds.

The banging on the doors was unrelenting, making the central area of the bunker unbearable. After speaking with Cross Fox, Stoat directed everyone who wasn't needed to the back of the shelter.

A small hallway led to a large mess hall and a series of dormitories—a whole world hidden under the earth. Bunk beds lined one room, each bed outfitted with a thin mattress without sheets or pillows. It was drab, but better than sleeping outside.

In the dormitory, the pounding was barely audible. "It'll stop soon," Gannet assured Cottontail as he held her hand. She kissed the foot on her necklace.

"Why don't you set up for the night here?" Stoat suggested, smiling. It felt forced, at least to Kestrel, but she was trying to calm them down.

Gannet claimed a top bunk, and Cottontail wanted one right next to him. He gave the little rabbit girl a boost, then climbed up into his bed. Stoat went off to find a linen closet or laundry room that might have sheets, pillows, and blankets.

Kestrel's hunch had proven correct—the older members had been there before.

He and Shrew set their packs down by the bunks, and Shrew took a water bottle out and finished it. His bottle was almost empty too.

The idea hit him.

"There's got to be a place around here to fill these," Kestrel said, shaking his empty bottle. He grabbed Shrew's too and wandered down the hall with Shrew following along.

The side corridor led down to communal showers. The line of chrome shower heads multiplied the avocado green tiles on the walls, assaulting Kestrel's eyes. Shrew hurried to one of the knobs and turned it on. A gurgle of air and a rattle-spurt brought the shower head to life. Brownish drops bubbled out first from disuse, but it finally ran clear and at full force.

Shrew put his hand in the water, retracting it quickly. The water was icy cold, as freezing as the snow outside. Running water was a good sign, though. Kestrel wondered if there was a water heater somewhere on the premises. If they had electricity, maybe they could get warm water.

"Let's find a sink," Kestrel said.

"And the water heater," Shrew chimed in as he turned off the knob.

Down the hall, they searched until they found the bathrooms, a kitchen, a pantry, and what was labeled as a control room. Kestrel tried the handle, but the door was locked. No keys were hanging around. Maybe the key was the one Hoatzin carried with her.

"I'm going to get everyone's water bottles so we can fill them," Kestrel said, changing course in hope of finding access to the room.

They passed Stoat along the way, who carried a stack of white sheets and pillows—clearly not the sheets they used in his initiation. Cottontail and Gannet had found a deck of playing cards under a mattress and were playing a round of Go Fish.

A groan of pain echoed through the hall. Cottontail and Gannet dropped their cards, Stoat froze, and Kestrel and Shrew hurried to see the source. Back in the main part of the bunker, Bowhead sat with his leg up, resting as best as he could; the two metal chairs he sat on looked too small and uncomfortable.

Thinhorn, hands bloody, finished sewing up his brother and turned to speak with Lynx. They said a prayer together, and Thinhorn took out a silver tag from his shirt and kissed it. Pronghorn was passed out on the table while Hoatzin and Cross Fox busied themselves cleaning the blood pool. Kestrel could smell the industrial cleaner from across the curved dome.

"I'm refilling water bottles," Kestrel announced.

One by one, they pointed him to their packs. Kestrel found Muskox's milk jug, along with the others, and Shrew took some of the canteens and bottles that Kestrel couldn't carry.

"Make sure to turn on the water heater. It's in a maintenance room between the kitchen and showers," Caiman hissed. His yellow eyes lingered on Kestrel as if he knew he was planning something. "Don't turn it up too high."

Kestrel nodded. On their way back, he wondered how Caiman knew this place so well, and how it had power. There could be a solar panel array like the one at the burnt cabin. Since it seemed to be a military base, there could be some underground cable system that ran to the nearby town or generators hidden somewhere in the building.

The bunker had seemed to be abandoned before their arrival, though Lynx and either Caiman or Pronghorn knew how to get in. Cross Fox certainly had a good sense of where the supplies were located.

Before they filled up on water, the two stopped at the maintenance closet and found the water heater. Cobwebs coated the cylinder; it was the first time Kestrel noticed any sign of animal or insect activity. Remembering Caiman's advice, they turned the temperature up, but not all the way.

Kestrel quickly looked around the closet, noticing the standard set of items—mops, buckets, cleaning supplies—but no keys, though there was an empty hook near the light switch.

The milk jug would have to suffice for now.

Kestrel walked into the kitchen with Shrew in tow, turned on the faucet, and began to fill the bottles they had. After half were filled, Shrew went back to the bunk to return the filled containers and get the rest of the empty ones.

Alone in the kitchen, Kestrel quickly washed off the muddy milk jug. The label became clear, and he tried to memorize the words, knowing he'd have to give it back and might not be able to see it again. He repeated the words on the jug until Shrew walked back in. Once the rest were filled, they left the kitchen.

Kestrel noticed that the gunshots and pounding had ceased. He wondered if the hunters were still out there, waiting and watching until they came out. Waiting to lodge a bullet in their chests or heads.

If heading to the sacred mountain was so important, then being trapped inside this bunker was not just a setback, but a disaster. Yet death surely awaited them outside—guns aimed at the door, waiting for them to step out. Another enemy in his way, an obstacle to his freedom—or were they the answer? Could he convince them he was a hostage and not a member of the thirteen? Would he be able to get close enough to explain it to them?

As Kestrel walked away from the wounded and back toward the bunks, he laughed. He didn't blame the hunters at the gates. He would aim a rifle at any of them for what they did. They all looked like beasts of the wild walking upright.

Monsters.

Shrew hugged him from behind as he stood at his bunk to unpack the rest of his things for the night. Kestrel bent his head to caress his cheek against Shrew's hand. Soft, gentle, right. He felt the arrows strike his heart. He was somehow falling in love with this stranger—with a monster.

Maybe he was becoming one, too.

THIRTEEN
CONTROL ROOM

"Shower's free," Stoat said to Kestrel as she guided Cottontail to her bed.

"Thanks," Shrew said as he took off down the hall.

Kestrel finished spreading his blanket over the thin mattress and imagined darkness settling over the bunker. The fluorescent lights couldn't convey such a thing, but he was tired, ready for sleep.

"Will you tuck me in?" Cottontail asked as she nestled under the covers. Stoat pulled the sheet and wool blanket tight and tucked it under the mattress. Gannet sighed deeply.

Kestrel looked over at him.

"What about me?" Gannet asked, giving Stoat puppy dog eyes.

Cross Fox rolled her eyes as she dried her hair with a towel. Stoat laughed and nodded. Gannet snuggled deep down, and she covered him.

Kestrel looked at his bed and wondered if his mother or father had ever done the same for him. The memories of his prior life felt foreign, as if they were just out of his reach, though a vague sensation of them brushed against his hand. If only he could grab hold of them and look at each.

Certain things *felt* familiar. Like the way Cottontail was tucked in or the way Shrew touched him. It was like his mind was trying to recall specific instances of his past, but it could only conjure shadows of feelings and moments.

"Good night," Stoat whispered to Cottontail and Gannet.

"Night," Gannet mumbled back.

"Night," Kestrel said as he got up from his bunk.

"Will you turn off the light?" Cross Fox asked.

Kestrel obliged, flicking the switch and then turning down the dimly lit hallway. He caught up with Shrew, who was already in the shower. Kestrel watched as the hot water beaded on his body, steam rising around him. Shrew was washing his hair with shampoo they'd found in a toiletries closet, the white suds foaming and stripping his scalp of caked-on dirt.

Earlier, Cross Fox had given everyone a fresh set of clothes from the supplies stored in the bunker. Most of the shirts were plain white; the camouflage green pants were military-issued, though there were a few pairs of blue jeans and khakis, as well as underwear and socks. None of them fit quite right, but it was better than what they'd been wearing.

Kestrel stripped off his bloody, sweat-stained clothes and threw them in a pile with the others. In the morning, Kestrel, Shrew, and Gannet would be responsible for washing them in the industrial laundry machines.

This place was a blessing from the gods.

"Hey, hey." Shrew grinned as he cleaned the remaining suds from his hair and face. After scrubbing behind his ears, Shrew moved on to the rest of his body. Kestrel said nothing in response, taking off his underwear and socks. He walked to the shower head next to his newfound partner.

Companion. The word was enough for now. It didn't imply anything more than what they were, but sounded better than friend or lover, more meaningful but not as serious.

Stoat had been less forthcoming in the last few days, and

Kestrel wished the three of them could be alone to discuss their future plans. He should've told her to stay up and meet with them, but that would be for tomorrow. They desperately needed to finalize their escape plan, but their current enclosure made it difficult.

"You're filthy!" Shrew laughed as he handed Kestrel a little bottle of shampoo.

Kestrel began scrubbing his head, making sure his fingernails got every molecule of dirt and debris.

Without asking, Shrew grabbed a clean washcloth and lathered it with a bar of soap. He stepped toward Kestrel and started to scrub around his neck and shoulders, careful to get the bits of dirt that clung to his collarbone.

"You don't have to do that," Kestrel said as his face grew warm.

"Have you seen how dirty you are?" Shrew laughed.

"I haven't even looked at myself in the mirror," he said with curiosity.

"You should." Shrew smiled as he wiped a few suds off Kestrel's face. "You're handsome."

There was an innocence in Shrew's eyes. Kestrel leaned in until they were nose to nose, brushing each other's skin. Inches away from a bliss as vast and deep as the ocean. There was a hunger within him —a different kind of desire. A longing to taste, to enjoy, to have.

Kestrel pressed his lips on Shrew's—gently at first—but when Shrew reciprocated, a certain ferocity came over him. Kestrel's tongue explored Shrew's mouth, tasting. Below, Kestrel could feel Shrew grow hard against his body. He reached down.

Shrew moaned.

Steam rose around the two as Kestrel sucked on Shrew's neck. Another moan. Then he bit. It wasn't a playful bite—it was deeper; tiny teeth marks accidentally drawing blood. Shrew winced, but Kestrel lapped at the blood and continued to kiss along Shrew's neck. Then he moved down.

The floor tiles weren't kind to Kestrel's knees, but his mouth was full and he was happy. As was Shrew, who ran his long fingers through Kestrel's soapy hair and held on.

After a few minutes, Kestrel stood, and they kissed again, deliciously violent. It took everything in Kestrel not to take another bite. He stared at the mark on Shrew's neck and wanted to do it again. To taste, to consume, to love. Kestrel licked the last bit of drawn blood.

Kestrel and Shrew dried off with itchy towels that smelled of stale air—the same scent as the rest of the bunker. They wrapped the towels around their waists and walked to the bench where they'd put their new clothes. When Kestrel put his shirt on, he noticed Caiman standing in the door, his scaly mask covering his face.

"What do you want?" Kestrel asked.

Caiman said nothing. His yellow, curious eyes narrowed on them, then he walked away. Shrew blushed, but Kestrel's expression turned into disgust. Not at Shrew—at the thought of Caiman watching them from the doorway. How long had he been watching?

"He gives me the creeps. I don't like him," Shrew said, sliding his shirt over his head.

"Me either," Kestrel said as he grabbed Shrew's hand. He peered out into the dark hall and led Shrew back to the small bunk room a few feet away.

Shrew climbed into bed as Kestrel dried off his hair. In the near darkness of the dormitory, he heard a sucking sound. After what he'd done to Shrew in the shower, he had no right to tell Stoat and Cross Fox to quiet down, though he considered it distasteful to fool around in the room where others were sleeping— especially a child.

Kestrel peered at the bunk Cross Fox and Stoat shared; in the dim light from the hallway, he saw they were both sound asleep. Gannet was curled up in bed and softly snoring, but Kestrel still heard the sound.

Then he turned and checked on Cottontail.

She was the source of the noise, the little rabbit trying to soothe herself. Even at her slightly unidentifiable age, she still seemed too young to be enduring such a thing. Kestrel approached her top bunk, where she was still tucked in.

He had to stop himself from gasping too loudly.

Cottontail sucked on the dried foot she wore around her neck. He took her small hand, bent all her fingers except her thumb, and grabbed the preserved foot. He pulled the toes out of her mouth and put her thumb inside. She made a noise, then went on sucking her thumb.

Tonight, his heart had been hit in different ways. Fear, passion, desire, horror, concern; a brutal, unrelenting pentad. Kestrel felt exhausted in a new kind of way, and his current situation was a kink in his plan to make it up the mountain and go beyond them.

Shrew was waiting for him in bed.

They kissed, then settled in.

Hours passed.

Kestrel's ears perked up at another sound—a mechanical whirl. Shrew snored softly, and Kestrel moved slowly to the edge of the bed, careful not to pull the blanket off him. From his bunk, he could see the others asleep. Was it dangerous to wander in the night with Caiman on the prowl?

The floor felt like ice on his bare feet as he slid out of bed.

Kestrel peered both ways down the hall. All clear. He turned to the right and headed toward the main area. In the medical room, Pronghorn was asleep on a makeshift cot next to the operating table. Thinhorn had fallen asleep on a mat next to his brother. Bowhead reclined on an old office chair, and Hoatzin snored in a chair outside the medical room.

Lynx and Caiman were nowhere to be found.

He wondered where they were at this hour, worried that Caiman might be watching him from some unknown, shadowy place. Kestrel stared at the military vehicle with the now flat tire. It looked old, something from a film he couldn't remember seeing. It certainly hadn't been used recently.

Kestrel ran his finger on the black glass and wiped the dust clean off. The mark was as thick as a snail's trail. He scrawled *HELP* in the dust, even though he knew no one would rescue him from the bunker.

On the way back to the bunks, he saw a door open down the hall. The doorway glowed, and a shadow moved within the frame. It was growing—coming closer—leaving the blueish bright room and heading right toward him. He scurried back into the bunk room and hid from the looming outline. It moved further down the hall as he lay back down and covered himself.

Caiman slinked down the hall, bobbing slightly, until he stopped in front of the bunks. His yellow eyes scanned the room. Kestrel heard him sniffing the air. Caiman *was* patrolling the halls after all. Kestrel uttered a prayer to whatever god would hear him lest Caiman realize he'd been seen.

"Get some sleep," Lynx whispered to him as she approached. "Call for me if you hear anything."

Kestrel could see her put a hand on his shoulder and kiss him on the cheek before she sent him off. Caiman hunched off in his scaly armor toward the entry of the bunker.

Guard dog was all Kestrel could think.

Lynx touched her bolo tie and hurried off in the opposite direction. Whatever was down at the end of the hall drew her back in. The light dimmed as if a door had been closed, but not all the way. A splinter of blue light still remained.

After waiting a moment for Caiman to put distance between them, Kestrel got back up out of bed and made his way toward the room. He had to move with precision and control each breath, to silence any noise coming from his body. The hallway was a treacherous corridor; it seemed longer and colder than before, each footfall threatening to betray him.

Kestrel pushed his body against the far wall opposite the open door, slinking along the pathway Caiman walked. Blueish gray light came from a room with numerous monitors. Kestrel saw the old screens before he noticed Lynx.

The monitors looked like old computer screens. They had an on/off knob and cutouts for a speaker, but that was it. The screens displayed images of the outside—the enormous metal front door, the slope down to the bunker, a road down the mountain, the curved dome of the building he was in, and the hallway where he stood.

Shit.

Lynx moved into view, gliding across the linoleum floor on an office chair, looking away from the screens. She stared down at a map spread across the desk and drew a winding line with her finger, tapping on the paper. It looked like she was scared of the map.

Then she looked up at the monitors.

"Kestrel—the Liberator himself," Lynx said. "Come here."

A chill ran down his spine. He was caught; there was no way of getting out of this. Pushing away his fight or flight response, Kestrel girded himself and went into the surveillance room.

"Can't sleep?" Lynx gestured for him to sit in the chair opposite her. A friendly upturned smile greeted him, but her eyes gave her away. Those catlike, glowing eyes mimicked the holographic shifting of the stone in her bolo tie. Sinister and searching.

Kestrel shook his head as he glanced at each monitor. On the far right screen, he could see Caiman settling down on a sleeping bag near the switch and intercom by the front door.

The two of them were the only ones awake, and they were alone.

"What is this place?" Kestrel asked as he sat down. The chair's padding had worn thin, and the plastic creaked. The control board was as old and unused as the monitors. Lynx moved the map she was studying to the side.

"It's an old military outpost. We believe this bunker was used for training and surveillance. The army was keeping the gods from bringing about their will." Lynx reached out and pecked at a button with her long fingernails.

One of the screens, watching a hallway that Kestrel hadn't been down, turned white briefly. A moment later, it came back to life, showing another door to the outside—this one smaller than the one they went through.

"What happened to them?" Kestrel asked.

"They're long gone. The government disbanded the unit that had been stationed on the mountain after the Cold War. I suppose they believed the gods no longer posed a threat," Lynx pondered.

"How do you know that?"

"I've been around almost as long as the hunters."

That wasn't the answer Kestrel wanted. "Who are they?"

"The hunters are not like us. They're mortal humans who serve themselves and do not belong to the gods of the sacred mountain." Lynx shuddered in disgust. "I once thought they were simply mistaken, that these foolish men believed we were the animals they hunted, but I soon discovered they've been after us for a long time. They've seen who we are, they know our mission, and they're trying to stop us at all costs."

"But why?"

"I'll be honest with you." Lynx reached out and touched his hand. "When Hoatzin spoke of your purpose, I was unsure what it meant. We each have a purpose that the gods give us. Yours is to be our liberator. I thought you were a threat to me."

A mist of sweat bloomed on Kestrel's forehead. Had Lynx figured out his plot and the alliance between him, Stoat, and Shrew? Did she know how much he wanted to kill her right now?

"You did?" Kestrel pretended to be unaware.

"It was my mistake. I believe you are to liberate us from the hunters, to find a way out, and guarantee we make it to the gods." She looked closely at him with those amber eyes. "That's what's called to you tonight, isn't it? The gods wanted you to see this, to be a part of this, to help me set our people free."

Kestrel nodded.

It was true. He would be the Liberator—but only for himself and anyone who would go with him. He wouldn't save Lynx from the hunters, but he needed to take advantage of her beliefs.

He smiled. He had found a way in. And like a torrent of water, he would exploit it until it broke the foundation in two. Kestrel would cleave the group in half, starting with Lynx. A schism within their ranks would break the fragile spine, and he could take those who wanted to go with him.

Their delusion would be tough to shatter, but he could do it.

"Will the hunters wait for us until we come out?" Kestrel watched the video of the front door. There was no one outside at the moment, but it was late at night and blisteringly cold on the mountain.

"They've gone for now, but they could be back at any time."

"Is there another way out?" Kestrel tilted his head.

"There is one, but I'm hesitant to use it." Lynx put her hand to her chin and began to lick the back of her palm. Her tongue sounded rough and scratchy, and she kept licking until she soothed herself.

"Tell me why," Kestrel demanded, trying to appear calm.

"There is a passageway. It cuts through part of the mountain to the other side, but puts us in peril. We're only a few days away from the sacred mountain. If we take the back way out, it puts us in the Northern Pass, which will shorten the journey. But the Pass is not kind."

"You don't think we can make it?" Kestrel asked piercingly.

Lynx bent her head like she noticed the threat to her assurance.

"It will be harder. The Northern Pass is blanketed with heavy snow. It's more exposed to the elements and open to the hunters if they're up that way. Cottontail already needs to be carried, as do the bones. Pronghorn and Bowhead are wounded, which will complicate the journey. I'm concerned that more days will slow us down or worse."

"That we'll lose one of the thirteen." Kestrel understood.

"Precisely. The gods have fulfilled their promises and completed the ranks of their servants." Lynx had a tinge of zeal in her voice. "We can't go back down the mountain."

"Right."

"There is one benefit to the Northern Pass," Lynx supposed. "There's a cave to take shelter in and rest. A few supplies are stashed there. It would be a safe haven."

Kestrel thought of Grouse, the one he replaced. Their group had thirteen people before he arrived. Had he not shown up, they would've finished their journey and been done with this whole charade.

While he couldn't remember why he'd entered the Hinterlands in the first place, he knew his current goal was to deplete their numbers, to be the adversary. In a way, he supposed, what was an adversary if not a liberator for the oppressed? If they took the Northern Pass, some of their strongest could be incapacitated— Pronghorn and Bowman might not make it. If the hunters showed up, then Caiman, Muskox, and Thinhorn would likely engage in a shootout.

"I think we should take it," Kestrel suggested. "It might be more difficult, but the hunters most likely won't traverse the higher pass. They could be outside the camera's view right now, setting up camp or waiting for reinforcements. We need to evade them at all costs. If they have no knowledge of the passageway, they'll be waiting for us outside the bunker while we're climbing to the top of the mountain."

Lynx deliberated.

"Stoat or Gannet could carry Cottontail. I'll take on any extra supplies to lighten the load for the others. I'm sure Shrew would do the same. Muskox can carry Pronghorn's load. If there is a threat, Thinhorn can pass his pack to Bowhead and go with Caiman to eliminate any hunters."

Kestrel was confident his suggestion would work. Stoat and Gannet wouldn't have to carry as much and would be able to protect Cottontail. He and Shrew would have the extra supplies they needed for their journey. Muskox would be weighed down.

The plan could work, he told himself over and over until he believed it. "We must fulfill the will of the gods," he added.

"I'll talk to Caiman and Hoatzin about it in the morning."

"Let me know what they say." Kestrel smiled back at her. The sense of power ignited his body; every bone and blood cell rang with resounding strength. He was gaining control of the situation.

His stomach roared.

Maybe this was the desire of the gods. Kestrel could liberate Lynx from her responsibilities and lead everyone out of the Hinterlands, never nearing the peak of the sacred mountain. For now, he would sow the seeds of doubt and finalize his plan with Stoat and Shrew.

"I should head back to bed," Kestrel faked a yawn and stood up, his duplicity sown.

"Rest well, Kestrel." Lynx dismissed him.

"You too."

Lynx returned to her map. On his way out, he caught a glimpse of their location and the charted path they were supposed to take. To the right was a rugged mountainscape, the ripples of the cartographers' map showing the drastic increase in elevation.

The Northern Pass. Kestrel held it in his mind as if it were a fragile spell, a way to break this curse.

FOURTEEN
INNARDS

Kestrel went to the kitchen to get some fresh water and maybe a midnight treat now that there was access to the food left in the bunker. The double doors to the galley swung open, and the faint hallway light leaked in. Someone stood at the end of the room, crouched over a table, watching him.

He reached for the switch. The fluorescent lights buzzed as they flashed on, and the intense white light stung Kestrel's eyes. He shielded them before he saw the man standing in the kitchen, caught in the act.

Thinhorn, hands covered in a white granular powder, sucked on his fingers. His curly hair was hidden under his wool hat, the tiny spiraling horns protruding from the side. Thinhorn's eyes were wide and scared.

"Sorry," Thinhorn said as he pushed away a container and brushed his hands on his pants. "I should go check on my brother."

Thinhorn ran out of the room, leaving the container open on the counter, and bumping into Kestrel as he slammed open the doors. As Kestrel reached out to stop the still-swinging doors, he hoped Thinhorn's startled outburst didn't wake the others. He walked to the counter, looked at the container, and laughed.

"Salt."

Of course.

The night and the people around him couldn't get any weirder. He went to search the cabinets, something he failed to do earlier, but they were sparse.

The search continued. There was dried meat in their packs, but they would need that for their trek up the Northern Pass. He spotted a brown cardboard box in the corner with *MRE* stamped on the side of it. Kestrel wasn't sure what it meant, but he untucked the flaps, took out a package, and tore it open with his teeth. Several things spilled out with a set of instructions. It was some sort of pasta in a tomato sauce. He followed the directions, prepared the meal, and stirred with his fork.

This was the first real meal he'd had in—how many days had it been? Kestrel had lost count. Was it a week or two? The days and nights blurred together; time was nothing now, a forgotten remnant of civilized society.

The food—now, that was *something*. Kestrel took the smell in as slowly and as long as he could. It was intoxicating. He stabbed the round pasta with the fork, ran it through the thick red sauce, and lifted it to his mouth.

The flavor coated his mouth, but not in the way he wanted.

Kestrel spat out the food into a nearby trash can. It tasted awful, somehow sour and bitter at the same time. Rancid, if food like this could go bad. He rifled through the packaging to find an expiration date. The little black printed stamp indicated that it still had a few years left.

Hunger rattled his stomach. Kestrel thought it was a bad package. He grabbed another and tried it. Awful—downright disgusting. Then another and another—all different types. Chili, a different kind of pasta, some kind of beef with barbecue, meatballs, chicken, and vegetables. All of it was bad.

But it wasn't expired.

Kestrel gave up looking for food and settled on the feeling of hunger. He looked at the emptied packages on the counter: spoons, small packets of salt and sugar, wet naps, hot sauce—and matches. Those could come in handy. Kestrel pocketed the matches and left the kitchen, turning off the lights as he left.

Either Lynx had closed the door or she'd gone to bed. In the dark of the showers, he heard a lapping sound. A faint glow from the hallway outlined an odious creature drinking from the wall to the nearby drain. Kestrel's shadow eclipsed Thinhorn's back, the strange man unaware of his presence this time.

Kestrel wandered back to his bed, slightly cold and hungry. Not the best way to sleep, but it was better than that first night out in the wilderness. At least he had friends, if he could call them that, a warm bed, and hot water. At least for one night.

Kestrel sat on the edge of his bed. Shrew adjusted slightly but didn't wake up, his arm above his head. It looked uncomfortable. Kestrel dug in his pack to see if there were any nuts or dried fruit left, but all he had was a slab of cured meat. There was no way to tell what part of person it was, but Kestrel didn't care. He took a bite. The flavor made his tongue rejoice.

Bite after bite, Kestrel savored the meat and swallowed when he wanted more. The little provision he had in his pack was enough to satisfy him for the night. In fact, that was the only thing that could satisfy him.

Flesh, he thought. That was all he wanted.

"I need some spirits," Kestrel chuckled, lying down next to Shrew.

Only then did he realize what Thinhorn was slurping up.

Kestrel dozed off with a full belly, and all was well.

The next morning was the first without a demand for them to wake up and go. Kestrel woke and saw that Cross Fox and Stoat were already gone, but Cottontail and Gannet still slept. Shrew stirred, barely opened his eyes, rolled over, and covered his head with a pillow to block out the light from the hallway.

When Kestrel sat up, he saw Stoat had returned for him and now stood staring at him. Her dark eyes were almost black in the shadow of the bunk, her braids tied up on top of her head, her slender frame even more gaunt. She pulled on her fur coat and got up, nodding for Kestrel to follow.

Stoat surveyed both ends of the hallway and turned to the left. Kestrel put enough space between them to avoid suspicion, checking the same way she did, but luckily, no one was in the hall. He saw her leave the showers with a bundle of clothes in her arms, heading to the laundry room.

Kestrel followed suit. She'd left him enough clothes to have his own pile. He gathered the dirty laundry and went into the same room she did. The space was away from the common areas, near the mechanical closet.

The lid to the washing machine was open. It was almost as old as the monitors in the control room, but mustard yellow with brown and silver accents. Stoat poured powdered detergent from an industrial-sized box into the tumbler without turning around.

It was easy to understand. Kestrel went to the second washing machine, opened it, and set the dials to their position.

"Could you please pass the detergent?" Kestrel asked.

Stoat passed the box, closed her lid, and pushed a button. The machine jittered and rumbled as water filled the drum. Then it was smooth sailing. The noise of the laundry machines drowned out everything else.

"I have a plan to get us out of here," Kestrel said. "Lynx is taking us through the Northern Pass. We'll probably have to stay in a cave. I'm thinking we leave when everyone's asleep and head back down the mountain."

"What about the hunters?" Stoat asked as she grabbed the box and returned it to the shelf.

"I don't think they'll be up that far. The tunnel will take us up to a higher elevation on a different side of the range. There's no way they know there's an alternate route out of here."

"Wasn't this their base?" Stoat asked. "They have to know about it."

"Lynx said it was abandoned a long time ago," Kestrel whispered.

"She told you that?" Stoat raised an eyebrow.

Footsteps caught Stoat's attention, and she glanced at the bottom of the door. The light was obscured by the shadow-feet. Stoat's left ear twitched, and her head tilted. Kestrel waited with her, their eyes fixed on the crack between the ground and the wooden door. The shadow moved away.

"Who will we take with us?" Stoat asked when she was sure it was clear.

"Cottontail, Gannet if he'll come, and Shrew," Kestrel left off Cross Fox on purpose. He wasn't sure he trusted Stoat's partner. She was too close to the top, too powerful, too needed, but by the look on Stoat's face, that was a mistake.

"Gannet will slow us down, but he shouldn't be here with them."

To his surprise, Stoat said nothing of Cross Fox.

"I had another vision of you," Kestrel changed the subject. "Like last time, it was hard to make out, but I think it's from our lives before all this. We were together, and you asked if we could go to a cabin. It looked so much like the burnt cabin, but maybe that's because that's the only one I've seen since I hit my head."

"Is that all you saw?"

"Yes," he lied. "Could you tell me what you saw again?"

"We were friends," Stoat whispered as if conjuring up the past in secret. "I remember we were driving and I asked if you were okay. Maybe we were heading to the cabin in your second vision. Then we got into an argument."

"And you left."

"Right." Stoat nodded. "I left, and maybe that's when...that's when we were separated."

"That's how you ended up here." Kestrel stared down at the

humming machine. Locked inside, the sweat and stains were being washed away.

"I'm sorry," Kestrel said.

"Don't apologize. I couldn't even tell you what we were fighting about. Besides, that's in the past now. None of it matters. The only thing we need to focus on is getting up the mountain. It's you and me. We'll get out of the bunker, escape the Hinterlands, and get back to our normal lives."

"And we will."

Once the laundry was done, they moved it to the dryer and set out to find some breakfast. Stoat went first, making sure the others couldn't catch on to their scheming. Kestrel stood surrounded by the clunking machines, waiting.

There was a pit in his stomach, begging Kestrel to listen to its cries. He tried to ignore it, but he couldn't. He couldn't even distinguish hunger from intuition. In some ways, they were the same.

Intuition was as natural as hunger, basic to human function, and it must be obeyed. Otherwise, it could cost him his life. Kestrel had to listen, to respond, in order to be satisfied. He wanted to trust his gut, but he only felt uneasy and unsure.

Dismissing the vague sense of disturbance in his gut, Kestrel left the laundry room and returned to the bunks. On his way, he saw Shrew in the kitchen setting out rations—preserved chunks of meat, a few dried fruits, and some nuts. The MREs were laid out, arranged by type, like they were about to have a feast.

Cross Fox was in the room too, instructing Shrew on preparing rations for the last portion of the trip up to the sacred mountain. She then took breakfast for those in the medical wing.

"Hey, good morning!" Shrew smiled, his red tooth prominent.

"Morning," Kestrel said as he hugged Shrew's waist. "What's for breakfast?"

"This is all the fruit and nuts we have left," Shrew said, handing Kestrel a portion.

Kestrel took the little pile of walnuts in his palm and tossed them into his mouth. He began to chew, but the flavor was off. He wanted to spit them out, but he wouldn't let himself, not after all the meals he wasted last night. He swallowed them and remembered the night of his initiation and how awful the flesh tasted then. The displeasure of the ritual seemed far away now.

"Something wrong?" Shrew glared at him.

"Nothing." Kestrel tried to smile, but the foul taste contaminated his mouth. He didn't understand. "Do these taste bad to you?"

Shrew took a few walnuts from his portion and cautiously bit one, slowly and methodically as if he would be poisoned by it. Kestrel couldn't find a trace of disgust on Shrew's face, which only made him worry more.

"They taste fine to me."

"I think something's wrong with my taste buds."

Lynx walked into the kitchen, retying her bolo tie. Her clothes were replaced with military garb. Her catlike eyes stayed fixed on Kestrel.

"I'd like to speak with you, Kestrel," she said with a serious look on her face. "May I borrow him, Shrew?"

Shrew nodded and returned to bundling up the provisions. Kestrel grabbed a slab of salted flesh and started to eat his morning meal.

Out in the hall, Lynx walked with Kestrel side by side. She stayed quiet, making it clear she wanted to move further down the corridor. As they passed the bunks, he saw Gannet making his bed while Cottontail tried to fix her rabbit ears.

"I don't want to go back outside," Cottontail sighed. "The wind is too cold. I don't like it."

"Let's stay here. Unless there's a place I could get some fish. There weren't any in the Snake when we were there, but I'm hungry for it." Gannet flopped on his freshly made bed.

Kestrel and Lynx continued their walk until they reached the main chamber of the bunker. Most of the blood had been cleaned up from the floor and the table, but Pronghorn was still lying down, his side wrapped in pink-stained gauze. Bowhead sat up with his leg propped up on a chair, talking with Thinhorn and Muskox.

Kestrel took a bite of the meat in his hand.

Thinhorn pulled his silver tag from beneath his shirt and kissed it again, looking at his brother and offering up a prayer with folded hands. What looked to be tags hung around their necks—if they were dog tags, their *real* names were etched on them. If he could take one, he might learn something about their former lives.

Hoatzin sat in a corner, her robe spread out, her hands tinkering with a brew of spirits. She added some water and took a bottle of what looked like blood and mixed it in.

Kestrel didn't flinch this time.

"You must be hungry," Lynx joked. Her eyes narrowed in on the meat in his hand.

It was almost gone. Kestrel had devoured it while they walked to the main room. He hadn't even noticed how fast he ate—he just knew that his mouth was thankful and singing the praises of the tender, salty flesh. Adding sap wouldn't make it any sweeter. It was enough. He almost didn't care that it was from a person.

Almost.

"You're changing," Lynx observed as if she peered into his soul. "It's taken some of the others longer than you, but in time you realize how delicious it is, how you've been missing out on it your whole life, and that other food will never satisfy you the way it does."

Kestrel took another bite.

"We'll leave once everyone is ready and head up the pass until we finally arrive at the sacred mountain. You will see the wonders of the gods!" Lynx said. "Trust me, by the time you get up there, you will be fully transformed. A feast awaits for all your hard work."

"I can't wait to see the gods." Kestrel smiled.

"And those who try to stop us will face your wrath." Lynx pulled out a large knife and gave it to Kestrel with both hands. He took it gladly and measured its weight. It would do.

Liberator.

He wanted to slice her neck open to free himself. His hand gripped the handle but didn't swing. Now was not the time. Not with the others so close.

The cycle would end soon enough. If he couldn't escape like he planned, he would ensure they all died up on the pass. Conviction steeled within him.

"The hunters won't survive you," Lynx said with a sneer.

Neither will the devourers, Kestrel thought as he tucked the knife into his belt.

"With Bowhead injured, let me take the end of the line," Kestrel suggested. "I know it's his responsibility, but he won't be as useful with his injured leg. I'll conceal our traces and keep watch from the rear. The gods will ensure our safety, and I'll slaughter anyone who tries to stop me."

Lynx nodded.

Kestrel couldn't contain his joy at the thought of taking Lynx down. The one who conjured this whole thing, who stole children and murdered people, melting the minds of countless others.

It was her turn to suffer.

FIFTEEN
MOVE OUT

The bunker's lack of windows and use of artificial light made it impossible to know what time of day it was. Lynx and Caiman watched the control room monitors to estimate when the light of the midday sun shifted the shadows of trees.

Stoat helped Cross Fox pack bags, take stock of supplies, and organize what they needed for the trek up the northern pass. Hoatzin had warned that the claws of winter were creeping up on them and would dig into their flesh until there was a chill in their bones. Kestrel was beginning to believe she was right. Lynx said that the monitors showed signs of snow, though Caiman thought it was static.

"Do you think it's snowing?" Cottontail asked Gannet in child-like wonder. Kestrel smiled before realizing what was to come. Things would get worse before they got better; if he had to kill to save the girl, then he would. He only hoped she wouldn't have to witness any more horrors.

Kestrel knew Pronghorn's injury was another crack in their armor. All the stars were beginning to align, pointing toward liberation. Confidence surged within him as he saw the way forward.

He could do this.

"I'm going to help Cottontail pack up," Shrew said after he finished refilling the water bottles and canteens. Despite his words, he lingered near the doorway.

"I'll be there in a minute," Kestrel said, separating and folding the laundry. He stored all that he could in the remaining space of everyone's packs, knowing they would need extra layers when the snow worsened. The smell of fresh laundry comforted him as he tucked an extra pair of jeans into his bag; the scent reminded him of a summer day. Summer seemed far away in the chill of the bunker.

Their time in the bunker felt otherworldly. Every moment they spent there was like sipping on the dregs of a former life—fleeting dreams of the past, memories they had all forgotten.

"Hey, can I ask you something?"

Shrew hopped up on the long table next to Kestrel and the folded laundry. Thin flakes of veneer were peeling around the edges, revealing the particle board. He picked at the edges with his fingernails.

"Yes?" Kestrel asked with a raised eyebrow as he folded the last shirt. He placed it on the stack of clothes and gave his attention to the man sitting before him.

"What are we?"

"Oh, so it's *that* kind of question," Kestrel laughed.

Shrew blushed, his eyes glimmering with anticipation.

Kestrel wrapped his arms around Shrew's waist and leaned against the table. He bent closer and kissed his partner. Shrew wrapped his legs around Kestrel and ran his hand down his back.

"I haven't said it out loud, but I think of you as my partner," Kestrel admitted as he pulled back, placing his hands on Shrew's thighs. He trembled so much that Kestrel could feel it.

"You have?"

"I have," Kestrel confirmed. "I'll be honest with you, this is new to me. I don't think I've ever been this close to another person."

"To be fair, you don't remember where you came from or who

you were with before," Shrew laughed. "What if you have someone waiting for you?"

"What if *you* do?"

"They would've come looking for me by now." Shrew laughed, but it seemed forced.

"You're right. But there's something between us I can't deny. A magnetism I can't control. Somehow, I found you in this awful place."

"I feel the same." Shrew grinned.

"Some might say we're moving too fast, but I don't think those around us have the best judgment," Kestrel laughed.

"I love you," Shrew said abruptly, his eyes wide.

"I love you, too."

Kestrel leaned in for a kiss, and they held one another. Their embrace felt as hot as the room they were in. Neither of them said it, but when they were together, it felt like home.

Home, home, home.

The words rang in Kestrel's ears.

A door slammed outside, breaking the spell.

"Aren't you supposed to be helping Cottontail?" Kestrel asked with a wink.

"I thought you were supposed to be doing laundry?"

"After you," Kestrel gestured to the door.

Shrew hopped off the table and pressed his pants down, hiding the evidence of their embrace. Kestrel had to do the same. They waited until they were able to step into the hallway without anyone noticing.

"There you are!" Stoat said as she ran to help carry the laundry. "We're gathering in the main room for a meeting. I think they want to leave soon. Does he know the plan?"

Kestrel shook his head and gave Shrew an apologetic shrug.

"We'll fill you in later," Stoat said as she led them down the long hall.

"Take a seat," Lynx said.

Everyone gathered in a semi-circle around Lynx like she was their guiding star. Pronghorn and Bowhead sat on the office chairs, with the others either on the floor or seated on boxes of unmarked, abandoned supplies.

"The gods have demanded our presence at the top of the mountain. It will take a couple of days, maybe more, to reach the summit. From our estimates, the snow has picked up, but it shouldn't impede our mission. Our biggest threat remains the hunters." She paused, gesturing to the injured. "You see what they did to Pronghorn and Bowhead. They tried to eliminate one of our strongest members and harmed the one who conceals us from them. These hunters don't want us going to the mountain and mean to stop us at all costs. They are afraid of the gods and will not hesitate to kill all of us."

Gannet held Cottontail as Muskox patted her on the back. Kestrel glanced around, realizing how animalistic they all looked now. Out in the Hinterlands, they blended in with their surroundings, but they stood in stark contrast to the man-made building. Even in the dated bunker, they were animals. Hoatzin put on her mask.

The longer Kestrel stayed with them, the more they seemed to devolve.

"Hoatzin, Caiman, and I have consulted the whispers and rolled the Gambit Stones," Lynx continued. "We will head out of this base, through the emergency tunnel, and exit onto the Northern Pass. We will make our way up from there. Bowhead, with your injury, you will be up front with Pronghorn. Kestrel will cover our tracks. Muskox will carry Pronghorn's pack. Gannet, I need you to carry Thinhorn's bag; we'll need him to make sure their injuries don't worsen. Stoat, can you take Cottontail?"

Stoat nodded.

"I can hop on my own!" Cottontail sprang up and hopped.

"I know you can." Lynx smiled at the little girl as she bent down to address her. "But the mountain is very, very dangerous. The snow might go up to your chin! I need you to ride on Stoat's shoulders and be our lookout."

Cottontail didn't seem convinced, but she agreed.

Cross Fox brushed her bushy hair and shot a side eye to Stoat before returning her attention to the list she was working on. She wrote something down and tucked her little notepad in her pocket. Gannet's stomach rumbled. Cross Fox shook her head as Muskox handed him what remained of his breakfast ration.

"May I speak?" Hoatzin said as she stood up. Lynx nodded. The woman made her way before them, wild hair bouncing as she bobbed in place. Her vivid eyes peeked out from behind the mask.

"The gods are ready for us. We must be ready for them. There will be one more ceremony, a purification for all of us, and then we will be blessed by the hands of the gods. The great feast will commence, and we will dwell with them forevermore!"

Almost everyone, save for Kestrel, Shrew, and Stoat, gave a resounding shout, eager to finally be rewarded for their pain. Kestrel wondered if it would be worth it. If they made it to the end.

He joined in.

Caiman stood up, and Hoatzin bowed to him as if to relinquish her podium.

"Be prepared," Caiman said in his reptilian voice. His thin, yellow eyes examined each person one by one until his gaze fixed on Kestrel. "War and death are upon the wings of the gods. The Hinterlands will be the center of civilization, and we will be the soldiers of a new world."

"Messengers of the gods," Hoatzin added.

"When the time comes," Caiman continued, "we will churn our enemies to dust. All will bow, and those who refuse will be devoured." He licked his lips.

Kestrel tasted blood in his mouth, sweet and metallic.

The others nodded in agreement, even Cottontail. Their shared delusion had poisoned them all; there was no way to undo it now. Kestrel knew the illusion of purpose would carry them up the mountain, and disillusionment would lead them back to the human lands.

"Let's get moving!" Lynx shouted as she raised her claws in the air.

Kestrel knew this was only the beginning.

Cross Fox busied herself opening a box with Thinhorn, who cautioned her as she removed something from within the crate. She carefully wrapped paper around the object and packed it, ensuring it was secure before moving on to the next item.

Back in the bunks, Kestrel and Shrew helped Cottontail and Gannet pack their belongings. Stoat led them back into the main area to set their packs against the curved wall, giving Kestrel and Shrew a moment alone. He explained the plan to Shrew in hushed tones.

"It'll be easy," Kestrel said, trying to sound convincing. "We've been isolated from the others over the last few days anyway."

"You're sure there's no other way?" Shrew asked. "What do you think is on the top of the mountain?"

"Does anybody really know?" Kestrel asked in response. He didn't know what awaited them on top of the mountain. No one did.

That was a problem. Without knowing the ritual or their collective purpose, there was no way to prepare. Knowing Lynx, Hoatzin, and Caiman, it could entail something horrible, though he wasn't sure anything could be worse than that night in the burnt cabin.

There had never been much detail given about what they would do on the sacred mountain or what would come after. A feast was mentioned, but what would they eat beyond dried flesh and MREs? Hoatzin gave no prophecies, Caiman no details, and Lynx gave very few promises beyond "they would abide in the gods' abode." And what would happen when the gods didn't appear? Would there be a ritualistic sacrifice to an empty sky? Would they wait around for nothing to appear? Maybe then the illusion would finally fade for the others.

"There's nothing on the mountain," Shrew confirmed.

Kestrel nodded in agreement.

"We need to get up there so we can find the village and head that way. It's our ticket out," Kestrel continued. Shrew agreed and finished stuffing his sleeping bag into his backpack. He took a long drink of water and offered some to Kestrel.

"You're sure?" Shrew asked again.

He couldn't be sure. Kestrel had seen the glimpses of the village in his vision, but they had been pieces from his former life. There was no way any of the rest of it was real. Seeing the milk jug confirmed his visions were leading him to the human lands. Somehow.

Before he could answer, Caiman appeared in the doorway.

"Be careful with that knife, boy." Caiman sneered at the glinting metal. "Don't want you to gut yourself halfway up the slope. The blood will make things slippery, and you'll have to crawl all the way to the top."

A violent stillness settled among the triad. Shrew muffled a nervous cough, and Caiman laughed, rubbing his rough hands together. Kestrel leaned against the post of his bunk and smirked.

"I'm not sure the gods would like that sort of talk. There needs to be thirteen of us, and if there's not, you'll be marching back down to the wastelands," Kestrel couldn't wipe the smug look off his face if he tried. "Winter will be a bitch, and *if* you survive that, the process will start all over."

"You're easily replaceable," Caiman said, dismissing Kestrel's claim. "I could track down a hunter, lead him away from his pack, and corner him. Then we wouldn't need you."

"I thought I was your liberator."

Caiman paused and put his hand on his holster, as though losing another member meant nothing to him. Maybe it didn't matter. Maybe he and Hoatzin were scheming this whole time. The Gambit Stones were nothing more than a parlor trick.

"Fuck off," Shrew said. He rolled his eyes as he picked up his backpack. He pushed past Caiman and made sure to bump into him as he walked out of the room.

Caiman let out a sinister belly laugh and leaned in the door-way. "Your little friend is feisty," he chuckled.

"He'll kill for the ones he loves," Kestrel shot back, playing it off as a joke.

Caiman did not take it as a joke. His back went stiff, and his eyes narrowed. He was suited up, ready for the fight ahead; he pushed up his sleeves to show off his scaly arms.

If it was meant to be a threat, Kestrel didn't notice.

"Let's get going," Kestrel said as he put his backpack on and headed for the door.

An outstretched arm blocked him from leaving. Caiman leaned in, his face close to Kestrel's ear. A cold, wet tongue slithered against his earlobe as Caiman hissed.

"Don't test me. I have made the Gambit Stones work in my favor before, and I will do it again."

There it was. Proof that everything was fake.

Caiman chortled, flipped the light switch off, and sauntered down the hall.

The lizard man was nothing but a pompous idiot. It seemed that he was afraid of Kestrel, maybe even jealous of his budding relationship with Lynx. A crack in his armor. It wouldn't take much to slice him open. In the dark, Kestrel inhaled. The thought of eating Caiman alive made him salivate.

So it begins, he thought.

Leaving the bunker was harder than expected. It had been the first semblance of normalcy since he awoke in the forest. Kestrel would miss all of it—the real beds, the pillows, the hot showers...especially the time spent away from the wilderness. But he was eager to get to the mountain top and head to the human lands.

Stoat greeted him, pulling him aside quietly before he met the rest of the group. Kestrel looked around her; the others were chatting and finalizing their preparations. Bowhead had found an old, long-barreled rifle to use as a walking stick. Muskox was practicing swinging his axe.

"Listen," Stoat said as she checked over Kestrel's shoulder for onlookers or eavesdroppers. "I remembered more of my vision, the one where I saw you from before. We were arguing, like I said. We were in a kitchen. It looked like the burnt cabin, but it was different. They couldn't be the same, could they?"

"That was in your vision?" Kestrel asked.

"Yes! I was thinking about all the details, running through it again, trying to figure out what was going on. I can't believe I forgot it." Stoat shrugged. "I'm not sure what it means exactly, but I know that all I have is you."

"What about Cross Fox?" Kestrel looked at Stoat's face, but it was void of emotion.

"My time with her was merely a transaction," Stoat said. "She knows that. I gave her what she needed, and she supplied me with the same."

Kestrel saw through the lie slipping through her teeth.

"I need you to promise me," Stoat leaned in, "that if it comes down to it, you'll do all you can to save me. Even if that means leaving the others behind, even if that means Shrew won't make it with you. I need to know you have my back like I have yours."

"Of course." Kestrel lied.

Two liars, two former friends, two people in love with strangers. There was so much they had in common, but none of it felt real. Kestrel wondered how they had been friends in their past, what they had in common, what hobbies they had enjoyed together.

He couldn't imagine it.

He likewise couldn't imagine leaving Shrew. His loyalty should lie with his friend, but his gut told him differently. Stoat told him to listen, but he wouldn't listen to her, not fully. His alliance had shifted to Shrew for some reason. Maybe it was the way Stoat ignored him for days, or the way she lied. Maybe it was the way Shrew made him feel.

At least Kestrel's lies were for freedom.

Maybe that's what everyone's lies were—avenues to freedom.

"Great," Stoat said, kissing him on the cheek before returning to help Cross Fox.

The conversation ended in a flash, dying from the poison in Stoat's words. Kestrel wasn't even sure *why* he felt like this, but there was something in her voice and the way she lied. It wasn't right. She cared for Cross Fox more than she let on, and that poked at him. Why lie about it? What else was she planning?

"Let's move out!" Lynx called, and the others fell in line.

Kestrel hurried back to the group, nodding at Stoat once more and kissing Shrew before making his way to the rear. Thinhorn and Muskox carried the large sack of bones. For whatever reason, they still needed them.

Maybe it was the will of the gods.

Maybe he would break the gods, crushing them into dust.

SIXTEEN
BURROW

Kestrel stood at the rear of the line near the curved wall, staring at a singular door sealed with an airlock. Caiman typed in a code on a pin pad. Had he watched others do it? Kestrel could imagine him lurking in the forest, waiting for a soldier to type in the code. The red light turned green, releasing the bolt. The door popped open with a groan.

Peering into the shaft, Kestrel could see the wooden plank walls, roots twisting through the rocks behind the slats. The tunnel was a mix of wooden slats and solid concrete, with steel beams reinforcing the rock above them. Dim yellow bulbs lit the tunnel, making the metal bars resemble a giant rib cage.

Without a word, the line began to move. Caiman held the door open while Lynx waited in the tunnel. As Kestrel stepped foot on the other side, Caiman followed, closing the door behind them. The old door locked back into place with an eerie screech. The lizard-like man tested the lock; it didn't budge.

No way back. Only up and out, Kestrel thought.

Caiman gave him a sinister look as he passed him to take his place behind Lynx. Kestrel wanted to rip out his snake tongue and savor his destruction.

Not today. He needed Caiman to get to the top.

Then he could gorge.

As they progressed, the tunnel began to curve and narrow. Muskox and Bowhead had to bend their heads to avoid low points overhead. Kestrel did the same out of instinct, though he wasn't nearly as tall.

"It feels like the walls could cave in at any moment. I don't like it," Gannet said anxiously.

"Hey, I kind of like this place. Feels like home." Shrew laughed.

Kestrel realized how far away "home" felt. The memories had only found their way back when he drank the spirits; the longer he'd been in the woods, the more he felt like he belonged in the wild. "How would you know what home feels like?" he asked.

"I guess I wouldn't," Shrew said with a shrug.

"What kind of feast are we going to have on the mountain? Will there be fish and meat?" Gannet asked.

"Just not rabbit," Cottontail said.

"Quiet," Cross Fox bit back.

She turned around lightning fast, listening with her hand cupped to her ear. Everyone else froze. Kestrel turned around to stare down the tunnel behind them.

A series of taps—soft at first, but steady and growing. Ticking like dripping water. The sound of a hand rapping on a metal door.

"Someone's in the bunker."

Kestrel didn't catch who said it. His vision narrowed, and the hall felt small as he thought of what might be at their backs. He turned to see Caiman standing next to him. Cross Fox rattled off numbers as she counted the group.

"All here," Cross Fox confirmed, nodding to Lynx.

"Who is it?" Gannet asked. His teeth chattered through his words.

"We didn't hide well enough!" Bowhead growled. "I tried and tried, but I failed."

"There's no way someone would be able to get in," Pronghorn said. "Only Caiman, Thinhorn, and I have the code."

"Someone from the military," Thinhorn suggested.

"Now turned hunter," Stoat chimed in.

"We don't know anything," Lynx said as she stood among them. "Let's keep moving. The tunnel is a few miles long, but if we hurry, we'll be well into the pass."

"Let's go," Caiman commanded.

Kestrel scanned the darkness, but all he could hear was the tap of a stranger on the bunker door in the distance. When he felt Caiman move from his side, he breathed a sigh of relief and returned to his position in line.

They spent the rest of the journey in absolute silence. Some held their breath as they rushed through the tunnel, the sound chasing them down. The corridor began to slope up, slowing them down.

"Keep moving!" Caiman shouted.

The tapping threat still echoed down the corridor, albeit quieter. The party had slowed down—Kestrel felt his calves burning, but he pressed on. Some had a fire under their feet, but others, like Gannet and Stoat, seemed to go at their own pace.

Something made him pause. He looked back at the passage and could've sworn he saw a hooded shadow chasing him. Reaching for him, tapping on his heart, making it beat. Was someone in the tunnel with them?

He couldn't shake the feeling.

There was nothing behind him—he needed to focus. He moved on and caught up with the group. The tunnel continued to bend and twist deeper into the earth. As it did, Kestrel thought of the twelve people in front of him as a backbone, snaking along. Each one would need to be broken to take Lynx down.

And that was his fear.

It wasn't long before the temperature in the corridor began to drop. Even the roots behind the planks that comprised the walls seemed to shy away from the exposed air. Kestrel adjusted his sleeves and wrapped the feathery coat around him. The incline and cold breeze seemed to signal that they were approaching the end. He couldn't wait to be free.

One step closer.

"Something's wrong," Kestrel said, furrowing his brow. A shiver went through him. The group moved as one slithering beast.

Still, he kept remembering they were about to climb the ice-drenched mountain, that hunters could be waiting for them. Death hung in the air like shards of crystal. A glacial wind snuck through the escape route, piercing Kestrel's skin, and cursed him with winter's breath. Chills bloomed on his skin.

"We should be close," Pronghorn said.

He was right.

Just ahead of them, the hallway ended as lights guided them to a small metal door. There was no keypad, just a simple hatch wheel.

"Ready yourselves," Lynx commanded. "It's going to be cold."

The others grumbled, but everyone pulled their coats tighter. Some put on hats or masks made of fur, feathers, or skin. Kestrel did the same, then helped Shrew adjust his cap.

Caiman walked up the incline to the hatch door and tried to turn the wheel, but failed. He puffed his chest, readjusted his arms and feet, dug into the dirt, and twisted. The veins on his scaly forearms protruded.

Kestrel stifled a laugh. The tough-as-shit provocateur couldn't open a door.

"Muskox!" Caiman bellowed.

The bulky man walked to the latch, put his outsized hands on the icy steel, and gave it all his strength. Two of their greatest warriors could not open a little door. It was winning even as it did nothing but remain steadfast. "Bowhead! Thinhorn!" Caiman shouted, demanding their presence. The quartet tried their hand at undoing winter's curse.

It became apparent, at least to Kestrel, that the old metal door was frozen solid. There was a small rectangle in the metal he assumed was once a window, but no light came through it. It had been frosted over—either dirtied or buried in snow and iced over after years of disuse.

Fear shot through him like an arrow. Kestrel wondered if the door would open at all. If it wouldn't, they were stuck. There was no way back into the bunker. Especially with whoever—whatever was tapping on the door. The hunters would be the least of their problems if they couldn't leave the tunnel. Hoatzin couldn't have foreseen this —otherwise, Lynx wouldn't have led them down this hall.

Hoatzin began to pray, calling upon the inhabitants of the mountain. Stoat, for the first time, seemed nervous. She paced in small steps, biting her thumb. Gannet plopped against the concrete wall and slid down into the dirt. A long sigh drifted from his mouth.

"What can we use to open it?" Lynx asked Cross Fox.

"I have the supplies, but we agreed only to use them in an emergency." Cross Fox tilted her head. "It would be unwise. The whole tunnel could collapse."

Lynx considered it carefully; she was running out of options.

"What if we boil water and try pouring it on the door?" Gannet asked.

"First, we would need a fire, but the smoke might choke us out. And we would have to boil our only water. The snow could be piled high enough outside that it wouldn't matter," Stoat told him.

Pronghorn lent his strength even though it hurt his side. The added muscle wasn't enough. They struggled to turn the hatch wheel. It was a stopped clock, signaling the hour of their demise. When Cross Fox exhausted all possible options with Lynx and Hoatzin ceased her prayers, Lynx turned to Kestrel with pleading eyes. He knew what she wanted. It was his time to try his hand.

"Liberator," Lynx whispered.

Her whisper grew into a chorus, an anthem of sorts, as everyone chimed in. First Gannet, then Cross Fox, followed by Stoat, Hoatzin, and Cottontail. Muskox, Pronghorn, Bowhead, and Thinhorn started to chant. Shrew did too. Their call shook the very walls. The rhythm made Kestrel feel powerful, as if he could truly liberate them, as if he were more powerful than their false gods.

Only Caiman remained silent.

They didn't hear the creak from the metal over their chanting. Kestrel walked to the front, feeling the power of their prayers, the chanting. He knew he would have Lynx in the palm of his hand. The others would follow.

Hoatzin bowed as he passed, which made Kestrel want to beg her to rise, but the others were doing it too. They began to sway, to cry out and shake as if the gods touched them.

Kestrel put his hand on the wheel, gripped the curved metal ever so slightly, and tugged. It was small—nothing powerful or divine. No otherworldly or godly strength was bestowed upon him. It was time, strength, numbers, and body heat. The door shattered the fragile ice encasing it and budged with a groan.

Icy wind shot through the smallest crack to overtake all it could. Colder than the air of the tunnel, it felt like a frozen death.

"You did it," Shrew said in astonishment.

Kestrel looked at the thin line of blinding white slicing through the muddied yellow light. The air was cold and burned his lungs, but he took in a big, greedy breath.

All eyes were on him.

"Liberator," several of them said at once.

The eleven hurried to gather around him. To thank him, to touch, some to gaze on him in wonder. Only Caiman, furious in shock and confusion, stepped away from the mob.

"All hail the Liberator!" someone shouted.

The others joined in.

"Quiet," Hoatzin said, trying to calm the others down.

Kestrel looked for Shrew to find an anchor in the chaos. He

needed to be tethered down so the noise wouldn't go to his head and convince him he was something more.

"I am your Liberator!" Kestrel shouted, playing into the group's delusion despite trying to remain grounded himself. He quieted them by raising both of his hands. "We won't find *true* liberation until we reach the sacred mountain and see the gods," he continued, redirecting their attention to the task at hand.

They nodded their heads, and Lynx took back command of the group.

Kestrel got in line, and the others followed, except for Caiman, who opened the door with a hard push of his shoulder. It slammed against the ice-clad earth, sending a fine powder into the air.

Kestrel wondered at the flecks of frost dancing above him. They spun like stars in the coal-gray sky. The wind whipped around them as the mountains stood like silent judges, the thirteen of them spectators in a pit. He felt the chill and adjusted his fur and feather hat on his head, pulling his coat closer as the others prepared themselves for the frigid temperatures—pulling on coats, hats, and scarves, lacing up boots.

Lynx, Caiman, Hoatzin, Muskox, Pronghorn, and Thinhorn slipped their masks over their faces, concealing their identities. Kestrel saw the dividing line between the group. Those who perpetrated the wicked wild, bearing the faces of the wilderness, and those who looked like wanderers in the Hinterlands.

The wind touched his face, and he felt something land on his cheek. He pulled it off, and in between his gloved fingers he saw a feather. Kestrel held it out and let the wind take it back.

Lynx gestured for them to follow with a knitted mitt. Kestrel watched as she put her hand above her eyes to shield them from the blinding sunlight. It was a stark shift from the muted cave. Her body braced against the gale, Lynx moved forward onto the ground beyond the tunnel.

Kestrel couldn't tell if they would be trudging through snow or if solid, mountain steps were just below the surface of the winter landscape. With a crunch, Lynx sank to her ankles. The snow poured through the hatch, filling nooks and crannies. Their path looked slippery, but she waved for them to follow.

One by one, they went out into the storm until it was Kestrel's turn. He urged Shrew to go ahead and watched as footprints began to pile up. It would soon be his job to start erasing the evidence of their presence.

He wouldn't.

Caiman begrudgingly held the door open for him and pointed with his sharp eyes for Kestrel to get out of the corridor. He took his sweet time, savoring the fading warmth of the bunker behind them and punishing Caiman for his earlier threat.

"Move," Caiman commanded with a hiss. His teeth clattered as he tried to stand tall, to jut out his chest and loom with fear, claws at the ready.

Pathetic. Kestrel laughed in his face.

Caiman lunged at him, hands out, and immediately halted when he realized the silver tip of a knife was pressed against his throat.

"You coldblooded fuck," Kestrel leered. "I hope you die out on this mountain, buried under the snow with your underbelly cut from top to bottom. Come for me again, and the flies won't be the only ones feeding on your corpse."

"Lynx needs me," Caiman said as his Adam's apple tested the boundaries of the blade.

"She does," Kestrel agreed. "But there will be a time when you're no longer needed."

Kestrel sheathed the knife, and Caiman let out his breath. Kestrel shook his head and climbed out into the blistering cold. Lynx was waiting on them, eyes locked on the antechamber and the two players within.

"The two of you need to settle your score," she demanded. "We *all* must make it to the mountain. Every. Single. One. Otherwise, this will all have been for naught, and the gods will *not* be pleased."

"Understood," Caiman hissed as he closed the door behind him.

That door was the last remnant of any semblance of humanity until Kestrel could reach the village on the other side of the range. There was no turning back now. Was there ever? Kestrel put his hand on his stomach. The thought of killing and eating Caiman excited his belly like sharp teeth protruding from his stomach. Nature would offer him absolution if he satiated his hunger.

To keep up the appearance of taking over Bowhead's duty, he kicked the snow drifts over the icy metal door until it was nothing more than white oblivion.

Lynx nodded, the fur around her face and neck already tinged with slivers of frost. The cold turned her nose and cheeks beet red. Her yellow eyes glowed in the chalky swirls. Caiman followed Lynx to the front of the line. A dangerous choice, but his only one.

If only Kestrel had the rifle to aim and fire point-blank at the back of his head.

SEVENTEEN

THE NORTHERN PASS

The blizzard pummeled them for two straight days. If this was the path to the gods' abode, the gods must be punishing them or testing their faith. The weather in the northern pass was far worse than anyone could've predicted.

After trudging through the snow for hours, Kestrel second-guessed his escape plan, his frozen limbs feeling like they might snap off. He was barely able to keep track of the others; the blizzard made them fade in and out.

Lynx found a rock face to camp behind when there was a break in the storm. Cross Fox had brought two large tents from the bunker, and they had packed extra wool blankets, but it wasn't enough to keep out the cold. Kestrel packed into the flapping shelter and buried himself under the blankets beside Shrew, Stoat, Gannet, Cross Fox, and Cottontail.

Kestrel watched as his breath roiled into fog and put his hands under his armpits for warmth. His portion of flesh was hard as a rock, and their water bottles were almost completely frozen. The thundering gale shook the walls of the tent as the night howled.

At some point, he dozed off, waking to find his face icy cold. Starvation clawed at his body. He wished death would take him, but quickly changed his mind. Death would be too easy—it would mean *they* win, and he wouldn't let them win. Monsters never win.

He watched the wind shake the tent. Shrew drew closer to him, as intertwined as they could be within their layered sleeping bag. A bit of Shrew's wrist showed between his cuff and mitt. Kestrel wanted to lick it, taste him, eat him.

No, no, no.

He held his tongue, trying to bury his desire. He wanted to steal back a memory, to claw it away from whatever accident made him lose them in the first place. There was nothing to grasp. Not even his name. What was his name?

Kestrel.

"No, not Kestrel," he said out loud. If the others in his tent heard him, they didn't move. Maybe they were frozen little popsicles of fur and flesh. Dead. Would that be liberation too? Kestrel shook his head, the delirium dragging him under.

Day two was just as unkind.

It wasn't possible to consider anyone else as they climbed. Kestrel was so focused on following in Shrew's footsteps as he meticulously traced Stoat's path, who matched Cross Fox's light imprints, who had the difficult task of mimicking Gannet's walking pattern. Gannet could never understand what he was supposed to do.

Kestrel wanted to step out of line and make a second set of footprints, but it was impossible to know what path was safe to walk in the storm. Following in the others' steps was his only option if he wanted to stay alive.

"Keep marching!" Lynx shouted.

Her command was nothing more than a whisper on the wind. Lost words in the Hinterlands, lost souls climbing in vain, lost hope eaten away by frostbite.

It was too harsh already. Kestrel moved glacially slow, and at that pace, it would take longer than expected to reach the summit. He knew they might not be able to survive another night if the conditions did not relent.

Shrew slipped, falling into the ankle-deep snow with a whimper. Kestrel panicked, running to him and making sure he was okay. Despite the snow clinging to Shrew's rosy face, Kestrel knew he would be fine.

"You've got this," Kestrel encouraged him. He wasn't sure Shrew could even hear him over the snowy static of the pass. In a normal situation, a kiss might've sealed the promise, but he was afraid their lips might freeze together. Shrew nodded and kept moving.

The ever-increasing altitude began its thievery. It first stole Kestrel's breath from the edges of his nostrils. After getting away with it several times, the trickster gained a newfound confidence and took from the depths of his lungs. His breathing rapidly increased without warning.

Cottontail, clinging tight to Gannet, kissed her charm and looked back at Kestrel.

The hairs on his neck that weren't frosted to his skin rose. He felt like someone was behind him, breathing down his neck. He whipped around but couldn't see much. The world had become like ivory, drained of every identifiable color. He looked down and saw the mashed snow where they had tread, the evidence he was supposed to erase. The trail led all the way back to the hatch—breadcrumbs for anyone to follow. No one seemed to notice, especially with Bowhead out of position.

That was the point.

Trudging along, they grew colder by the second, their bones stiffening, their joints slowing—the mechanics of their bodies locked in frost. It was like a virus chasing them down, freezing every cell, icicles stabbing their innards. A fever would be nice. At least it would be warm.

Cross Fox stared up and around as if she were trying to find something. Kestrel looked too, but it was all static, white, and buzzing. Her head tilted, ears alert, eyes as thin and piercing as a sword's edge. Her mouth fell open. Then Kestrel heard what put fear on her face.

Gunshots rang out in the flurried air. Bullets eliminated the flakes in their path, colliding with the powdery snow around them. Little puffs bloomed like nuclear clouds.

One, two, three, four, five—maybe more.

Kestrel searched the pass, but nothing was visible.

Stoat pulled Cottontail off her shoulders. "Stay low," she instructed.

The unrelenting storm made it hard for the hunters to aim. Hoatzin continued with Gannet, Cross Fox, Stoat, and Cottontail, waved on by the rest, who would deal with the hunters. Gannet took Thinhorn's pack of bones as he passed.

"What did you do?" Bowhead yelled when he met Kestrel and saw the tracks in the snow. "You were supposed to keep us safe, to hide us!"

Kestrel stepped back, the hulking man in his face. Bowhead tightened his fist and pulled back his arm. Kestrel flinched, but Lynx grabbed Bowhead's bicep and pulled him back, shaking her head.

Caiman shot a scathing look at Kestrel and drew his gun. Pronghorn unholstered a pistol as Thinhorn pulled out a sniper rifle. They took the second bag of remains and placed it on a small ridge to their right to stabilize their weapons. Bowhead covered the tracks as best he could and piled snow on the pack of bones to hide the army green fabric. Then they all hid behind the ridge.

"Ready yourselves," Caiman commanded.

Muskox brandished himself with his hefty axe, Bowhead had a large knife similar to Kestrel's, and Shrew was handed a small blade no larger than a butter knife. It was all they had. They closed in on each other, a half circle turned outward, arms ready for a fight.

Where are they? Kestrel thought.

More shots, the sound of feet crunching ice, and voices rang out in the distance. Kestrel looked around and realized they blended in with their surroundings—their coats and hats were white with snow. That's why the hunters kept missing.

The hunters were as snow-blind as they were. They emerged from the blizzard like phantoms crossing through the veil. They were closer than any of them realized, guns raised and ready. Fire and ice collided as more shots hit the snow banks.

Caiman, Pronghorn, and Thinhorn peered through their scopes, aiming carefully before pulling the triggers. Kestrel counted—so far, four hunters were gunned down.

"How many could there be?" Lynx asked as she searched the horizon. She tugged on her bolo tie, fiddling with the amber stone, and praying under her breath.

"Four already. Two summers ago, I saw the largest group I'd ever seen. Six total, but there could be more now," Caiman said.

"More?" Shrew asked. "They would come up this far to hunt us?"

"They would pursue us all the way up," Lynx said, "if it meant stopping us."

Wind and the sounds of breathing filled Kestrel's ears. The hunters were silent, unmoving behind the thick snowy curtain. Kestrel wondered if it was over, or if they were regrouping.

"Do we move? Keep going up the mountain?" Lynx asked Caiman.

"Not yet."

Caiman adjusted his rifle and aimed. He fired once, listening carefully for any movement. In the groaning wind, Kestrel heard footsteps.

"They're coming for us," Kestrel said.

Fright and anticipation bloomed across the others' faces. Shrew moved closer to Kestrel and stared into his eyes, crystals frozen to his lashes. Kestrel shook off the premonition like it was a fly zipping around him and not a warning.

EIGHTEEN
FIRESTORM

From fifty feet away, a figure rose out of the chalky oblivion, perfectly camouflaged until he rushed toward them. Kestrel's heart began to race as Caiman turned to shoot. Another appeared through the fog of white, stealing his attention. Thinhorn fired. Pronghorn aimed and pulled his trigger, but his gun jammed.

The hunter pummeled toward them, gun ablaze. Muskox ran out to fight off the intruder. Lynx shouted something unintelligible as Thinhorn ran after Muskox. Bowhead hobbled after them, but it was no use.

"Beside you!" Kestrel shouted as he scouted the blizzard for hunters.

A hunter with a machete in his hand came out of nowhere. Muskox swung his axe but missed. Kestrel tried to shout a warning, but it was too late. The man hit Muskox in the side, felling him. Thinhorn swung his knife, nearly hitting the hunter, but the assailant dodged.

Muskox got up and tried to help Bowhead, but the first hunter had closed the gap, his gun locked on the man in front of him. Muskox froze with a deathgrip on the axe—locked in a stalemate while Thinhorn tussled with the second one. Kestrel watched, his pulse throbbing in his ears.

Caiman took down the hunter in front of him in a volley of fire. Pronghorn abandoned his jammed gun and pulled out a baton resembling a nightstick. He groaned as he raised it, wincing.

Bowhead finally gained the upper hand, slitting the throat of his opponent and decorating the mountainside with crimson confetti. Bowhead licked the blood from around his mouth and turned to the hunter who held Muskox hostage.

The hunter watched, his face shielded by a mask, the weapon in his hand shaking. Pronghorn and Bowhead closed in, their steps so slow no one noticed.

Until someone did.

Kestrel saw it first, but gave no warning as the hunter barreled out of the wintry gale, using his body weight to take down Pronghorn, who collided with Bowhead. Overpowered, they fell like dominoes. Kestrel concealed his glee, but as soon as they fell, Caiman and Thinhorn were at the pile of tangled bodies.

"Get on your knees!" Caiman shouted at the hunters, his gun aimed and ready.

"We must ask the gods what to do with them!" Lynx shouted from the small outcropping. Kestrel looked at Shrew warily. Two extra men meant Hoatzin would roll the Gambit Stones, and two would be sacrificed and eaten. Which two would be up to chance.

Kestrel remembered Caiman saying he could work them to his favor. If that were the case, he would ensure Kestrel was chosen. Then it would all be over. He felt a flood of fear for the first time and began to rise. If it were between him and the hunters, he would have to kill them himself.

As he stood, weapon in hand, Caiman pointed his gun upwards and marched them off into the static flurry. Kestrel bent back down and concealed his knife. He tried to see where they had gone, but the group had disappeared. He sprang up, trying to keep them in his sight—this might be his chance to kill Caiman in the chaos—but as soon as the figures became clear to him, Caiman pulled his trigger. Blood and brain matter splattered out the back of the first hunter's head, and his body went limp.

Fuck, Kestrel thought as Muskox took his axe and plunged it into the second one's chest, sliding down until it split open his gut. The bodies lay on the pristine white snow like a sacrifice on holy ground.

Kestrel watched the bloodshed, but he soon forgot that their deaths benefited him. All he could think of was their flesh. He put his hand on his belly as hunger raged inside him. He wanted to run, to snatch and devour their bodies.

"No!" Shrew yelled.

Kestrel turned to see another figure arise from the craggy face behind them. The last phantom had come to drag them down to the pits of hell. Kestrel ran as fast as he could. The hunter slashed at Shrew, cutting across his face. Shrew screamed, and Kestrel burned with fury.

"Caiman!" Lynx shouted, so loud and guttural the mountains seemed to shake.

Kestrel shrieked, brandishing his blade, and pushed Shrew behind his back. He fought the urge to check on his partner; it was life or death now. The silver edge of the hunter's knife clashed with Kestrel's. He held his own as they battled—a flash of mirrored metal and white flurries.

The hunter slammed a fist into Kestrel's stomach so hard he couldn't breathe. He fell back into the pillowy snow. He picked his head up as the hunter tossed Shrew aside. Lynx tried to run, but slipped on the ice, falling to the ground.

Shrew cried out in agony.

Kestrel forced himself up. Lynx was on her back, scrabbling away like a trapped animal. She backed against the bag of bones, the skeletons surrounding her. The hunter stood above her, pistol drawn and aimed at her forehead. Her cat eyes widened as large as saucers as the killer cocked the gun.

Blood spouted from his head.

The hilt of Kestrel's knife slammed into the hunter's skull. He pulled the long knife from the man's head, bits of brain and blood sliding out as the hunter's body fell to the ground at his feet. Lynx gazed up in astonishment.

Kestrel licked the blood off his knife and grinned, his teeth stained red, his eyes darkened. He examined the shrouded face, wanting to rip the mask off the mysterious hunter and take a deep bite. To eat the soft, warm, fresh flesh. The blood on his tongue was not enough.

Kestrel extended a hand to help Lynx stand and turned to his partner.

Shrew had been shot—friendly fire from Caiman or Thinhorn, most likely. A stray bullet intended for the hunter who attacked them. His shoulder was bleeding. Kestrel pressed on Shrew's wound as he cried. Kestrel held him, comforting him with soft words, trying not to pull his hand away to lick the wound.

Even Shrew could be a feast. He remembered the bite mark he left on his shoulder.

No, no, no. Kestrel tried to remember what was left of himself.

The last of the hunters eliminated, they could go on. Or so he thought. From the blizzard's blight, Caiman, Muskox, Pronghorn, Thinhorn, and Bowhead emerged. A sixth man was with them. Caiman couldn't control his devious smirk.

Kestrel clenched his jaw. He was wrong. Caiman would surely ruin him now.

"This one came after we killed the other two," Muskox said.

"The gods must decide," Caiman beamed as if he were honoring his own traditions and strictures. His eyes were fixed on Kestrel. Those sickly yellow eyes were hungry for flesh, ready to liberate Kestrel from his earthly form.

"Kestrel saved us!" Lynx shouted. She ignored the others and ran to Kestrel, wrapping her arms around him.

"The Liberator!" Lynx continued, and the others joined in.

Kestrel saw Caiman steam with fury, a burning coal in the cold.

"We must keep moving," Pronghorn interrupted, sensing Caiman's simmering anger.

"The others are ahead," Lynx assured them. "I told Hoatzin and Cross Fox to lead them to the cave. When we reach the cave, we'll deal with this one."

The hunter's eyes widened. Thinhorn and Muskox searched the man, stripping him of his rifle and knife. Pronghorn passed the gun to Kestrel.

Caiman glowered, pulling ropes out of the bag of bones and wrapping the bodies together like packages.

"Carry what is left in the bag," Lynx said to Shrew. "Thinhorn and Pronghorn will be responsible for keeping guard over the prisoner. Kestrel will guard me and provide backup."

Caiman and Muskox tied the ropes around their waists and across their chests. They would drag the dead bodies up the mountain to the cavern. Lynx reformed the line, but Bowhead insisted he remain in the back to erase any evidence of them. It would be quite the task, especially with his wounds and the bodies they carried with them. A trail of pink slush. Bowhead had no branch to destroy evidence, but he was more determined than ever.

Kestrel's plan had failed.

Not only had the hunters failed to kill off the thirteen, but they had also sacrificed themselves for naught. They were now nothing but frozen slabs of meat bound to be consumed. Then there was the matter of the survivor. Caiman would use him as an excuse to roll the Gambit Stones and—somehow—manipulate the results so that Kestrel would be ousted before they made it to the peak.

Death lingered ahead, beckoning him forward. He remembered the vision he had, how he walked out of the dark cave to see the bodies of the dead, the flies consuming what the vultures could not.

"We will feast!" Lynx shouted with glee. "The Eidolons provided one more meal to help us endure to the end. Bless the gods."

The others cheered as Lynx led them toward the cave. Kestrel couldn't stop thinking about the hunter they had with them. The march was worse than before. They were weighed down by the bodies they dragged, by Bowhead's need to clean, and by the still-raging blizzard hammering them from all sides.

As he walked, Kestrel tried to determine how Lynx knew where to go in the bleak, whitewashed landscape. She often looked to the stars and the others to help guide her, but with the ashen clouds above them, she couldn't see them. How did she know where to go?

The night set in as they climbed higher. The incline began to hurt his feet, and Kestrel winced as his boots rubbed against his ankle. Red sores bloomed on his skin. He wanted nothing more than to take off his shoes. If he did, he might end up like Cottontail.

Kestrel realized he didn't know how the little rabbit girl lost her foot. There was *so* much he didn't understand. Why had none of them regained their memories? Why did Lynx call them by animal names? How had he ended up there? The mysteries swirled like the falling snow, impossible to pin down. Even if he could hold a question in his hand, it would melt before he found an answer.

Maybe that was the point.

Kestrel walked slightly behind Lynx, like a guard protecting a queen. The procession came to a halt when the hunter fell to his knees, unwilling to go on. Pronghorn hit him in the head, and he fell over. Thinhorn glared at his brother, pushing him away.

"Keep moving," Thinhorn said, dragging the hunter back to his feet.

"How much farther?" Kestrel asked Lynx.

There was uncertainty in her narrow eyes when she looked at him. She huffed, and the fog of her breath filled the silence.

She never answered.

Kestrel wished he had a watch. At least then he would be able to estimate how much longer they had. Hours had to have passed. The idea of a manmade timekeeper on his wrist felt alien. The others were no help, and the weight they carried all but stopped them.

"We need to cut the dead weight," Kestrel suggested, then inwardly winced. The metaphor was a little too on the nose.

Lynx continued to ignore him.

"It's slowing us down. Nightfall has already come, and who knows if there are more hunters behind us. The longer we're out here, the more we risk dying either by gunfire or freezing."

"We are almost there." Lynx straightened her back like she was convincing herself of it, too. She certainly wasn't convincing him. Kestrel rolled his eyes and sighed through his teeth. If he weren't severely outnumbered, he would take the gun off his back and shoot Caiman, Lynx, Pronghorn, Bowhead, Thinhorn, and Muskox. In that order. Then he and Shrew could make it to the cave, lie to the others, overpower Hoatzin and Cross Fox, and escape by morning.

It wasn't necessary in the end.

"The cave entrance is just ahead," Lynx announced. To the right of it was an arrow made of bones, almost lost in the snow if not for the single red thread tied around the end.

Cross Fox.

Kestrel knew she was key to the whole operation. If Lynx wasn't around, he assumed she would be the leader. In fact, he wondered why Lynx was chosen in the first place. Caiman was the warrior, Hoatzin the seer, Cross Fox the planner, and Bowhead the concealer. Was leading her only purpose?

To be fair, the others' purposes weren't as clear either. Sure, Thinhorn had medical knowledge and Pronghorn's military training helped—especially since he had access to the bunker—but what of the rest?

What about me? Kestrel thought. Was he simply there to be a "liberator" or would he outlive them? Was it just the first word that came to Hoatzin?

The path veered to the right, and within a couple of hundred yards, they saw the entrance to the cave. It was a gloomy, dark maw on the side of the mountain, a hollow wound of rock and emptiness. The perfect hiding place for them. Silent rejoicing surged through them, and they picked up the pace. The group uttered huffs of relief as they reached safety.

NINETEEN
GANNET'S PURPOSE

The mouth of the cave was dark as the starless night in the Hinterlands. Kestrel looked at Lynx, worried. The cave appeared devoid of any signs of life.

"We hid here a long time ago," Lynx said. "The cave is a complex system of halls and chambers. They're farther in."

Kestrel gazed into the dark abyss before him. If the darkened door of the burnt cabin was a lion's jaw, this was the gaping maw of something far more threatening. For a moment, he swore that eyes stared back at him, as if the cave entrance were the face of a shrouded devil. He swallowed as he walked forward.

"I'll stay here until all are inside," Lynx assured him. "I need to get the bones they put out. We can't leave them behind. They deserve to meet the Eidolons on the mountain, too."

Kestrel turned around as Lynx stared off into the impenetrable storm clouds.

Shrew ran to his side, touching the bullet wound in his shoulder.

"How far do we have to go?" Kestrel asked as they walked down the inky black corridor. Warmth began to tease the two of them as they went further into the earth. They turned once more to see faint firelight dancing on the walls, creating little picture shows of shadows. Crackling wood and the heavy scent of pine and birch guided them.

"Until we're as far from the wilderness as possible," Shrew shrugged.

Following the twisting path that smelled of woodsmoke, they arrived at the chamber where the others had set up camp. A small fire burned, big enough to warm the space without smoking them out. A simmering pot of Hoatzin's brew boiled over it. Gannet leaned against a wall, gulping down the last of his rations. Cottontail was already fast asleep, burrowed beneath a pile of blankets.

"You made it!" Gannet said, his mouth full.

Stoat sighed with relief. She got up from her spot beside Cross Fox and Hoatzin and hugged Shrew, then Kestrel. "What of the others?"

"They're fine," Kestrel said.

"Are any of you wounded?" Cross Fox asked as she dug into a pack of extra medical supplies.

"Muskox has a small wound. The others are fine," Shrew answered.

"You were shot in the shoulder," Kestrel chimed in when Shrew failed to mention his wound.

Shrew turned red as Stoat pulled off his coat and checked the spot of his wound. "Cross Fox, could you hand me a bandage?" she asked, pressing gauze on the mark. Shrew winced.

"There's no exit wound," Cross Fox said. "It'll have to stay in for now. Thinhorn might be able to remove it later."

"There's one more thing," Kestrel said. Before he could say more, Caiman and Muskox walked in without their ropes or the bodies. They sat down, exhausted and breathless. Pronghorn and Thinhorn arrived with their guest shortly after, and everyone stared at the hunter.

"Oh my," Hoatzin said as she touched the container holding the Gambit Stones. She looked at Kestrel, then to Caiman, who confirmed her curiosity with a nod. Kestrel felt a bead of sweat on his forehead.

After a few moments, Lynx appeared with a broken-down Bowhead. Bowhead set down the bones and rope used to mark the path.

Cross Fox and Stoat handed out water and portions to all of them. Lynx pulled Cross Fox aside, and Kestrel listened carefully as Lynx told her that there were bodies in a different chamber of the cavern that needed to be taken care of at some point. There wasn't a rush since they were frozen solid over the course of their journey.

"We have some salt stored in an antechamber down the way," Cross Fox said. "I can start the process tonight. If needed, we could smoke them first and then preserve them. There's some coal rock in the far cavern as well as the cache of wood we left here from the spring years ago."

"No need to preserve them," Lynx said, holding up her hand. "We leave for the sacred mountain in the morning. It is only a day's journey, maybe more if this storm continues to worsen. Let's prepare a fire and roast all of them for a holy feast."

"There are some coals, I believe, down a hallway. I can start a fire and stoke them until we're ready."

"First, we must roll and see who the gods choose to take up the mountain and who is to be sacrificed for us." Lynx sighed.

"I hope it's Gannet," Cross Fox scoffed.

"Do not hope for such a thing," Lynx shot back. "You do not get to hope who the gods pick. They choose, and you obey. We do not pray for a choice."

Cross Fox nodded, rolling her eyes as she turned to Kestrel and the others. She gathered a few things before leaving their camping spot, Stoat following after her. The hunter was forced to sit, still bound in rope.

For the first time, Kestrel noticed how bulky the man was. He did not speak, nor was his pure white disguise removed from his face, but he was alive. His eyes flitted to and fro as he tried to understand what was happening.

Kestrel recalled the feast from his first night. Time was a circle. The vision of Grouse on the altar returned to him again and again. Kestrel had taken his place, and maybe now it was time for Kestrel's to be taken. Maybe his purpose had been fulfilled by saving Lynx, even if it was for selfish reasons. Maybe it was justice—penance for what he had done, even though it wasn't his doing. But he couldn't let himself be sacrificed. He had to save the others.

Kestrel downed his water bottle and ate half of his portion of meat. It wasn't enough. As the others gathered around the small fire, he thought of roasting flesh, the fresh bodies of the hunters dripping fat, their skin crispy. Kestrel joined the others and sat next to Shrew, acutely aware of his knife's weight on his hip. Beside them, Gannet woke up Cottontail for the coming festivities.

A feast.

Kestrel thought of all that was to occur. Would the Gambit Stones work in his favor, or would they pick another? There was the option that the hunter would be chosen, but how could he tell or sway it in his favor? If he lost the roll, then at least he wouldn't have to eat more flesh, but then he thought of the other possibility.

He could feast.

Caiman stood to talk with Lynx and Hoatzin. Kestrel watched their every move, trying to read their lips as Caiman had purposely turned his back. They spoke for a few minutes before disbanding. The warrior then turned to him, flashing a wicked grin.

"From the beginning," Lynx extolled, "the gods have asked me to help fulfill their purpose. To gather the thirteen, to initiate the new members into our people, to lead them to the sacred mountain. But there can only be thirteen of us. Whenever we cross paths with another, we let the gods decide their purpose. Some join our ranks to help us on the journey, while others serve us another way."

Kestrel noticed the others nodding along. Believing and agreeing.

"We are at such a crossroads again. At our last juncture, Kestrel joined our ranks, and the gods named him liberator. We all have our own purpose. Some have answered the call of the gods and others await their destiny, but rest assured, we will all serve the Eidolons in the end."

"Hoatzin," Caiman interrupted, eager to move on. "Are you prepared?"

Kestrel could see Caiman give her a curious and knowing look. Hoatzin nodded. The trap had been set, and Kestrel was about to fall victim to their scheming. He held his breath.

"We roll the Gambit Stones!" Hoatzin shouted. She took the six objects out of their canister and shook them in her hands. Each second passed dreadfully slowly for Kestrel. The sounds of the stones hitting against each other were like cannon fire. Tattering and splintering all his thoughts, sinking into the depths of his churning stomach.

Hoatzin released the stones, and they rolled on the rock floor until they came to a stop. The silver house key stopped short and pointed toward Kestrel. There was no way it could know he was there, no way to fake that. The eye rolled off toward the fire, stopping before getting too close. The gemstone shot little specs of light on the cave wall, the compass spun endlessly, the half wishbone clanked on the stone, and the die landed on a two—the black dots like eyes watching him.

Hoatzin raised a shaking, bony finger to Kestrel.

Just as they planned.

"No," Lynx shouted. Everyone turned to her, shocked and confused. "Kestrel is our Liberator. Read them again."

"The gods have spoken, Lynx," Caiman said, trying unsuccessfully to hide his smirk.

Kestrel stood up, unafraid.

Stoat and Shrew guarded him, watching what would happen next. Even Gannet stood up and positioned himself in front of Kestrel. Three stood with him, but it wouldn't be enough. All the brute force was on the opposite side.

"You are mistaken, Hoatzin." Lynx's voice dripped with desperation. "Look at them again, and you will see this is not the will of the gods. I'm sure this is a mistake."

"The gods have spoken. Do you doubt *my* purpose, or are you questioning the gods?" Hoatzin screeched. She bowed low to the Stones and picked them up, returning them to their container.

Caiman brandished a knife and charged at the four who stood in opposition. Pronghorn wasn't far behind. Lynx spread her arms to stop them, creating a stalemate. No one was sure what to do, especially since their own leader commanded them to halt.

"You can't change this one's fate," Caiman said, slinking slowly along the wall.

"As if you haven't stripped others of their chance to join us," Kestrel spat. "Lynx commanded you to stop on the mountain, but you killed the others. Their bodies are piled up in the caves because of you, and you think *she's* ignoring the wishes of the gods?"

It was good reasoning and self-preservation, not belief, that gave Kestrel the conviction behind his words. And if the looks on the others' faces were any indication, they were beginning to question Caiman too—particularly Thinhorn and Bowhead.

Everyone began to shout. It was as if an organ ruptured—a violent outburst, a chaotic undoing, a body fighting against itself. Caiman leapt at Kestrel, but Lynx caught him by the collar. Stoat and Shrew stood at the ready, but Gannet seemed to vanish. Pronghorn stepped back, and Thinhorn grabbed his shoulder, trying to reason with him.

Muskox tried to grab Kestrel himself, but Kestrel dodged him. The Gambit Stones fell to the floor at his feet as he saw Cottontail pull the container away from Hoatzin. Cross Fox came at him with a knife, but Stoat grabbed her by the wrist. The two began shouting at each other. Shrew held onto Kestrel, extending his machete to guard him.

The whole cave devolved into animalistic rage. Bodies thrashed, screaming and punching, as they fought each other. Amidst the riot,

Kestrel noticed the hunter struggling to his feet, working to undo the tied ropes.

He wasn't the only one to notice.

The shadows moved as the blur overtook the hunter. Relief and sorrow swept through Kestrel as the hunter writhed on the floor of the cave, blood spurting from his neck. The killer's weapon clattered to the cave floor, silencing the fight. The raging storm that compelled them to fight each other seemed to quiet into a calm sea—even if the current pulled beneath the surface.

Kestrel gulped and released a breath.

Another death that spared his life.

"What did you do?" Hoatzin shrieked.

"What I had to do," Gannet stood tall and proud with the long knife at his feet. "None of you remembers my purpose. You think I'm too stupid, incapable of fulfilling it."

Lynx started to rebuff his statement, but Gannet held up his hand.

"I hear you talking about me. I know what you say about me. He's lazy, he's dumb, he's worthless, he's a burden, he's a glutton. Maybe I am. But does anyone remember my purpose?"

Silence.

"Preventer," Hoatzin said slowly.

Kestrel let the words sink in. He choked back tears of gratitude as he watched Gannet examine the blood on his hands. Then Gannet looked at all of them, one by one. He locked eyes with Kestrel and nodded. Confidence puffed up his chest. He was proud of himself.

"I prevented the death of our Liberator. That was my purpose all along. Some of you seemed to think I was preventing you from getting to the sacred mountain, preventing you from eating, since I ate so much. But that hunter would've killed us given the chance, and I prevented you all from dying before we reached the top."

"And in doing so," Stoat chuckled, "you fulfilled your purpose."

And saved my ass, Kestrel thought.

"You can thank the gods at your leisure," Gannet said as he sat down beside the hunter.

"Let's put this behind us and prepare," Hoatzin said with a forlorn sigh. "The gods have *clearly* chosen who they want to be a part of the thirteen. Pronghorn, Thinhorn, please set the next chamber up for the rite."

Caiman's jaw was tight.

Kestrel waited. It was hard to imagine that the threat of sacrifice was over. Pronghorn and Thinhorn left the room, dragging the bones with them. Hoatzin enlisted Cross Fox and Stoat to help her with the spirits. Caiman, Muskox, and Bowhead were sent to ready the fire, and Shrew took Cottontail by the hand as they set off with a few supplies Cross Fox gave them.

"Thank you," Kestrel said to Gannet. Warmth nestled within him, a kindness bloomed, and Kestrel realized that Lynx and Gannet both saved his life.

"Why did you do it?" Kestrel asked.

Lynx stood nearby—not too close but within earshot.

"You showed me mercy," Gannet said. "I'm meant to prevent. Maybe my mistakes helped us in the end, saved us from crossing paths with the hunters. Maybe I can prevent the worst."

Kestrel's stomach roiled. If it was his purpose, then Kestrel was eternally grateful for the strange rituals. Now they were bound together, corded in a life debt, only to be unbound in death. Gannet had to be freed. He was too good to be out here.

Lynx didn't say anything, only watched and waited.

"I'll fill them with snow. It should melt into water by the morning," Gannet motioned to the water bottles, taking as many as he could carry as he left the room.

Lynx moved over to the body of the hunter and removed his mask. She gasped.

Kestrel hurried to her side. The hunter was a woman. She was wrapped in heavy gear, all but hidden. Much like them. But the huntress maintained her humanity, had not given in to the darkness that lingered out here. Her face looked more real than his own.

Had she known?

The question raced through Kestrel's mind. Had she known what they were? If they'd been hunting animals, they would've stopped once they realized they were humans—unless they knew the whole time. Maybe Lynx was right. Maybe they were trying to stop them. But why?

Kestrel wished he could wake her up to ask her the questions that haunted him. When Lynx began to strip her down, Kestrel decided to leave out of respect for the dead.

It was just like the first night he awoke. Only this time, he was responsible. This time, he was hungry. Starving.

Before he left the chamber, he heard Lynx singing softly to the woman, her voice dripping with sorrow. The hall was long, but Shrew came to guide him down deeper into the cave system.

Following the noise, Kestrel arrived in a huge room that reminded him of an amphitheater. Rows of rock seemed to slope down to one central spot. In the middle, a pyre had been assembled to hold and cook the hunter's body, and alongside it, a small fire.

Above him hung the bones of those who came before. The red cords appeared almost rust colored in the dim light of the earthen auditorium. Kestrel didn't question how Pronghorn and Thinhorn managed to get up there, but he could see that each bone-cord was tightly wrapped around a stalactite, and extra rope was suspended between the pointed rocks. A spiderweb of crimson intertwined in the soot-colored formations, dirtied and permanent spikes that felt like teeth. He was in the mouth of a dangerous and foreboding god, the tongue below him, the throat full of fire and ready to consume.

A monster of their own creation.

In a moment, he would become the monstrous creature himself. Kestrel tried to resist the hunger, to step back from that precipice before it was too late. But he'd already partaken. There was blood in his stomach, dried flesh between his teeth, and the bodies of others intermingling with his own. He'd communed with the wild, and he'd *enjoyed* it.

The coals Cross Fox and Stoat prepared stoked a few pieces of wood under the altar constructed for the feast. In a moment, the hunter's body would be placed there, prayed over, and painted with flicks of fire—gleaming amber, vivid carmine, and simmering yellow.

Hoatzin stirred her brew one final time before announcing she would need everyone to join her in the procession. During the last sacrifice, Kestrel was just coming to, uninitiated and sick to his stomach.

How fast things change, he thought.

The others finished their duties and proceeded back to the chamber where Lynx was still preparing the body. Kestrel trailed them, and when he arrived, he noticed the bare body on the floor. Lynx had stripped the woman of her clothes, cleaned her body, and trimmed her hair.

Seeing the look on his face, Stoat whispered to Kestrel, "So it doesn't ruin the taste. Burnt hair is the worst."

"Especially without sap to sweeten it," Shrew added.

Kestrel didn't need the syrup of the trees. He would even be willing to eat the hair, as long as he got to taste fresh flesh. He remembered his disgust at Hoatzin's gift during his initiation. It seemed so far away now. Would a bite of her taste any better now?

Lynx invited everyone to take their position. She stood at the head and waited for others to surround the body. Kestrel followed the lead of those around him. They bent down and all grabbed the hunter's body. His hands held the hunter's soft flesh, and when commanded, he lifted the vacant frame to his waist. Her body smelled of musk, and Kestrel felt insatiable.

TWENTY
SILENCE

The path back through the cavern hall felt claustrophobic, like the walls were closing in on Kestrel. The procession was slow, almost sacred, as if grief had placed a hand on their shoulders and sung a dark lament, soft and fleeting as the moment before death.

Death—holy, sacred, ceremonial.

They ferried the bodies down the corridor like Death himself. If they were death's couriers, Kestrel wondered who the god of the underworld would be. Lynx? She had certainly claimed her fair share of souls—but was she the ruler or the messenger? He supposed in the end it didn't matter. Either way, there was a dead woman who didn't deserve this fate, didn't deserve to be cut down, only for her bones to be tied up in crimson cord and hung from whatever lofty place someone could find.

Down to the altar they marched. Lynx sang her dark lullaby—a hymn of the Eidolons, Kestrel supposed—to soothe the living and the souls that lingered with them. He felt her presence behind them, watching her own funeral. He prayed she would find peace, that her soul might escape the cave and find paradise.

A tear fell from Kestrel's eye, but he didn't know if it was shed for the woman or himself, for who he had become. Because he wasn't just sad—he was hungry.

The bearers took the woman down to the pyre, set her on the altar, and moved away. The bodies of the other hunters were already there. Lynx and Caiman arranged coals next to her body, stoked the flames, and her skin started to crisp. Hoatzin found her brew and stirred it once more. The other ten stood a few feet away, a semicircle of wolves ready to pounce, to rend flesh asunder, and tear it apart in their jaws. He couldn't stop looking at her tender flesh.

Devourers.

Kestrel remembered how he thought of them that first night.

I am one of them.

"This is the sacrifice," Lynx said as she bowed before the woman's body. When she rose, a strange light glimmered in her wide, round eyes. She turned to Caiman, who bowed in response and called out, "The time is now!"

"Hoatzin," Lynx said, turning to address her. "Have you prepared the spirits?"

"The spirits are ready," Hoatzin trilled as she bowed to Lynx. Her eyes were eerily distant behind her feathered leather mask.

They were three stars exalted: Caiman's eyes shone with power, Hoatzin's eyes flooded with insight, and Lynx's catlike eyes beamed with harmony. As they stood on high, the others bowed their heads. But Kestrel kept his head up, observant.

A sweet scent filled the chamber as the masses waited for their morsels. The smell of roasting meat and crisping skin wet Kestrel's mouth. He tried to dismiss it, to wish it away, and be someone better. The duality waged war within him, but his old self, whomever that may be, was about to lose once and for all.

Were the others like him, too? Could Shrew and Stoat be cursed with the same affliction, or was he alone in feeling the immense desire to consume human flesh? How could he return home like this?

The questions were wiped from his mind as the scent of meat tickled his nostrils.

"Thank you, hunter, for your sacrifice," Lynx said as she raised her arms high in the air. "We are able to go on because of your death. Your blood will be our blood, your flesh our flesh, and your life our life. We are one."

Hunter.

The word sat heavily on Kestrel's chest. They didn't even know her name. The woman had only been with them for a few hours, and the last moments of her life were spent hiking up a sharp incline and freezing through a blizzard, only to be met with the horrors that surrounded her now. She hadn't even spoken, her voice cut from her. Silence was her name.

The smell soon overpowered his thoughts.

His hand trembled, as if he were a puppet pulled by strings, and the puppeteer was his belly. Lynx, Caiman, and Hoatzin stepped forward, and the rest mimicked their leader. Lightheaded, Kestrel's mind fled him, and instinct took over. He reached for the hunter's body.

Kestrel clawed into her thigh, ripping through the crispy skin, her carrion under his nails. Her flesh was soft and tender. Bringing the handful to his mouth, he salivated over the pink and white meat before he nipped at the shreds. Juice and blood flowed from the corners of his mouth. He wiped it and licked his fingers.

Something woke within him—an ancient spirit, a creature with a hundred teeth—and he devoured the rest. Bits of flesh hung from his mouth. The smoky, sweet flavors of oak, hickory, and coal teased his senses.

The others dug in. Cottontail sank her little teeth into the woman's leg, Gannet sucked on her fingers, and Lynx ate from her collarbone. Caiman leaned over the hunter's body and cleaved her chest, eating bits off the ribs, but hunting for the heart.

Within minutes, the hunter, whom Kestrel had named Silence, was almost nothing but bones. Her gray-white frame had been left exposed, her heart shared by Caiman and Lynx, and her other organs divided among the rest.

Bowhead went for the liver, but Kestrel pushed him out of the way and stole it from him. It was his. He ate it like fruit, supple and sopping wet. As if they were the pinnacle of the god's creation, the Hinterlands their garden, and organs their forbidden fruit. Kestrel worked the last flecks of meat from under his fingernails after he shared a lung and kidney with Shrew.

Kestrel should have felt different. He should've regretted what he'd done, found himself naked in the garden, fled from their presence, hidden himself with fig leaves, and waited for the gods to find him. But he didn't feel guilty or ashamed.

He felt satisfied.

Silence hung on his lips. Kestrel tried to use his tongue to get out the bits of flesh lodged between his teeth. He tasted her again and smiled. There was a part of him that wanted to pretend he didn't have a choice, that he had to blend in with the thirteen, to ensure his position until he could escape, but that would be a lie.

He tried to shake the feeling, but it wouldn't flee. He was content, for now, to be among the devourers.

Shrew wrapped his arms around Kestrel and leaned against him. Kestrel kissed his partner's head, smelling his hair. Shrew nuzzled in, and they relished in their love. Their love was not a monstrous thing —it was divine and pure. It was good.

Even if Kestrel was not.

Hoatzin stirred the spirits and pulled a ladle from the depths of the pot. Cross Fox helped her fill bottles and passed them out to each person. Each container was half full—more spirits than he drank during his initiation or on the day of the first snow.

Kestrel took his first sip. The elixir was strong, so potent he heard Gannet cough after he took a swig. Shrew threw his back, but Kestrel took his time.

"How long will it take?" Kestrel asked.

"Minutes," Shrew answered, looking up at Kestrel with an infinite kindness in his eyes. "You might trip a little, see colors or hear music, or you might see a vision of the gods."

"All I want to see is you and me," Kestrel whispered in his ear, "free from this place."

He kissed Shrew's lips, the taste of him like the sun breaking the clouds. Rays of indulgence and heat shot through him. Whatever happened next, he wanted to experience it with Shrew.

Kestrel wanted to take in his partner, to breathe his scent, to taste him, to bite him, to consume him in the way only a lover's hunger can. He bit Shrew's lip.

Nothing was said between them, but the spirits began to take their effect. With each kiss, each touch, streams of ecstasy flowed, their senses heightened by the drink. Everything seemed to sing. The bite on Shrew's lip struck a chord, the kiss on his collar played a key, and a touch on his chest sang a melody. Hands and bodies collided in a harmonious song that lovers and bards could have played on for all time and through the ages if only they had heard it. Kestrel lay down and stared at the bones above him.

The bodies of the dead made beautiful music.

Kestrel felt his mind slip, felt his essence rise skyward, but before he left this body, he turned his head.

Cross Fox kissed Stoat, their hands running over each other's bodies. Lynx joined in, kissing Cross Fox on the neck and grabbing Stoat's breast, rubbing softly. He looked away to the other side of the room. Gannet had a hand behind his head like a pillow, Cottontail resting on his stomach, and both stared off and smiled. Thinhorn and Pronghorn laughed together until Pronghorn's side hurt too much. Bowhead cupped Muskox's face in his hand and nipped at his chin as Muskox leaned against the cavern wall. Hoatzin appeared asleep.

Kestrel saw Caiman staring at him, eyes wilder than ever, fury and green fire scorching his irises. A hiss came from his split tongue, and the scales on his body seemed to shine iridescent in the glow of the embers. His lips pressed together, his brows furrowed.

He exhaled. A greenish-gray smoke expelled from his mouth and clouded all that was around him. The air turned foul and toxic. Kestrel began to choke, his eyes filled with acrid tears until he could no longer see.

Then he was in the village.

Red cords tied to each building held them suspended like a web. From there, the ropes jutted out and plunged into the earth, extended like roots. Kestrel went to the nearest building. There was no door on the rusted hinges, so he entered. The rooms were nondescript, painted bone white, but the floor was squishy, made of pink and scarlet fibers. With each step, it pulsed with light.

The house led him to a back bedroom. Inside, a shrouded body lay on the bed. The floor urged him to approach; the walls asked him to unveil the body. The whispers that stirred through the house wanted him to listen.

He obeyed.

Kestrel threw off the sheet and couldn't breathe. It wasn't the stench, the maggots crawling about, or the flies that repulsed him. It was the face of the departed.

It's me, Kestrel whimpered. He wanted to leave, to run far away, but a great earthquake shook the room, preventing his escape. The roof broke open above him. He moved out of the way and hid in a corner. A giant hand reached through the crack of the ceiling and felt around before picking up the house. Looking out of the window, Kestrel could see that he was being lifted high above the mountains of the Hinterlands.

The walls began to crumble and fall away, shattering and falling to the ground like snow until all that was left was the beating floor, the body, and himself. The red cords tying it to the earth had loosened. He was ascending in the skeletal palm of a hand.

A shrouded face appeared before him. He could not make out who it was, but the veiled being opened his mouth. Kestrel expected to see teeth, but no teeth protruded from the gums. Instead, mountain peaks rose, icy rock sharpened to slice.

Hollow sockets for eyes glowed like Lynx's amber stone, and flies swarmed the creature's nostrils. Kestrel, his own dead body, and the room around him fell into the shrouded one's mouth. A tongue of freezing water lashed against him, strong as a river.

Kestrel got caught in the undercurrent and tried to surface for air. He struggled until he broke through the thrashing waves. Before him, his dead body tossed and turned. He tried to swim for it, but no matter how hard he kicked and paddled, the decaying corpse floated further away.

The flood plunged him into absolute darkness. He tried to find his corpse—whether to use it as a life raft or to somehow save it, he wasn't sure. The water around him smelled of the spirits, fermented and past its expiration date.

He could see light above him, so he swam up. Churning in the inky oblivion, stars appeared.

He inhaled sharply as someone grabbed his ankle, tugging him below the surface. Kestrel fought and kicked against the assailant, but couldn't see who had him by the foot. The struggle went on until he was fully submerged. When he could no longer hold his breath, the salty water stung his throat and nostrils.

Kestrel opened his eyes in the murky depths and saw who dragged him under. It was a former version of himself he no longer recognized. They sank like cement blocks.

The dark water wavered, melting into another vision.

The sun beamed brightly. Kestrel's blurry eyes focused, and he realized he was under a wide tree on a summer day. He sat up and caught his breath, feeling his body and the velvety blanket beneath him.

Shrew sat up beside him and placed a hand on his back. He examined Kestrel, his face etched with concern. He had no words as he tried to understand what he was seeing.

There was a lake in front of him, and kids swam in the water as their parents sat on a dock. To his right, two young girls played with a Frisbee, and to his left, just past Shrew, a man and his dog walked down a paved trail.

"Where am I?" Kestrel asked as he tried to orient himself.

"The lake," Shrew said, laughing softly. He took Kestrel's hand and squeezed it before resting his head on Kestrel's shoulder.

Kestrel's chest rose and fell, faster and faster. The sounds were too much—too right, too confusing. He fell backwards, taking Shrew with him, and the people around him became buzzing flies and swirls of snow. He was back on the mountain now, climbing higher, almost to the top. His hands were bloody and raw, and his fingernails looked more like talons.

Snow pelted him, and ice-hard shards sliced into him. His feather coat was not enough to protect him. Kestrel began to run from the coming storm, from pummeling spears of frost, but there was nowhere for him to go. He wanted to go back to that memory, to the lakeside.

A knife flew past him, tumbling hilt over blade, and struck a tree heavy with snow. Another came, clipping his cheek. He held his hand to it and turned around. Someone stood in the blizzard shining like a light. They approached, hidden behind the hunter's mask.

Kestrel couldn't see their eyes, but they bent down and kissed him on the cheek where he had been sliced. He noticed a foot around their neck—just like Cottontail.

The mysterious figure took a third knife and raised it above their head. Kestrel kicked the concealed person in the leg, slipping on the snow as he got up and tried to run away. The killer advanced on him, but was losing ground.

Before him stretched an endless runway of white. Kestrel put his arms out to shield himself; when he did, he felt the wind swirl under them, lifting him ever so slightly. He tried it again. The gale caught on his coat, and he began to fly. He flapped his arms and rose above the onslaught.

Kestrel soared high like a bird in flight. A house came into sight— familiar, but out of place in the Hinterlands. He flew toward it, curious if it was a safe place to nest. It was a short distance away, but the wind began to whisper around him. It spoke in an unknown language, reminding Kestrel of a poem. It was deep and spiritual, speaking truth while leaning into the beauty and devastation of the world. The wind beckoned him back, to turn away from the house, to return to the mountain range behind him.

The wind was hungry.

Violent, emptying, unnerving hunger.

A current carried him to the left, back toward the pinnacle of the sacred mountain. From this height, he could see several people standing there, covered in shrouds and watching the skies. A gust blew around Kestrel, funneling down to the peak. The shrouded ones dispersed, their clothes caught on the wind—nothing but fabric on the breeze.

The whispers called to him, and he landed on the sacred mountain. He spread his wings and screamed. The whole world melted into a singular point. The burning heart inside his chest released a plume of black smoke, flies, and splatters of blood. Even the whispers were obliterated.

He was alone.

Kestrel blinked, back in the cave.

"You had a vision of the gods, yes?" Hoatzin asked as the smoke receded.

"What did you see?" Lynx said, staring into his eyes. Kestrel looked past her as he tried to find Shrew's face in the onlookers. Caiman grit his teeth and fumed. The others must've been free of the spirit's effects. Shrew stood nearby, his brows raised in worry, while Stoat drank water, watching him with curiosity.

"Silence and liberation," Kestrel said.

TWENTY-ONE
A SLIPPERY SLOPE

estrel sat on his mat, sipping the last of his water and watching as Shrew discarded his bandage. He took fresh white gauze from Cross Fox's stash and reapplied it. Kestrel saw the dried blood on the wrappings and wished he could take Shrew's pain away. He looked at Stoat and mouthed "tonight." She nodded and looked at Gannet and Cottontail.

They were all close to the exit of the chamber. Gannet sorted through the hunter's belongings and folded her clothes. He set the stack next to Cross Fox's sleeping bag so she could stow it away, but there was one thing Gannet didn't place on the pile. He slid something into his pocket and made sure that no one saw him—except Kestrel. He looked from Cross Fox to Stoat and raised an eyebrow in question. Stoat shook her head, pursing her lips.

It was a curious thing to Kestrel, how Stoat was willing to leave her partner behind. Even after a couple of weeks, he knew he wouldn't leave Shrew.

"I'll keep watch," Kestrel said, ensuring his plan would go off without a hitch. He wished they could take Bowhead with them, have him erase their trail, but it wasn't worth the risk. They had to hurry to the top of the mountain and start down the other side. Even if Bowhead were on their side, he would slow them down.

"No," Caiman challenged..

Kestrel saw the knife in his hand—the same one he used to cut the red cord for the hunter's bones. "More could come once they realize the others are missing."

"Caiman is right," Lynx said. "He will protect us. That is his purpose. We need him now more than ever."

Kestrel chewed on his lip, and Caiman smirked. While the others prepared for bed, Thinhorn and Pronghorn brought in a heap of hot coals from the other cavern room to keep their chamber warm through the night. The men piled the coals in a heap where the small fire had been.

Shrew and Kestrel curled up next to each other, and Kestrel found himself wishing for a hundred more nights like this, but safe in the human lands. It frustrated him that he still couldn't remember any details of his former life. Where had it all gone? Why were his memories stripped from him when he woke that first night? He begged the gods to give him just a piece back. What was a dream and what was a memory? Shrew was there with him... How could that be?

Stoat finished repacking her things, careful to steal a few essentials here and there, making sure Cross Fox didn't notice. Kestrel felt sorry for her. She was about to abandon the woman that she loved in order to help him.

He threw his arm over Shrew, kissed him on the cheek, and lay down. Shrew rolled over, but Kestrel stayed wide awake. Even now, he felt Caiman's eyes scanning over him, the predator carefully tracking his prey.

Time was viscous—thick and slow that night, like sap threatening to sluggishly consume him and fossilize him in amber, forever lost in the mountain. Kestrel had to begin their escape soon. He sat up and looked around the room. The embers cast a dim glow, and Caiman's yellow-green eyes were on him.

Kestrel nudged Shrew and pretended to stumble as he got up, kicking Stoat in the shin. Down the corridor, he went into an empty chamber and relieved himself, the sound distracting him from the man who crept up behind him.

When he turned, Caiman stood behind him. Kestrel zipped up his pants and pushed past Caiman, making sure to bump into him on his way back.

"Watch it, boy," Caiman said, brandishing his knife in his hand, the silver glinting in the midnight blue of the cavern. Kestrel rolled his eyes and kept walking. Caiman hissed and followed him, but Kestrel didn't walk back into the room where the others slept.

The walls of the amphitheater room were coated with soot, and the stalagmites dripped with the savory flavor of the hunters, even though the bones had been taken down and tucked away. Kestrel walked all the way to the remnants of the altar, its wood ashen and crumbling into the cinders below.

"Why are you following me?" Kestrel asked.

"I don't trust you," Caiman said, slithering closer. "You may have saved Lynx, but I can see the deceit in your eyes. You don't belong among us, and if we weren't moments from the mountain crest, I would gut you and slurp on your intestines."

"Too bad you can't," Kestrel said, and laughed at Caiman's crooked smile. He dismissed him with a wave of his hand. He walked around to the other side of the altar and glared at Caiman.

"Your little friend saved you. You're lucky I didn't slice his neck the last time he ruined something for the rest of us."

"It must be hard," Kestrel said with a smirk, "to feel that you're being replaced."

"I'm not!" Caiman shouted. "I have a purpose, and I will keep carrying it out until the end."

"And yet you would jeopardize and delay your eternity to kill me?"

Caiman narrowed his eyes and waved his knife by his side like an excited dog. He was a vicious hound, ready to hunt, rabid with hate and jealousy.

Kestrel put one hand on the hilt of his own knife. Lynx was a collar around Caiman's neck, pulling him back when he got too ferocious. Kestrel wondered if it was time to let the dog off its leash.

"You don't even believe in the gods of the *fucking* sacred mountain. You're a blasphemer using them for your own benefit," Caiman said, pointing the knife at him. "When we get to the abode of the gods, they will smite you for your deception."

"Not before I kill and devour you. Though you don't look very tasty," Kestrel sneered. "I bet you taste as good as you smell."

The taunt worked. Caiman stepped sideways and moved in line with Kestrel, knife held out. He inched closer, but Kestrel did not move. There was no reason to; he had the upper hand.

Caiman charged. Kestrel dodged the knife, pulling out his own blade. The warrior stumbled, then crouched low and fortified his stance. He swayed back and forth to find the right angle for his next attack.

Kestrel snorted. It was almost too easy. He backed up slowly, knife out, until his heel bumped into a large stalagmite. He quickly glanced behind him and grinned at the rock pillars, tall and sharp.

Caiman lunged for him again, leaping off the ground with immense force. Kestrel stepped aside swiftly, letting fate take its course. He watched as Caiman fell forward, skewered by a stalagmite —a holy punishment for a wicked man.

The fall didn't kill him—not instantly. Blood trickled down the conical rock formation as its tip penetrated Caiman's abdomen. He struggled to free himself, but his leg was lodged on a smaller stalagmite. His limbs twitched like a bug.

Kestrel laughed and picked up a piece of simmering coal. He stood over Caiman, leering at him as he tried to call out for help. The coal singed his fingers, but he felt no pain. Caiman rallied his strength and began to scream, albeit weakly. Kestrel leaned over the man, pressing the coal to the lizard man's lips. His flesh sizzled, mimicking the hiss that Caiman so often uttered.

"Hush," Kestrel commanded as he pulled the coal away.

Caiman's mouth was sealed by fire, a plea in his eyes, his voice silenced. Kestrel stood like an angel above him—monstrous, shining, and horrifying. He saw himself as a savior—a servant of the light who would purify any darkness from the world. He tossed the coal back into the heap.

When he returned to the chamber, Stoat and Shrew were lining their packs in the hall outside. They moved back into the eerily quiet chamber to get the rest of their supplies. Stoat cradled Cottontail in her arms, carrying the sleeping girl out into the hall. Gannet walked out into the hall with a yawn.

Kestrel picked up his pack. Together, they snuck out of the cave. Before they reached the entrance, Stoat grabbed his shoulder. He slung his rifle around to his back as she passed Cottontail off to him and ran back into the darkness.

When Stoat returned, she took Cottontail back from Kestrel, her knife in her hand. They moved through the caverns, silent and tired. The air grew colder as they approached the entrance of the cave.

Oh no, Kestrel thought.

If the trek up to the cave was bad, this was worse. The blizzard continued in the onyx night. Snow dotted his face as the wind whipped it around the craggy rocks.

"We're getting out of here," Kestrel said, trying to encourage the others as they began to walk. "We can't go back through the tunnel to the bunker, so we have to go to the top of the mountain. There's a village on the other side. If we can make it there, we'll make it out."

His confidence inspired their weary, bleak outlook. Shrew nodded and grabbed Kestrel's hand. Stoat, holding Cottontail, proceeded to walk, while Gannet gripped the hilt of his knife and adjusted the straps of his pack.

"Gannet," Kestrel said, looking at the young man. "Will you keep watch at the back?"

Gannet agreed, standing up tall and proud.

"We have a few hours on the others as long as they don't wake," Stoat assured them. "If they do, they'll be on us in a blaze, and I wouldn't put it past Caiman to slaughter us all."

"We don't need to worry about him. I took care of that," Kestrel said. He kept moving, refusing to allow the others to ask further questions. He recognized the look on their faces.

"If you hear or see anything, don't hesitate to shout," Stoat commanded the others.

Blistering snow and hail made their journey painfully slow. Combined with the lack of sleep and no noticeable path forged for them, Kestrel fought to get ahead of the eight who remained hidden beneath the earth.

Seven, he thought. There were only seven now.

Either Muskox, Pronghorn, or Thinhorn would likely be the first to reach them. If they did, Kestrel would unleash his simmering fury. As he climbed, his long-suppressed emotions emerged. Tears froze in the corner of his eyes. He had been through so much, and now freedom was a slippery slope before him.

Hours went by in silence. Only the mercurial wind continued to whisper and roar—some moments furious and raging, others calm and delicate, but always cold and unforgiving. Hail pelted them, the little orbs of ice shattering like a dropped snow globe.

Cottontail woke for a bit when Stoat switched places with Gannet, and he took the little girl on his back. She kissed the foot that hung around her neck for good luck and said a prayer to the gods for safe travel. Gannet had to hold tight to her little hands locked around his neck.

"Can we stop for breakfast?" Gannet asked. "I'm hungry."

"Me too!" Cottontail said.

"We can stop for a few minutes, but we have to keep going," Kestrel replied as they halted and circled.

Stoat dropped her pack, and it slumped in the snow as she pulled out a few MREs and put them to the side for when they'd make camp. Kestrel wasn't sure they would stay still for that long. She searched through her pack and found four satchels of nuts and fruit. She offered to share a portion with Cottontail.

Gannet took his portion and ate quickly, almost choking on the food until Shrew told him to slow down and savor it. He nodded and ate one half of a walnut. Cottontail munched on a dried apple and hopped around to stretch her legs.

"I need to relieve myself," Stoat said. She left her pack and wandered toward the tree line.

Kestrel watched her walk away. Something in him wanted to mimic Bowhead, to follow her and erase her from existence. He ignored it. Being unseen wasn't important anymore. He would risk it all to get out.

"Want some?" Shrew asked as he held out a little bundle. Kestrel kissed him on his cold, flushed cheek and took some nuts. He juggled them in his hand before throwing them back. He spat them out immediately.

"Are they bad?" Gannet said, looking up at him.

"Try them," Kestrel said as he pointed to Shrew's bundle.

Shrew sniffed it, nibbled on a nut, and ate it. He shrugged and ate a few more.

"Tastes fine to me," Shrew rebuffed. "Want some fruit?"

"What else do we have?" The thought of nuts and fruit made him wince in disgust. He rummaged through Stoat's pack. Pulling out the white cloth, he turned it over and realized it was the hunter's mask.

Why does she have this? He thought. Stoat already had her fur hat on, but maybe she thought someone might need it later. Kestrel kept digging and found some dried meat. The smell of smoke and salt was like a perfume, sweet and luxurious. He took a bite. It was delicious and he needed more, but he wanted to savor it, to make sure he had enough for later.

"Gannet, what did you take from the hunter?" Kestrel asked curiously.

"Nothing!"

"Gannet, I saw you."

"Well..." Gannet looked away.

"I'm not mad. I just want to know."

Gannet opened his jacket and pulled out a black rectangle wrapped in a cord, passing it to Kestrel. It was an old cell phone—at least ten years old—with a short antenna. The screen was as small as a matchbook.

"I thought it looked cool, but I'm not sure what it does." Gannet shrugged.

"Can I hold on to it? It might come in handy." Kestrel smiled.

He took off a glove and pressed the power button. Nothing happened. The screen didn't light; it was as dead as the person it belonged to, though the cable was coiled around it. If only he could find a way to charge it.

Shrew, distracted, looked around at the mountains and trees. "This reminds me of a vision I had once," he said as he tightened the laces on his boots. "It was when Wapiti killed a hunter who was chasing us, or maybe when Vole passed. You didn't know them, Kestrel, but I think you would've liked them."

Vole. Another to add to the list.

"What was that dream about?" Cottontail asked.

"I was standing in the snow, in a place that resembled where we are now, but the trees were on fire, and the sky was painted pink and purple and orange. It was eerily beautiful. Some of the others were with me, and we danced around, celebrating the fire that was raging out of control. I was worried we would burn too, but Lynx, Hoatzin, and Caiman assured me we would be safe. And we were."

Gannet finished his satchel of nuts and fruit and sniffed the bag.

"Then a great bird soared over us, and from it poured hail and snow and shards of ice. Icicles rained down, extinguishing the fire. The thirteen of us put on our sheets to hide from it. We threw the red rope we used for the bones and pulled it down."

"Why didn't you tell me about this one?" Kestrel asked, chewing on flesh.

"It didn't seem that important," Shrew laughed.

"What does it mean?" Cottontail asked as she tilted her head, her bunny ears leaning.

"I don't know." Shrew chuckled. "I was never good at interpreting dreams. Especially the part that didn't make sense."

"What part was that?" Kestrel asked.

"I was driving a car—it was really old, from what I remember. The radio was playing, and I was laughing, going around a corner. Someone was in the passenger seat. I can never remember who it was. That's the weird thing—the person with me in all my dreams is erased, like a blur of light. Whoever it was was singing along, and the summer sun was shining."

Kestrel's ears perked up. His eyes narrowed, and he stared at his partner as Shrew continued his story.

"I asked the person next to me if they were okay. I had to turn down the radio to hear them—it was like they couldn't speak. Something was preventing them from talking, from telling me the truth, like they were keeping a secret. Then the vision ended."

"Weird," Gannet said dryly.

"Have you ever told anyone this dream?" Kestrel asked.

"Yeah," Shrew said. "I told Stoat when we started to plan our escape."

"When? Exactly. I need to know."

"I told her when we were waiting for Muskox and Grouse to come back. The day you showed up."

Kestrel didn't know what to think, but before he could ponder it, he heard footsteps approaching. Stoat returned from relieving herself and started to repack. Shrew rubbed his shoulder and took a deep breath.

A cleared corridor guided the offshoot group up to the mountain-top. Kestrel took the lead while Shrew brought up the rear. Walls of trees stood on both sides like guardrails up to the top—pillars as white and gray as tombstones. Kestrel wondered aloud how this came to be.

"It was cleared," Stoat said as Cottontail woke back up. "Years ago, Lynx roamed the land alone, the first of our group to be chosen by the gods. You wonder why the Northern Pass wasn't our first choice? This is holy ground. She spent her first spring culling the trees around the top of the mountain. It's a pathway for when the gods descend to claim the land. Lynx was found worthy and given her purpose—to gather and lead the thirteen."

"A pathway?" Shrew asked.

"From the mountain, through the Hinterlands, to the world," Stoat recited. "The gods will devour all, but the faithful will enter into the home of the gods after the feast."

Kestrel thought about the story Stoat told, about the myth that upheld Lynx all these years. It was a vision of death, hunger, and destruction for those who didn't believe in the shrouded deities. And as far as he knew, there were fewer than thirteen who believed. Lynx had wandered the Hinterlands for some time, it seemed. Lost, trying to survive, maybe trying to build something—alone, insane, hungry.

"Lynx is a monster," Kestrel said.

"But you saved her life," Shrew scrunched his face.

"That was for you, not her. If that hunter had killed Lynx, she might have gone for you next."

Something seemed amiss, but he shook it off and continued on. The hail and frost began to ease up as they trekked on. The air was sharp with ice, but the wind backed off its assault. The flurries felt like a gift, the calm in the eye of the storm.

Light rose behind them. But it wasn't the sun. Not yet. Kestrel turned and saw a beam sweep across the trees, spotlighting them in the swaying, unsteady light.

Someone was chasing them.

TWENTY-TWO
TURNCOAT

"Run!" Kestrel commanded in a low voice.

Shrew grabbed his pack, Gannet picked up Cottontail, and Stoat readied herself. Kestrel took the rifle off his shoulder and loaded it. He let Shrew lead Gannet and Cottontail to hide behind the trees.

"How many are there?" Stoat asked.

Kestrel shook his head. There was no way to tell. Flurries fell faster now. The light seemed small—like a flashlight.

"Let's move slowly along the tree line," Kestrel said. There was no time to hide their tracks. He prayed to the gods that the snow would cover any markings—then questioned his own utterance.

The light closed in on them, but the storm whipped up a veil of snowflakes. The forest provided some cover, but the shadows grew, and the sounds of rustling branches and shredding evergreens distracted them.

Kestrel kept watch as they moved. When he glanced back, he saw Cross Fox in the midst of the blistering white. She shielded her face, scanning the treeline with her flashlight. Her fox hat caught in the wind and blew back, revealing her pale face.

"She's searching for me," Stoat said as she stepped out from behind a tree.

"No," Kestrel pulled her back.

"Stoat!" Cross Fox's voice was loud and painful. She yelled again, her siren-sound a desperate call to come back home.

She was alone as far as Kestrel could tell. Stoat tried to twist from his grasp and run to her, but he held her arm, squeezing as tight as he could.

"We can't be certain," Kestrel said as he tried to read Stoat's face through the blizzard.

"She won't hurt me."

"There could be others."

"Trust me," Stoat pleaded.

Kestrel suppressed his protest.

"Please," she added, her eyes heavy with tears.

Kestrel took an icy breath, his face flushed. He knew he wouldn't have left Shrew.

A flicker of light hit them and then went out as Cross Fox's flashlight died. When Stoat stepped out of cover, Kestrel didn't try to stop her. Cross Fox ran toward her in the heavy snow.

"Cross!" Stoat shouted, embracing her as they drew close.

All at once, it clicked, and Kestrel raised his gun, jaw set. Cross Fox went rigid in Stoat's embrace and pulled back, eyes wide.

"What's wrong?" Stoat cried. Cross Fox flicked her eyes to Kestrel, who now stood behind her, rifle pointed at the back of Stoat's head.

"Don't move," he said through gritted teeth.

"Put the gun down, Kestrel," Cross Fox said.

"Kestrel?" Stoat asked with a tremble.

"Friend," Kestrel recalled. "That's what you said the first night. You made me believe we were friends in our other lives. Pretended you remembered me, but that's the funny thing—you didn't. No one remembers anything from their old lives, not clearly."

Cross Fox clenched her jaw. Kestrel nodded at the flashlight, and she dropped it. Stoat remained with her hands up, still trembling. Kestrel pushed the barrel of the gun through her hair until it hit her skull.

"What are you doing?"

"You lied to me. You made me think you were my friend."

"I am."

"You're not. How did you know?"

"What are you talking about?" Cross Fox asked as she sized up Kestrel. Her eyes shot to Stoat's, then off into the distance. Kestrel heard it too—a distant howl on the wind—but he ignored it.

"How did you know?" he demanded, hitting Stoat's head with the cold metal of the rifle.

"It was easy," Cross Fox admitted.

Kestrel narrowed his eyes. Stoat stepped forward and turned to face him, her hands still raised. Cross Fox adjusted her stance, and Stoat moved ever so slightly closer.

"That morning, Shrew and I were alone, and we talked about what memories we still had. We all have them, but they're never clear. I knew how they found him. I knew someone would come looking for him eventually," Stoat said with a smirk. "When Grouse and Muskox came back with you, Cross Fox and I emptied your pockets before we burned your possessions. I looked through your wallet and found a picture of you two."

"That's how you knew. That was your way in," Kestrel surmised. "Why?"

"My purpose is discernment. I test everyone—become close with them, determine their true intentions. The way you showed up in the wilderness was suspicious. Grouse and Muskox reported to Caiman, and he asked me to befriend you."

"What do you mean? How did I show up?"

"You were hunting," Cross Fox chimed in.

"Not exactly," Stoat interrupted, shooting a glance at her partner. "You were searching for him. They said they ran across you, but you clearly weren't a hunter. If Caiman had been there, you would've been dead, but Muskox has a soft spot for people who aren't hunters. They spent days observing you, watching from a distance to see what you were doing, and decided you seemed harmless. Muskox wanted to leave you, but Grouse said they had to bring you back. Especially since you would likely die out in the Hinterlands."

"What was I doing out here?" Kestrel asked. He lowered the gun slightly to look into her eyes.

"You don't know? I thought you would at least suspect why the two of you were so close."

Shrew, Kestrel realized. His breath turned ragged; he blinked as he began to understand. He had been out here searching for Shrew the whole time. Why was Shrew missing in the first place? Was this all a lie to throw him off?

If it was a lie, it worked. Kestrel's hands shook, and he pointed the rifle away from the women. Cross Fox whipped out a handgun and pointed it at him. Stoat grabbed the rifle's barrel, disarming him in a flash. Both weapons were aimed at him—one at his head and one at his heart.

The betrayal was brutal. Kestrel watched as the turncoat silently coordinated with her partner. He never trusted Cross Fox, but Stoat —she had manipulated him into trusting her. He now understood why she seemed so detached when she decided to leave Cross Fox behind. It was never the plan.

"Why?" Kestrel bared his teeth.

"You can't escape," Cross Fox said. "We need all of you."

"Bullshit!"

"Despite what you *feel*, you were chosen by the gods," Stoat said with a nod. "We would never let you leave. We just had to convince you that you needed us to get this far. Had you known earlier, you would've tried to flee. While Lynx might have sympathy, Caiman would've killed you, and that would set our plans back."

"Caiman is dead," Kestrel spat.

"He's not," Cross Fox dismissed him. "We attended to him after you left. Thinhorn wasn't too happy with your little stunt. He's wounded, but he'll make it—at least until we get up the mountain."

Kestrel was incredulous. "Why even let us get this far? Why not stop us when we left the cave?"

"Hope is an accelerant. It puts a fire under you. You're almost to the top of the mountain, and you did it all on your own." Stoat smiled. "You had to believe you were the liberator—at least until you saved us, which you did when you took out the hunter. Had he killed Lynx, it would've been over, and you could've escaped. At least until Caiman tracked you down."

"We didn't know," Cross Fox admitted. "She only told me that you were escaping when she woke me. She said to look for Caiman within the caves and that you all would be running up the mountain. The others aren't far behind."

"Let's go get the others." Stoat gestured toward the treeline.

Kestrel was forced to turn around and march up the slope as Stoat held the gun to his back. He could feel her eyes following his every move and hated himself for giving them the upper hand while he got lost in the dream of his former life. Now he would never be free of them.

"Why was I searching for Shrew?" Kestrel asked as they climbed.

Ahead of them was the spot where Shrew had taken Gannet and Cottontail. He prayed Shrew had the foresight to keep going, to take them as far as he could and keep them safe since Kestrel couldn't. He had failed, but if they could get away from this place, then at least he could say that they made it home.

"Years ago, Shrew got into an accident, and the gods chose him. We saved him. Other hunters came looking, but we moved on. Then you showed up."

"But how did you know?"

"You carried a wallet with a picture of him inside. It wasn't hard to figure out," Cross Fox explained again.

"What was his name? What was *my* name?"

"That doesn't matter," Stoat bit back. "What's past is not ours anymore. You belong to the gods on the sacred mountain. Kestrel the Liberator—that is your name and your purpose. Nothing from the human lands belongs out here."

Something rustled in the treetops ahead of them. Kestrel waited for a great bird to take flight, like the one from his vision, but nothing scoured the sky of the white oblivion.

Cross Fox, Stoat, and Kestrel arrived under the canopy and followed the tracks.

Kestrel prayed they would disappear after a few paces, but they didn't. Not quite. One set of footprints veered off while another seemed to wrap around a great tree. Cross Fox investigated and looked up. A snap of twigs came from the left, and they decided to follow it.

As they walked, the crunching snow concealed the trap laid for them. Kestrel searched for a sign of the ambush to come, and glanced up, careful not to tilt his head. He ducked.

Without warning, Gannet leaped from the dense evergreen branches above Kestrel and landed on Cross Fox, a knife in his hand. In one blur of limbs and metal, he held on to her and stabbed as many times as he could. They fell to the ground.

Kestrel bent and kicked Stoat in the leg. She buckled but held the rifle. Kestrel grabbed it, trying to take it back from her. He had no time to see if Gannet was okay, but he did see Shrew step out from behind a tree with a machete in hand. Cottontail peered out from behind the large pine.

Shrew lunged at Stoat and sliced her across the belly. Her white coat turned crimson, the snow around them a slosh of pink and red. Cross Fox screamed for her partner, but Kestrel wouldn't let Stoat go.

"Fuck you," Gannet spat as he rose to stand over Cross Fox. "I've been wanting to do this for so long." Gannet grabbed her pistol and put it on his belt.

Stoat knelt in the snow, holding her stomach. The wound was shallow but long, bleeding enough to cause concern. Kestrel held the rifle at her, cocked the gun, and licked his lips.

"Stop!" Shrew commanded.

Gannet froze with the knife lifted high, his hatred for Cross Fox clear on his face. Kestrel believed she deserved it for every insult she had thrown at Gannet.

"Why?" Gannet demanded.

"We are not like them. They would slaughter us, but we have to be better. We have to get out of this place and leave these horrible things behind."

"What do you propose we do?" Kestrel asked his partner.

"Tie them up," Cottontail suggested.

Kestrel considered the idea. He wanted Stoat to be punished for her betrayal. It cost them precious time and could have cost them their lives. But Cottontail hopped toward them. She didn't deserve to be out here, to be tortured, to watch people die over and over, to be conditioned into believing lies and eating people.

"Fine. We tie them up."

Gannet huffed. Kestrel worried his newfound sense of purpose was going to his head. Then he remembered what he had done to Caiman in the altar chamber, his hunger for flesh and the change that had already taken root.

Shrew and Gannet dragged Cross Fox to a tree and propped her against it, the bloody trails in the snow like a sanguine Christmas ribbon. Kestrel used his gun to point Stoat toward the large evergreen, and she obeyed. Shrew dug through their packs and found enough red rope to tie them up like a little present for the others.

Kestrel wondered what they were planning to use the rope for.

"She'll bleed out if you don't let us go," Stoat pleaded.

"If the others are really behind us, then Thinhorn will stop the bleeding."

Fury flashed in Stoat's eyes, and she lunged forward, trying to take the rifle back. Kestrel lunged toward her in turn. The gun slipped from his hands, and Stoat reached for the trigger. Gannet tried to pull Stoat away, but the rifle fired.

With a whimper, a body hit the ground.

"Kestrel!" Shrew screamed.

Kestrel felt his entire body for the bullet entry, but couldn't find a wound. Tears welled in Stoat's eyes, and Gannet screamed. Kestrel turned to find Cottontail on the ground. Gannet sped past him to the little girl.

"No! No! No!" Gannet screamed.

"Go! I've got them," Shrew said to Kestrel as he finished securing Stoat and Cross Fox.

Cottontail had been struck in the side, her body trembling in pain. She reached her tiny hand out, and Gannet held it. Kestrel hurried to her side, packed snow on the wound, and felt around her back to see if it had exited. The bullet was lodged in the ice beneath her.

"Get me the gauze from Cross Fox's bag!" Kestrel shouted at Shrew.

The light in her eyes was fading, her skin turning bluer by the minute, in contrast to the soft pink snow all around her. Cottontail grabbed the foot that hung around her neck and kissed it. Gannet said a silent prayer over her as he held her. Kestrel shook his head.

"I'm cold," Cottontail said.

Shrew took his jacket and placed it over her. "She needs blood," he realized. "She might bleed out."

"Blood! We can't get her blood. We don't have anything like that!" Gannet shouted.

Kestrel stood. Stoat stared up at him, but Cross Fox hung her head. He bent down and lifted her chin. Her wounds dripped with blood.

"Where?" Kestrel asked Cross Fox.

"Where what?" Stoat responded.

"Don't fucking play with me. Where can we get medical supplies? There has to be something. You know these lands better than anyone. There has to be a stash of equipment somewhere."

"There," Cross Fox tried to get the words out, but struggled. Kestrel held the barrel of his rifle at her throat and pressed hard.

"Say it."

"The village. On—" Cross Fox winced in pain. "On the other side of the mountain. There are supplies there. More bandages. No blood, but maybe something to stitch her up."

When he took the gun away, two circular imprints remained. Kestrel returned to the others. He wouldn't let Cottontail die, not now. They had come too far to let her become a victim of the wilderness, of Lynx and her sycophants.

"Let's get her there," Kestrel demanded. "Gannet, you take the rifle. Shrew, take the handgun. I'll carry her."

"No," Gannet said. "I want to be the one to take her. She's my friend."

Kestrel, seeing the tears in the young man's eyes, agreed and strapped the gun to his back. Shrew picked up Gannet's backpack as well as his own. Gannet gave Cottontail a drink of water, then carefully picked her up in his arms, wrapping her in Shrew's jacket.

Shrew found another coat in Cross Fox's bag and put it on. He nodded for Kestrel to look inside, and Kestrel's eyes went wide. He decided to take the contents with them, packing them in his own bag.

"Hurry. We have to get her to the village," Kestrel urged as they walked toward the edge of the clearing. "Let's stay in the trees until we reach the top. It shouldn't be too far."

"What if the others come?" Gannet asked.

"I'll stop them."

TWENTY-THREE
THE SACRED MOUNTAIN

Trees became sparse, and rocks split open the frost-coated ground as they reached the peak of the mountain. The slant of the land decreased until it wasn't visibly apparent, though Kestrel could still feel the incline in his burning calves. The path ahead led directly to a clearing. No peak in sight.

Cottontail was bundled up, blood soaking through the cloth, but Gannet made sure she was breathing steady and not turning the granite blue of a corpse. Shrew complained that his boots were wet, his feet freezing, but the air up on the sacred mountain was strangely warm.

Kestrel wasn't sure they would make it.

"What's that?"

He turned around and stared into the distance to see the others speeding up the mountain.

From the looks of it, they had reached the two tied to the tree. It would take time—Thinhorn would have to tend to their wounds, and they would have to gather their strength.

"Look," Kestrel said as he saw three people stray away from the group. He couldn't be sure, but he assumed Lynx and Caiman were two of the three. The third could be Hoatzin or Muskox, maybe Pronghorn. He had to get his friends across the mountain faster.

"Let's move," Shrew said.

"You keep going," Kestrel told them. "I'll catch up."

"No, you have to come with us."

"It'll be okay. Go with the others. I'll be right behind you," Kestrel held Shrew's hand and kissed him on the cheek. Shrew looked hesitant but nodded.

Gannet and Shrew hurried to the very top. It wasn't far—less than a mile, if Kestrel had to guess.

The others approached, running fast, their weapons in hand. There was no way out. Kestrel could use the rifle to try to pick them off, but without a scope, it would be nearly impossible until they were closer. He needed to put distance between them, to make sure they would fall back and keep away at all costs.

He put down his pack and pulled out a matchbox. He carefully removed the two cylinders he had taken from Cross Fox's pack. They were reddish orange, and the sound they made echoed in his head before he lit the fuses.

Burn it down, Kestrel thought, laughing. *Blow it up.*

Two sticks of dynamite. Why Cross Fox felt the need to keep explosives was lost on him, but he held them in his hand and felt their immense power. Kestrel set one down and put the other between his legs. He tried to strike the match against the box. The first matchstick didn't ignite—but the second did.

Kestrel touched the match to the fuse. It caught quickly. With a burning stick of dynamite between his legs, he realized this was no time to second-guess. He threw it in the air.

"No!" yelled a faint voice from below. Whoever said it shouted when they saw the orange tube fly through the air.

A gust of wind extinguished the fuse. Kestrel realized his first attempt had been eliminated and proceeded to his backup. If this didn't work, it was all for naught; he would have to run hard to catch up with the others.

He lit the third match and begged for disaster.

The explosive tumbled through the air. Time slowed.

Kestrel thought of it all and hoped it would burn, begged for it to be wiped clean from the face of the earth. When it landed, it stuck straight up out of the snow, the sizzle of the fuse like the great beam of a lighthouse.

One.

Two.

Three.

Four.

That's how many seconds it took.

Right before the boom erupted, Kestrel saw the second stick of dynamite just inches away from him. Fate was on his side. The eruption grew from a ball of fire and smoke to a squall of wind and snow. The entire mountain trembled. He lost his footing and slipped as the snow and boulders became a frozen tidal wave.

Before it was too late, Kestrel caught himself on a nearby outcropping of rock just the right shape for him to grasp onto. The ice scraped beneath his outstretched boot heel. He pulled himself up, feeling the snow sift like sand around him. Then he slipped, losing his hold.

The darkness swallowed him.

And in the dark, he collided with something that stopped his freefall.

Kestrel sat up and saw the snow flying down the mountain. Shards of frost like diamond dust sliced down trees, sheets of verglas shattered and rolled—winter's apocalypse. When he looked for the others, they were nowhere to be seen. The avalanche had either buried them or rolled them further down the mountain.

They couldn't survive that, right?

The cloud of ice settled, like frosty mist falling, glimmering like the stars.

Silence rang through the Northern Pass. There were no more

trees along the walls of the valley. It was clear as far as his eye could see—a pathway.

A thought crossed Kestrel's mind—the consequences of what he'd done—but he shook his head. He walked away, feeling like the victor of the earth, the champion of the sky. He felt powerful as freedom coursed through him. A storm was gathering around the mountain—the peals of thunder a raucous rejoicing.

Kestrel the Liberator!

All the world seemed to sing his name.

"Up and out," Kestrel said as he walked to catch up to the others.

They weren't that far ahead. The path was solid rock, jagged edges rising up higher and higher until the walls met in a ring. The sacred mountain was an amphitheater. The others huddled against a wall, shielding themselves from the wind.

Cottontail whimpered as Gannet sang a soft song to soothe her. Shrew was repacking their gear and making adjustments. When he saw Kestrel, he looked as if he'd seen a ghost. Kestrel marched forward, proud of what he'd done.

"You're alive!" Shrew ran to Kestrel and wrapped him in a hug.

"Of course I am."

"We didn't know what happened." Gannet rocked back and forth with Cottontail in his lap.

"I set off an avalanche," Kestrel said coldly. "They won't be chasing us anymore."

"Your head," Shrew said as he touched the marred flesh of his scalp.

When Shrew pulled his hand away, it shone ruby red. Kestrel touched his wet head, and bits of rubble fell from his scalp. He could feel the blood matting the hair around the open wound.

"What is it?" Kestrel asked.

"Kestrel," Shrew stepped back. "It looks like you hit your head on a rock. Are you sure you're okay? The blast shook the entire mountain."

"I'm fine." He dismissed Shrew's worry with a kiss.

Shrew pulled away.

The air there was warmer than the rest of the mountain, the snow falling away from the top like an invisible dome hung above them. Kestrel looked over the shorter edge to his right. In the distance, he could see the end of the road and the shells of buildings—the village.

"There," Kestrel said and pointed. "We're almost there. There are medical supplies and places to shelter. Likely other things we'll need. Maybe other people will be there too."

"I need to rest," Gannet said as he brushed Cottontail's head. "She does too."

"Why don't we take a break and eat?" Shrew suggested.

Kestrel agreed, noticing the sun setting in the west as they settled in the center of the jagged circle.

Gannet checked Cottontail's bandages and let out a heavy sigh. Shrew handed Gannet the rest of the fruit and nut rations, then unpacked two MREs and prepared the meals. They came together rather quickly, though their quality was dubious.

Kestrel's stomach rumbled. The craving crept up on him, grabbing his shoulder with its claws and whispering in his ear. Shrew gave him a brown plastic pouch of indistinguishable pasta in red sauce and a flimsy plastic fork. He stabbed the food, brought it to his mouth, and inhaled.

Ugh. Kestrel pushed it away.

"What's wrong?" Shrew raised an eyebrow.

"It smells off."

Shrew took the pouch and sniffed. He put his fork in, snagged a few pieces of pasta, and put them in his mouth. He chewed without incident. Kestrel was surprised; he expected Shrew to spit it out and say it was spoiled.

"It tastes fine to me."

"Is there anything else?" Kestrel asked.

Shrew rummaged through the pack and pulled out a pack of cured flesh. Before he untied the strings that bound it, Kestrel reached for it, teeth bared. His hunger raged.

"I don't think we should be eating this anymore."

"Why?" Kestrel asked as he took it from Shrew. "We need to eat, and we can't afford to waste any."

"It's not right."

"That didn't stop us from eating before." Kestrel ripped into the tender flesh.

"We had no choice," Shrew said with a furrowed brow.

"And we still don't have one."

Kestrel ate another piece, ending the conversation.

Shrew handed the others their meals.

Cottontail ate what she could and drank some water. She was weary, but she hung on long enough to kiss her foot before going to sleep. Gannet checked her wounds while Shrew finished his meal and packed the trash into his bag. Kestrel propped himself up on one arm and stretched out his legs. Shrew finished up and lay nearby—but not as close as before.

Kestrel looked down at him, remembering what Cross Fox and Stoat told him. He had been looking for Shrew out in the Hinterlands. They had known each other before. Kestrel wondered if the man in Shrew's dreams was him and vice versa. Had they been in love before? Why was he missing in the first place?

Shrew sat up and kissed Kestrel—deep and slow, like he was searching for something within the kiss. Without Shrew, Kestrel believed he would be lost—a boat unmoored, no anchor to keep it close to the shore.

The kiss was laced with desire. Kestrel bit Shrew's lips—they were as delicious as a ripe strawberry. Shrew pulled away and touched the pad of his finger to his lip. He had drawn blood.

"Sorry," Kestrel laughed lightly.

Shrew dismissed his apology, but stopped kissing him and inched away. Shrew curled up next to him and placed Kestrel's arm across his body, his fingertips falling around his waist. In the warmth, Kestrel grew weary.

"Do you think there were ever gods on the mountain?" Shrew asked.

"Does it matter?" Kestrel responded. "There's nothing up here now."

"I know, but I think it makes a difference. Someone had to believe there was something up here. People don't start believing in gods out of the blue, right? There's got to be some *reason* for it all."

"Not really," Kestrel dismissed. "Humans have been doing this forever. The script is always the same. A person believes they're in communion with a god they craft from their imagination. They find others and persuade or manipulate them into believing their story. Over time, it grows and shifts and alters. Atrocities are committed for the salvation of the group, and the god returns to free them."

"You think that's what happened with Lynx?"

"I do." Kestrel nodded. "Whatever happened to her is beside the point. She found others, stole missing children, murdered and ate people, and put us all through hell for what? An empty mountain at the end of the world."

"I'm glad I found you," Shrew said as he moved in closer. "If we don't have our own personal memories or homes of our own, at least we have each other. Whatever happened out here, whoever we were, we'll find our way back and be our old selves again, right?"

"Right."

Kestrel looked around the mountain top at the bowl-like walls that shielded them from the rest of the world. A little haven. The mountain was indeed sacred, but not because there were gods dwelling on its peak. It was where they found a slice of peace.

The peak was hollow, but filled with those who loved one another, who cared for their kind, who wanted to be home.

Gannet offered to keep watch while the others rested. Then they would switch. Kestrel and Shrew agreed, and the two eventually dozed off as the sun rose.

TWENTY-FOUR
SHROUDED

Kestrel wheezed as a booted foot hit his stomach. The bright midday sun and the hard impact to his gut blinded him, stealing his breath. He struggled, desperate to reach any weapon he could find.

"Up!" a man shouted.

Another kick accompanied the harsh, hissing voice. Kestrel scrambled to his knees, the cold metal barrel of a gun on his forehead. He saw three figures before him; his ears rang with throbbing pain.

The hunters, he thought.

He was wrong.

It was not a hunting party. It was his worst nightmare come to life —Caiman, Hoatzin, and Lynx. Caiman held Kestrel at gunpoint, a sinister grin on his face. Bandages wrapped his abdomen and leg where the stalagmite had pierced him.

Hoatzin held Cottontail pinned to her chest, a knife at her throat, keeping Gannet and Shrew at bay. Lynx knelt, praying.

"We've made it to the abode of the gods," Lynx said. "Even though you tried to delay the inevitable. Kestrel, I thought you were on our side. I thought you believed in our mission, but I suppose it doesn't matter now. We are here, and the others aren't far behind us. Everything will be fine in a few moments."

"How?" Kestrel asked. "There was no way you could survive the blast."

"The avalanche," Hoatzin corrected.

"We survived the same way you did." Lynx looked up. "By the grace of the gods. They had a mission for us, and we've completed it. The feast will begin shortly. Tie him up until then, Caiman."

Kestrel glanced over and saw that Gannet and Shrew had their hands and feet tied with the red rope, but cloth was tied around their mouths so they couldn't speak. Caiman retracted the gun slightly, leaving an imprint in Kestrel's skin, but kept it trained on him. The enforcer pulled out a length of cord to secure Kestrel.

"The others are alive?"

"Of course they are," Lynx shook her head. "You still don't get it. We all serve a purpose. We are all chosen to fulfill the will of the gods. They cannot be stopped. We are bound to them, and nothing gets in their way."

Caiman bumped Kestrel's skull on purpose. The pain was a sharp slice through his head. He winced.

Something was wrong. He didn't understand what Lynx meant.

"There are no gods on this mountain," he panted.

"Kestrel," Lynx said, squatting in front of him. "They are already here. The feast is about to begin. You need only look and see they're with us now. Waiting to be given a form."

The others arrived, fury on their faces. Muskox held Cross Fox in his arms. Bowhead aided Stoat. Thinhorn and Pronghorn carried the sagging bags of bones on their backs. They stopped short of the inner circle, setting their things down, and stepped forward.

"We begin the final ritual," Hoatzin shrieked with glee. She issued commands as she passed Cottontail off to Bowhead. "Muskox, make a small fire in the center of the clearing. Thinhorn, Pronghorn —the bones."

Muskox unbound the firewood from his pack and used a matchbook to strike the blaze. Thinhorn and Pronghorn unsheathed the bones of all the bodies the group had burned and eaten. The countless corpses were carried and placed carefully, stacked as if the skeletal remains were precious relics. Kestrel counted six piles of bones—six little altars surrounding the fire.

Kestrel looked at each stack of white bones, then up to the sky above them. He expected to see open air, wisps of cotton clouds—maybe the yellow light burning—but there was something more.

Dust gathered, and snowflakes formed solid crystals, silhouettes forming in the sky.

He swore he saw a frayed hem billow in the warm breeze.

Thinhorn took the red rope and interlaced it through the bones, tying them together like strings of muscle and sinew.

"Look!" Hoatzin shouted as she raised her arms.

The abyss revealed the outlines of figures. Human-like, but altogether not human. Faces as absent as vapor, bodies of smoke shrouded in tattered cloth like mist falling from a sky of oblivion.

The gods of the mountain, Kestrel thought. His mouth hung upon. He couldn't believe what he was seeing.

Death lingered in the strangely warm air—the fresh scent of rot, the tang of blood, sweat, and musk. The bodies of the gods became more opaque by the second.

Their faces were concealed by their hoods, their worn ash robes from an ancient kingdom, threadbare cloth not fit for a pauper. The hems of their garments were shredded to pieces and blew in the breeze. Their hands opened, outstretched, as they waited for their offering. The whispers grew around them.

"What the fuck?" Kestrel uttered under his breath. He looked to Shrew, who appeared both mesmerized and afraid. Gannet and Cottontail, too. The little rabbit girl began to cry, as did some of the others. But their tears seemed happy, like their lives were now fulfilled.

"Behold!" Lynx shouted. "The gods of the Sacred Mountain. The Eidolons of the Hinterlands. Shrouded in darkness, forgotten in the human lands. Remnants of ages past. Together, we will release them from their prison and give them flesh. Their formless power called to us, choosing each of us for their purpose. Now we give of ourselves that their glory may be made manifest through their feast!"

The others bowed down to the earth, their hands out in front of them. Some openly wept; others praised. Kestrel could hear the whispers around him becoming distinct, separate voices speaking into the world, screaming for form, shrieking.

"Hoatzin," Lynx called. "It's time for the Gambit Stones."

Hoatzin stepped up and bowed low, her long robes flowing behind her like a priestess. She emptied the Gambit Stones into her hands.

"Eidolons," Hoatzin approached the first pile of bones. "Here are the minds you have graciously let us borrow on our journey. They have guided us well, choosing the thirteen that stand before you and making impossible choices, but the Gambit Stones have saved our lives. Now, I will return them to you so that you might be made."

The bird woman held out the first stone—the die. She opened her clenched right fist, and the god bowed low to take possession with its vapor-clad hand. Six sides, bright spots on the black faces, fate, and odds. The second god swayed as Hoatzin handed it the wishbone. Stark white, structure and frame, strong and steady.

Green light reflected off the gemstone as Hoatzin handed it to the third. Facets, manifold potential, beauty, and permanence. The fourth was given their key and swirled with joy. Hard and sharp, unlocking the unknown, a door opening.

Kestrel understood what each element was, why it belonged to each god, as if they were whispering to him. Were they speaking to him this whole time? Did they lead him up this mountain?

Hoatzin presented the compass to the fifth god, who grabbed it quickly and held it out. The needle stopped. Direction, clarity, the pathway they were meant to be on. The path he was meant to be on.

Lastly, Hoatzin gave the eye to the sixth and graciously nodded.

The god took the eye. The whispers were clear to Kestrel—knowledge and foresight.

All at once, they crushed the items in their shadow-hands, shattering each object until it turned to dust. What remained of the stones was released and reabsorbed into the essences of the gods.

"Now we begin the feast." Lynx looked up with wide and amazed eyes. "We have all been chosen, our purposes have been fulfilled, and we are to become one with the gods before us."

Shrew tried to speak but was muzzled by the cloth over his mouth. Gannet furrowed his brow and jerked to break loose of the ties around his hands. Cottontail made a silent wish on her foot as Bowhead held her. Kestrel didn't know what was left to do other than plead with his captors.

"There's still time to stop this," he said. "You don't have to do this."

"Quiet!" Caiman hit him across the face.

"You saved me. You liberated us from the hunters, and therefore, you served your purpose. Now you will be given up to the Eidolons for a feast, to give them a body so they might reclaim the earth. They have been unbound for so long, they have forgotten what it's like to have flesh, to feel the earth, to rule over the human lands and be praised," Lynx told him.

"They aren't real," Kestrel said, lying to himself.

"You foolish boy," Hoatzin said. "Look and see! They're here before you. They've been speaking to you this whole time. Who do you think laid claim to you? Who called you to the wilderness and gave you those dreams? It has been them!"

"Does anyone else doubt?" Caiman said, still brandishing his gun.

Heads shook in response. No one dared to speak, but no one denied the deities before them either.

"We begin," Lynx said.

"Who will be the first to offer themselves to the gods?" Hoatzin raised a knife, waving it in the air.

Muskox took a step forward. The gods seemed to undulate above them, swaying and whispering.

"Blessed be Muskox, the bravest among us," Hoatzin said and ushered him toward the fire.

"Kneel before the Eidolons of the Hinterlands, the ancient gods of the Sacred Mountain, who will raid the world and end the reign of humankind. Offer your life and your body, and when they feast, you will live on in them," Lynx extolled.

"Don't do it!" Kestrel screamed.

Caiman hit him with a right hook to the jaw. Kestrel tasted blood as a tooth loosened.

Hoatzin raised her knife high and plunged it into Muskox's heart without hesitation. Blood sprayed out of his chest and splattered across her face. Only a small whimper escaped his mouth as he fell to his knees and closed his eyes. Hoatzin removed the knife and licked the edge.

"Thank you for your sacrifice," Lynx whispered as she placed a hand on Muskox's right cheek, kissing his left.

Another life taken.

The first god bowed low and reached out its hands. Muskox's hand and arm began to dissolve, warping into hundreds of little particles, and vanished like a mist in the midday sun as he became one with the first god.

Violently, the bones in the first pile began to rattle. The first bone, a tibia, was dragged across the ground, the red cord tied around it followed behind, along with the rest of the bones. They began to take shape in the cloud of dust that was the god, building a frame. Bones swirled with red threads intertwined with the dust and Muskox's shimmering remains.

Kestrel began to shake as he saw ribs align along the spine, and two jaws jutted out from a mismatched skull. Finger bones fused to the head like spikes. The creature jittered and tried to scream. The whispers turned harsh and tangible, the body spiked with bits of flesh.

Yet, it was unstable, incomplete.

"Who is next?" Lynx asked.

Kestrel looked to Shrew, fearful of what might happen to him.

The flood of volunteers came, eager to join with the gods. Cross Fox went next, dropping Stoat's hand and leaving her behind. Hoatzin stabbed her knife directly into Cross Fox's heart, and she dissolved, merging with the second. Stoat's mouth hung open. She placed a hand over her heart as the others walked away.

Thinhorn and Pronghorn offered themselves up to the feast. The other gods came forward, and all three shifted, cracked into flesh and bone and disfigured monsters, the dust around them binding to their new bodies. Bowhead released his loose grasp on Cottontail, and the little girl hopped weakly to Gannet and Shrew. Gannet nodded for Cottontail's help, and Kestrel hoped she understood to untie him.

Stoat did not move.

"The first will be favored," Caiman said, shoving Kestrel to the ground. Kestrel felt the cords that bound him loosen as he shifted his hands. Caiman sat in front of Hoatzin, spread his arms wide, and readied himself. She plunged the blade into his heart as he grinned. The sixth god came to him, a bastard of bones in an inhuman shape. A skull with four femurs hung from its jaw, toe bones for hair. It absorbed Caiman into itself.

"Now begins the last phase," Hoatzin announced. "The Eidolons need the second bodies to leave their spectral forms."

"Will they devour us, too?" Stoat asked. Fear pooled in her eyes.

Kestrel watched as she stared at the Eidolon, who had eaten and absorbed Cross Fox. Her mouth twitched, her breath ragged.

"We will become them," Hoatzin said in a sing-song voice. "The Gambit Stones gave them their minds, the first six their spirit, and we will offer them our flesh. They will take our bodies and join with them, becoming corporeal."

"Gannet," Lynx said with a leer. "You're next."

TWENTY-FIVE

HUNGER

Hoatzin and Lynx dragged Gannet in front of the fire. All the bones were in the air, stark white against the buzzing blackness and shifting bodies of the deities—an amalgamation of death and resurrection, the exhumed bodies reuniting in the sky. Gannet brought his hands to his lap as he looked up at Hoatzin.

Kestrel noticed, but she didn't.

When Hoatzin raised the knife above her head, Gannet lunged. She fell back, her arms flailing as she tripped over her robe and fell backward into the crackling fire. She rolled around in the flames, trying to crawl her way out, and screamed in horror as her skin blackened. Lynx ran toward the fire, shielding her face as it grew. Hoatzin reached out, begging from burning lips, but Lynx couldn't reach her in time. The flames consumed her. The smoke smelled of rot, fermented fruit, and body odor.

Stoat stayed utterly still.

Kestrel watched as her body roasted, the juices bubbling under her cracked skin. If she hadn't smelled so awful, he would've been hungry for her flesh.

"What have you done?" Lynx asked as Gannet stared down at her. She picked up a discarded gun and pointed it at him. Kestrel sprang up, tackling her to the ground. Gannet grabbed her shoulders as Cottontail untied Shrew's ropes.

"Stoat!" Lynx screamed, but Stoat could only look at Cottontail with a lump in her throat.

The gun lay on the rocky ground. Gannet twisted Lynx's arms behind her back, holding her prisoner. Kestrel made his move. The gods did not react; their unfinished forms still jutted and shifted sporadically, their eyes beginning to glow. They turned to one another, and they began to alternately whisper and shriek.

Kestrel picked up the gun and aimed it at Lynx's head.

"Do *not* do this," she pleaded. "They need our bodies. The gods cannot survive without our sacrifice. They need us so they can return and rule. Kestrel, you need to do what's right. We lost Hoatzin, but there are still six of us. Don't ruin this. Remember, you will be rewarded. After the feast, Paradise awaits you."

Kestrel cocked the pistol. Lynx flinched.

"Lynx," Stoat said softly. "If Hoatzin hadn't...what would become of you?"

Shrew armed himself with a knife, slowly inching into an attack position behind Stoat. Kestrel saw Stoat raise an eyebrow.

"What?" Lynx responded as if she didn't understand.

"The Gambit Stones were for their minds. The first six were sacrificed for their souls. Hoatzin said the next six were to give their bodies to the gods. Minds, souls, bodies." Stoat counted on her hands.

Gannet shuddered.

"What of it?" Lynx asked.

"That leaves one," Stoat chimed in.

"After the rest of us were devoured by the gods, you were going to be the only one left," Kestrel surmised. "What were you going to do?"

"The same as I've done this whole time—serve the Eidolons in whatever way they desire. That has been my mission from the beginning. From the moment I arrived in the Hinterlands, I have always and only served their needs. Their will be done, not mine."

And yet, Kestrel thought.

"So, any one of us could be the last one standing?" Stoat asked, eyeing Lynx.

"If no one else is sacrificed," Gannet thought out loud, "the gods don't get their bodies."

"They don't terrorize the earth, no one claims their twisted heaven, and it ends," Kestrel said.

"But you don't believe that," Lynx asked. "Do you, Stoat? You're still faithful to us. You've always believed that the gods were good and would reign over the world and you would be blessed for your sacrifice. They've promised you that. Don't you want to be with her in paradise?"

Stoat shook her head but didn't say a word. She looked to the Eidolon that had stolen Cross Fox away from her, searching it for a sign that Cross Fox was still in there, still alive somehow, but there was nothing. She was gone.

"There's still time," Kestrel offered with sincerity. "You don't have to do this, Stoat. We can still get out of this, leave the wilderness, and return to the lives we once had."

"We can end this and return to normal," Shrew urged.

"Don't listen to them, Stoat," Lynx cried. "Take the knife at your side and shove it into your heart. Offer yourself to the gods, and you'll be with Cross Fox again, joined with her forever. The two of you will go on after this, and you will be honored."

"What will happen? Tell me. How will they conquer the world?" Stoat undid her knife sheath and held up the serrated blade. Its teeth glinted in the daylight.

Lynx began to speak, but gasped. The gunshot was so sudden that the others barely registered it. She fell to the ground and sputtered as she reached for the gods above her. The hole in the back of her head oozed slick and red.

"What did you do?" Stoat didn't look him in the eyes.

Kestrel bent down and smelled Lynx's sweet scent. He stuck out his tongue and licked the crimson liquid, lapping it up, savoring it. This was not like the other bits of preserved meat. Those bits of dried flesh were hearty and salty, but Lynx's blood tasted of honey and delight. Kestrel, unconcerned about the others, sucked her syrupy blood from the back of her head. Better than any sap-drenched meat.

There was a certain hunger in the pit of his stomach. Kestrel put his teeth on the nape of Lynx's neck and bit—not too much, but enough to rip her skin and pierce sinew. Like her blood, her flesh was delectable, far better than anything he had tasted before. Kestrel took another bite and then another, faster, like a child rushing through their dessert. Rabid.

"Kestrel," Shrew said as he placed a hand on Kestrel's shoulder. "Stop."

A command that rang hollow. It was not forceful, but sorrowful. Kestrel peeled his tongue and teeth away from Lynx's neck and looked up at Shrew's distressed face. Blood dripped from Kestrel's chin. He noticed Gannet looking on in confused horror, Cottontail hiding behind Gannet's legs, and Stoat bewildered by his actions. They all watched with bated breath.

"She tastes so good," Kestrel cried. He pulled away and wrapped his arms around Shrew, and began to cry. "I'm so hungry! I'm starving. I need something!"

Shrew held him, offering small platitudes of comfort.

"This is not who you are," Shrew said as he kissed Kestrel's head. "You've been through so much. We all have, but you can't let yourself become them."

"We need to get you out of here," Gannet told them. "Cottontail still needs her wound patched up. Why don't we get down to the village?"

Kestrel nodded, blood dribbling from the corner of his mouth. He looked at his hands, saw the scarlet stains, and began to lick his fingers clean. Stoat stepped back and went to rummage through the other packs. Gannet picked up his backpack and held Cottontail in his arms, shielding her in his chest from the scene.

"Here," Stoat said, handing him a parcel of dried meat. "This will hold you over until we get you to the other side."

Kestrel clawed at it and took a bite. It wasn't as delicious as Lynx.

"We need to go now," Gannet urged.

"What a waste," Kestrel said, forlorn.

"It's not a waste. Look at what she's done to you." Shrew said. "If these gods can resurrect the dead, then we need to put as much distance between us and Lynx as we can. I don't know how long we have, but you need to leave her behind."

Kestrel looked once more at his hands, one holding a bit of preserved flesh, the other still drenched red. He closed his eyes as tight as he could and winced. The salty-sweet taste of Lynx turned bitter like a penny in his mouth. His breath sputtered, and he swallowed hard, his hands searching for Shrew's to help him, his eyes drowning in tears.

"What have they done to you?" Shrew asked, looking as though he were looking at a stranger.

The Eidolons began to speak to Kestrel, whispering and shrieking, their voices overlapping like the sound of rattling bones, chiming wind, and shifting sand. Some begged, but all demanded that Kestrel finish what was started. He looked at Shrew and the others.

"They speak to me. Can you hear them?"

The others looked at Kestrel and shook their heads. Stoat hung her head; Gannet walked away with Cottontail in his arms. The jingle of his pack was the only sound Kestrel heard.

Then the voices of the Eidolons returned.

"Let's go," Shrew said as he lifted Kestrel up.

The voices of the gods were violently loud, pounding in Kestrel's ears. But their words were indistinguishable—as if they were all shouting at the same time.

Stoat caught up with Gannet and Cottontail. They went to the side of the mountain, and Gannet pointed toward a cleared pathway down to the human village. It was the same type of clearing Lynx had made on the other side. Kestrel realized it was true—the gods did intend to march from the sacred mountain into the world.

Looking back, Kestrel noticed they still shifted between their physical and ethereal forms, unable to stabilize themselves or step from the other side of the veil. They were clouds of shifting flies humming on the wind. Kestrel watched as all six reached their hands toward him, calling him back, demanding their sacrifices.

One bent low to examine Lynx's corpse and began to sing over it. It was the most dreadful song he'd ever heard, an ululation meant to resurrect the dead. The other five, shattering in their animalistic and monstrous forms, joined in. The small fire, which had roasted Hoatzin's body plumed, a pillar of fire from the bowl of the mountain.

The Eidolons began to pour their power, their howling voices, and their essence into the bodies on the mountain. Shrew took Kestrel by the elbow and led him down the path toward the village.

TWENTY-SIX

DOWN

The trek down seemed far less treacherous than their upward climb. The storm had ceased, and the abnormally warm air from the peak made the snow less severe.

Stoat, Gannet, Cottontail, and Shrew trudged as fast as they could ahead of him. He hoped to get far ahead of any lingering threat, but one thought plagued his mind: what if Lynx rose from the dead? Kestrel thought of the avalanche that should've killed them, Caiman's injuries, and the wound on his head.

The day passed quickly. Above him in the vault of the sky, the sun began its descent. Soon it would be dark. Kestrel shuddered.

"Do you think it's possible?" Gannet asked no one in particular.

"I don't want to think about it," Shrew answered.

"What if she comes after us?" Stoat asked coldly.

"We should've finished off her body," Kestrel said.

"Burn it, you mean," Shrew said to ward off any other thoughts lingering in Kestrel's mind. Kestrel looked at him and nodded. They walked as close to each other as they could.

"We died in that avalanche," Stoat confirmed. "The gods brought us back."

"No, you didn't. Don't you dare say that," Kestrel shouted. "You might have been buried in the snow, but none of you died. It isn't possible to come back from the dead. Death is final—it's permanent, everlasting."

"Don't pretend," Stoat scoffed. "Cross Fox died from her wounds! I saw the onslaught of ice and rock and trees hurtling toward me. Within minutes, I was buried under the snow, frost filling my lungs, and I couldn't breathe. You died on that mountain, too, but you won't admit it. You died, and you're here with us now, just as I am."

"I didn't die," Kestrel said through gritted teeth.

"You have a gash in your head! How do you think you got it?"

"Stop it!"

"Kestrel," Shrew said gently.

"I'm not dead!"

"You're not. Not anymore," Stoat said, huffing a breath. "The Eidolons are the Gods of Death. They brought you back, as they did for all those who were chosen. The hunters were trying to destroy us completely, to make sure there was nothing left to bring back. As long as there's a body, it can be raised from the dead. Just as you were. You're more like us than you realize, Kestrel."

"You're a liar," Kestrel shot back. "You lied to me from the beginning! You betrayed *all* of us. You were never my friend. You used Shrew's vision to trick me, to test me, and all of this is because of you."

"I can't stand you."

"Then why don't you go back to your death gods? Climb back up that mountain and be with Cross Fox! I'm sure the two of you would be happy bringing destruction into the world as long as you're together. All you've ever cared about was the gods and being with her. So go!"

"Don't you dare speak her name," Stoat yelled. "I lost the love of my life to those things!"

"And I almost lost mine because of you," he retorted.

"Well, I'm here now." She threw her arms up. "I could've stopped you from getting away. I could've sacrificed myself and set loose the gods on the mountain, on the whole earth, but I didn't!"

"And you want my thanks? After everything you've done."

"No!"

"Then what do you want?" Kestrel demanded.

Stoat stopped in the snow, undid the buttons on her jacket to let out the heat, and took off the mask that was perched on her head. She threw it down and opened her mouth as if she was about to unleash wrath upon Kestrel, but instead turned to the mountain.

"What is it?" Gannet asked, holding Cottontail tightly.

"Is it Lynx?" Cottontail asked, shivering.

"No," Stoat said with a tremble. "Do you hear that?"

Kestrel studied the others. They didn't know what she was talking about. Shrew approached her and cupped his ear. Kestrel could hear the wind, the rustling trees, and shuffling feet in the snow, but there was nothing else. Stoat tilted her head and smiled.

"It's Cross Fox. She's calling me."

"Stoat," Shrew touched her cheek. "She can't. She's gone. We have to keep going, okay?"

"I need to go back for her!"

"Hey," Shrew said, trying to comfort her. "It's getting dark out here. Why don't we get to the village and camp there for the night?"

"But she needs me!" Stoat locked her eyes on the mountain.

"I don't feel good," Cottontail cried.

Gannet adjusted her in his arms and opened her coat. Kestrel saw the blood-soaked bandages before Gannet closed it back up. Stoat looked at the little girl. Shrew tugged on Stoat, and she began to follow in his footsteps, but she looked back again.

"We have to get her there," Gannet said as he started to walk off.

"You really don't hear that?" Stoat asked.

Kestrel heard the whispers, but wouldn't let Stoat go back. He kept the rear guard, hand close to his gun just in case she tried to make a break for it. There was no way he was letting anyone back up the mountain, lest one of the gods get their sacrifice and become flesh.

Gannet, Cottontail, and Stoat walked ahead while Kestrel and Shrew walked together a short distance away.

"I thought she was your friend," Shrew put his hand on the back of his neck.

"So did I," Kestrel scoffed. "Stoat was testing me, gathering information for Caiman. She figured out who I was, she saw *my name* from before, and she threw it out. But not before she found out who you were to me and pretended your visions were hers."

"We knew each other?" Shrew's voice grew quiet.

"I didn't have time to tell you," Kestrel stopped walking. "She told me that when Muskox and Grouse found me, I had a wallet on me. It had my ID and a picture of you. Caiman and Cross Fox realized who I was, and Stoat decided to exploit it. She claims that I was searching for you, that we were together before—"

"Before all of this," Shrew laughed, the sound tinged with sadness and relief. "We were together *before*. That's why you found me. That's why we clicked so quickly."

"We found each other. I was lost out here, but somehow we found our way back to each other. Without our names, without our memories."

"We found each other," Shrew repeated.

"It's the only good thing out here," Kestrel smiled and grabbed Shrew's gloved hand. He wished he knew more about who they were, where they met, and what their lives looked like outside of the Hinterlands. What were the odds they would meet again in a place like this?

Kestrel paused, imagining it all. Dreams upon dreams—a real life with Shrew.

They'd have a little cozy kitchen with a sun room off to the side, where Shrew would water plants and play with their cat in the summer sun. Kestrel would work on fixing up the old house they bought, the roof would leak on rainy days, and the floors would creak if stepped on the wrong way. Friends would come over for dinner, and Shrew would insist on board games while Kestrel made drinks for everyone, their favorite songs playing on the stereo.

That life would be wonderful, he thought. It was funny how he could imagine so much but remember so little, like something held his memories captive.

They followed the others' footprints. Kestrel knew they would have to catch up, but he enjoyed the moment of levity. He was ready to be done with the wilderness and find his life again.

Screams sounded ahead of them—short and piercing, a cry for help.

They ran.

The trees grew thick around them. After another turn down the path, the snow and tracks became muddled by a burst of chaos. The emptiness of the straightway struck fear into his heart.

"What happened?" Shrew turned to Kestrel.

Fuck, he thought.

Kestrel ran to the spot where the footprints disappeared into the trampled frost. Looking to the left, he noticed a set of tracks descending from the hill, cutting through the evergreen trees.

"She attacked them," Kestrel said, pointing to spots in the snow. "She ambushed them!"

"Look," Shrew bent down and touched his finger to one of the footprints. Within the icy crater was a gray substance—soot. It smelled of smoke and body odor.

"Hoatzin," Kestrel said as he pulled the rifle off his back.

Shrew armed himself with the machete.

Kestrel bolted down the soot-marked path. The trees blurred as he went, faraway shouts urging him to hasten his arrival. The starless sky hinted of danger. What they had escaped was now chasing them down.

The trees began to spread out, and a small, isolated brick building came into view. The village was now within reach. Gray stone and dried grass peeked up from shards of ice that still clung to the ground.

Kestrel halted, and Shrew was there a moment later.

Gannet stood with the pistol in his hands, Stoat holding her knife out, with Cottontail hidden behind her two guardians. There was another—a shadowy figure with a shroud. For a moment, Kestrel thought it was an Eidolon in the flesh that had come after them. The creature spread her arms and shrieked, the familiar rotten smell worsened by smoke and burnt wood.

Hoatzin turned around. Crispy, charred bits of her flesh cracked and fell off, wafting with ash around her body. She stood naked with her arms outstretched, a phoenix from the hellfires of the abyss.

Kestrel would make sure she stayed dead this time.

"The Eidolons of the Hinterlands have sent me for you!" Hoatzin shrieked. Smoke rippled from her throat, her teeth stained tar black, her hair singed to the root. She was alive, though deep fissures ran through her charred skin as it cracked and peeled.

"What do we do?" Shrew asked quietly.

"We can't let her go back," Kestrel said coldly. "Gannet! Take Cottontail and Stoat and go to the village."

"No one is going anywhere!" Hoatzin shouted. "You are all coming back up to the mountain with me. The gods demand it. You have a purpose, and you will serve it until the end."

"Hoatzin, you are outnumbered," Kestrel said as he aimed his gun at her head. "We won't let you return to the mountain."

"You can't kill me," Hoatzin cackled. "They've brought me back time and time again. Death belongs in their hands. None of us will die until their will is fulfilled and they rule the earth. We will outlive the very ground we walk on."

Cottontail began to hop away, hobbling in the snow until Stoat put the little girl on her back. Gannet kept his handgun at the ready as he stepped backwards slowly. Hoatzin was torn between them— unable to let the other three go but aware Kestrel was watching her.

She leapt.

Two shots rang out. Hoatzin was down.

Black blood pooled on her shoulder and seeped from her head.

Gannet, Stoat, and Cottontail kept going while Kestrel and Shrew dealt with her body. They stood over her, frozen with inaction. She would come back if what she said was true. And so far, it had all been true. Kestrel knew what needed to be done.

"We could bring her to the village," Shrew suggested. "Maybe there's a place we could lock her up—an old storage room or another bunker."

"I don't want to take the chance."

"Then what do we do?"

Kestrel put his rifle on his back and took Shrew's machete. Without flinching, he plunged the blade into her knee. He sawed back and forth, slicing between bone and marrow, undoing the threads of sinew and muscle that held her together. Inky blood spurted from her foul body.

"Kestrel?"

"I'm taking care of it."

"Like this?"

Hoatzin's charred flesh cracked and flaked as he finished cutting off her leg at the knee. Kestrel threw the left leg as far as he could before moving to the next. Shrew bent down beside him, trying to take his attention away from her corpse.

"She can't come after us if she's scattered in pieces across the forest," Kestrel said sternly. "That's what Stoat said! The Eidolons need an intact body." Kestrel *knew* he was right. Hoatzin had already come back twice that he knew of, and she said it had been more than that. If she were nothing but a head buried in the snow or a torso thrown to the wilderness, then could she come back?

"We need to hurry," Kestrel said. "Lynx likely isn't far behind. We need to finish this, dispose of Hoatzin, get to the village, and get the fuck out of here. If Lynx returns, then we'll have to get rid of her too."

Shrew nodded, then held his hand to his mouth, retching. He ransacked his backpack, found another knife, and got to work on her head. Kestrel watched her eyes for movement and listened closely for a heartbeat in her charred remains.

"I'll take it," Shrew said as he decapitated what remained of Hoatzin. He stared into Hoatzin's dead eyes. Kestrel stared too, afraid she might blink awake any moment. There was more to cut up.

Shrew walked off further into the woods with her head.

Kestrel spread the rest of her pieces as far as he could go without leaving the perimeter. He buried pieces under the snow, hid her arm under a rock, and threw her chest into a small ravine to the south. He watched it roll and settle into a cranny between two rocks.

Shrew had returned by the time Kestrel got back. He stared at the coal colored slush under his boots. Kestrel touched his chin, and Shrew looked up, a thin smile spreading across his face.

"Let's go," Shrew said and turned to walk toward the village.

"I doubt the gods can piece her back together," Kestrel laughed. Shrew gave him a weary glance. Kestrel felt his savagery multiplying and unfolding, a prism of death that only belonged to the wilderness. If there was a cure for it, he wasn't sure he wanted to take it.

As they arrived at the village, Kestrel gave Shrew a sideways glance and saw crystalline tears rolling down his cheeks.

TWENTY-SEVEN
THE VILLAGE

Desolate, Kestrel thought. Or maybe "abandoned" was the better word. The village was nothing but hollow buildings, given over to dead ivy, buried under the weight of their collapsed roofs.

An overturned military truck lay off to the right, the back canvas ripped, the boxes inside rifled through. Beyond the truck was an array of solar panels. Some of the panels were buried under drifts of snow, but it would be easy to clear them off. Kestrel headed that way with Shrew at his heels. He found a panel on the back of a garage with the symbol of the sun printed on it, and pushed the handle up into the "on" position.

"It'll take time," Kestrel said. "The batteries might be drained."

"If they work at all. How long do you think this place has been abandoned?"

"I don't know how long, but I want to know *why* it was."

A faint hum coursed through the air as the electricity came to life. Kestrel couldn't wait to see what would happen, but he also knew it might take hours—or nothing would happen at all.

"I'm sure the others found a safe place to camp for the night,"

Kestrel said and reached for Shrew's hand, but Shrew pulled back. Kestrel raised his eyebrows.

"Sorry," Shrew stuttered. "I'm just on edge."

"Don't worry. I'll keep you safe from anything out here." Kestrel put his arm around Shrew's shoulders, and they walked back to the main path that wound through the buildings. The fresh footprints in the muddy slush veered off toward a building at the far end of the encampment. They passed three bunkers, a water tower, a garage, the mess hall, and what appeared to be four sleeping quarters. Stoat, Gannet, and Cottontail had chosen the last building. Kestrel wiped his boots halfheartedly on the front steps and entered.

"You're here," Cottontail muttered. Her voice echoed softly through the half-empty space. She sat on a cot, her legs hanging over the edge while she ate. The sound of bending plastic on the bed made Kestrel flinch.

"Is she gone?" Stoat asked, looking up from her work. She had wrapped Cottontail in crisp white gauze, and a sewing kit and a bottle of hydrogen peroxide sat beside her. Stoat finished stitching and pulled Cottontail's shirt down.

"How did you know about this?" Kestrel asked.

"We've been here before," Stoat said quietly.

Gannet walked into the room and dropped a set of faded, cream-colored linens on the cots. Cottontail started to hop up, but Stoat put a hand on her shoulder and made her stay down. Kestrel looked at her and remembered the bloodstains on his hands, the bodies of the dead, the things he'd done out in the wilderness, and the hunger inside of him. If it meant keeping that little girl safe, it was all worth it.

"We'll stay here for the night," Kestrel said. "I've turned the solar panels back on. Hopefully, we can get some power and find our way out of here."

"How are we going to do that?" Gannet asked.

Kestrel pulled out the cell phone and tossed it to him. The cord uncoiled as Gannet caught it. Up until now, it had been useless, though if the solar panels couldn't generate any energy, it would remain so. Stoat packed up the sewing kit, peroxide, and bandages in a bag and stood, then quickly turned her ear.

"What is it?" Shrew asked as he turned around.

"Nothing."

Kestrel raised an eyebrow but remained silent.

"This place smells like the bunker," Cottontail huffed.

"It's a military outpost," Stoat said before she went through a door leading to a small storage room. She put the medical supplies back on a shelf and returned, closing the door behind her. "The bunker once belonged to the hunters, as did this village. They left them to rot years ago."

Kestrel kept a careful eye on the traitor as she moved around the room.

"Why?" Shrew asked as he began to unpack and set up a bed close to the wall.

"This is where we lost some of the others," Stoat said. She sat on a cot, the mattress squeaking under her weight. "We were circling the mountains—it was the first time we had thirteen people. The hunters were roaming, watching us, following us for days. No one knew. When we got too close to the village, they attacked. We lost two that day."

"Who are the hunters?" Kestrel asked, taking a drink from his canteen.

"A branch of the military, right?" Gannet guessed.

"Not quite," Stoat replied, her general annoyance with Gannet showing. "As far as I know, they are former military who once had base stations across the mountains. The bunker where we took shelter once belonged to them. Pronghorn and Thinhorn were stationed there before they joined us. Caiman and the others said there was another camp far from here, closer to the human lands, but I've never seen it."

"If they're not with the military anymore, why are they still here?" Kestrel asked.

"To stop us. That's all I know."

Kestrel stared at Stoat, his eyebrows stitched together.

"Here," Shrew said, handing him a sheet for his cot. Kestrel touched the soft cotton and ran his finger along the thin gray lines in the fabric.

Stoat rose and walked to a counter, taking a few pouches out of a bag. She distributed the MREs to each person and sat down cross-legged on the floor. Cottontail opened her meal, squealing with joy. Gannet shoveled food into his mouth even though he didn't seem to enjoy whatever the meal was.

"When I get back to the human lands, the first thing I'm eating is seafood," Gannet said, smiling at the thought.

"A cheeseburger. Extra pickles." Shrew opened his MRE.

"Chicken nuggets," Cottontail said, her little face beaming.

"I want steak," Stoat said quietly.

They all looked at Kestrel.

Poking at the mystery meat with a fork, Kestrel stared at the food, the red sauce reminding him of blood, flesh, and sinew. He sniffed, scrunched his face, but didn't answer.

"Not hungry?" Shrew asked.

"I don't know." Kestrel dropped the meal on this cot. He rubbed his hands on his pants. "Are there flashlights?"

"We didn't find any," Gannet said, "but there are these."

Gannet handed Kestrel a large opaque tube and made a bending motion with his hands. Kestrel mimicked him and cracked the plastic, the liquid inside glowing bright orange. The glow stick made Cottontail perk up, so Gannet gave her one too.

"I'm going to look around."

"Do you want me to come with you?" Shrew asked and sat up on his cot.

"No, no. Get some rest. I want to be alone for a minute." Kestrel kissed Shrew on the forehead. A mix of emotions danced across Shrew's face, and a little piece of Kestrel's heart broke. It looked like worry, fear, and love jumbled together—but more than that, it looked like distrust.

Alone, Kestrel walked the long way to the front door, his footsteps echoing loudly on the squeaking floor, the orange glow illuminating his path. Looking back, he watched the little group settle into their makeshift room. They were so close to getting back to normal, back home. He wondered if their memories would ever come back.

There was a boisterous hunger in the pit of his stomach.

He wondered if *he* would ever come back.

Outside the bunk house, there was no light except the glow stick Kestrel held in his hand. He raised it slightly above his head and searched as far as he could see.

Ahead of him was a command post. Kestrel walked across the wide path to the front porch of the building. He turned the knob, and the door opened with an unwelcoming groan. A stale smell tickled his nose as he crossed the threshold into complete darkness. His rifle shifted across his back as the glow stick guided him.

With an errant step, his knee collided with metal. He grunted in pain and recoiled, holding his light out to find an old metal desk. Kestrel examined it closely. Rust grew up the steel legs like moss on a tree. There were papers scattered about, and at the edge of the desk sat an oil lantern.

Kestrel searched his pockets until he found the matchbook. The old hunter green lantern had enough oil to last for a bit. He turned the knob to raise the wick and struck a match. With a whisper of smoke, the lantern lit.

What is this? Kestrel thought.

A topographical map of the Hinterlands lay on the desk. Its lines shifted like bends in a river, the colors fading in and out as the land demanded. The sacred mountain was marked with a sticker in the shape of a flag, with another marking the bunker. A dotted pencil mark followed the course of the tunnel to the Northern Pass. A thin circle surrounded the cave, but the burnt cabin was crossed out. Boundary lines dashed across the map in red.

There was a manila folder on the desk too, photographs peeking out from its edge. Kestrel flipped it open. The first picture was a man standing just in frame on a ridge. The next was a closer shot, followed by another, zoomed in on the area. Four shots later, Kestrel realized the target. She emerged from behind a tree with her head turned toward the photographer.

"Lynx."

Kestrel flipped to the back and found a detailed file on the person who led the thirteen, another portrait shot paper-clipped to the top. The photograph looked like Lynx. Her face was younger, less feline, and her smile seemed genuine. She wasn't wearing her usual attire, save for the bolo tie with the amber stone in the center. She wore a cowboy hat, her hair falling past her shoulders.

A photocopy of an ID with a name highlighted was also included. Kestrel realized it was her real name from before. He said it aloud, but it felt wrong. He flipped through the document and read as quickly as he could. There wasn't much about who she was now—just the story of her disappearance from a crash, statements from her family, and a police report. There was even less on the Lynx he knew. The file mentioned that she led the group, but that was all they could decipher.

It wasn't the only folder. There were others—Caiman, Hoatzin, Muskox, Pronghorn, Thinhorn, Cross Fox, and Bowhead. There were even files for Wapiti, Grouse, Vole, Jackal, and two he didn't know, Coati and Albatross.

Some of the files were labeled with the day they died and their cause of death—several were from missions carried out by the hunters to slow down the thirteen. Kestrel moved them out of the way, searching for his file and the ones for Shrew, Cottontail, Gannet, and Stoat, but the files ended at Bowhead.

Kestrel cursed under his breath.

There was, however, an unmarked red folder. Kestrel ran his finger along the edge, anticipation sending a shiver down his back.

He flicked it open. There were no pictures—there couldn't be—but there were stories, witness sightings, and relics of the past. Evidence of the gods.

"Eidolons," Kestrel read the name out loud.

He shuddered, as if the utterance gave the distant gods more power. He wondered what they were doing now, their forms unfinished. Were they still plotting their return?

These hunters, whoever they were, had been tracking them. They knew of the gods and the legends of the Hinterlands. They'd been working to stop the Eidolons from returning.

Kestrel had to find out more. He picked up the lantern by its handle and carried it through the rest of the building. Down the long hallway was a filing cabinet next to some crates. He opened the filing cabinet and found another stack of folders. He set the lantern on top and opened the first file. Kestrel's eyes bulged. He skipped to the next, then the next, until he went through the rest of the stack. Seventeen folders in his arms—seventeen names he'd never heard. He opened the second and third and fourth drawers—they were full of files too.

So many others.

Kestrel put them back, closed the drawers, and walked back down the hall. The sheer volume of people Lynx had taken possession of was unfathomable to him. He could hardly breathe. Kestrel returned to the metal desk, set the lantern on the edge, and stacked the file folders of the thirteen back together. The door behind him opened with a creak. Kestrel turned around. In the dim glow, he saw a figure step forward.

"Stoat," Kestrel laughed. "You scared me."

The orange glow stick that Stoat held inched closer, dimmer than his own, as if it had gone bad years ago. As she moved into the light of Kestrel's lantern, he realized it wasn't Stoat.

"Hello, Kestrel," Lynx said dryly.

Before he could draw his rifle, she was at his throat—a lightning-fast blur of blade and amber. Her knife split the skin of his neck, his blood dribbling on the steel.

"Lynx..." Kestrel tried to control his breathing and determine his next move.

"The Liberator who usurped me, betrayed the call on his life, who gave up the abode of the gods for the fleeting vanity of the human lands. The demented man who slaughtered our prophetess to pieces and discarded her in the woods," Lynx said with a bite.

"You won't kill me," Kestrel said, staring into her eyes. "I know you need me."

"Don't you realize? You've served your purpose. You liberated me and the others from the hunters. The gods have raised me to find you and dispose of you for good. Then I'll take the others back to the mountain, and we will finish this."

"You'll need another. I know you won't give yourself up."

"The gods can wait." Lynx grinned. "The others will sacrifice themselves for the Eidolons, then I will venture back out to find one more. They've been patient for thousands of years—a few weeks won't hurt."

"You're wrong." Kestrel pushed back, feeling the knife's edge nick his skin. Fear flickered across Lynx's eyes, and in a flash, he caught her arm and twisted it, the knife slipping from her grip. The blade fell through the air. He tried to grab it, but Lynx pushed against him. He missed.

Kestrel slammed into the desk and knocked the lantern over. The knife clattered across the concrete floor out of sight. He went to reach for his gun, but Lynx wrapped her fingers around his throat. A knee to the stomach made her release her chokehold and cough.

The lantern rolled off the desk and shattered, extinguishing the light.

Lynx pounced on him, and Kestrel dodged haphazardly, colliding with the wall and sending a picture frame plummeting. Everything crashed to the ground around them. Kestrel knew if he didn't win this fight, then the world would meet the same fate. Lynx fell on the chair beside the desk and toppled over it, bringing the map and the glow stick with her.

Kestrel pulled the gun off his back, cocked it, and fired as fast as he could—a warning shot. Lynx climbed up from the floor and held her hands out.

"You don't want to do this, Kestrel," Lynx said.

"After everything you've done to me, done to all of us, why shouldn't I kill you now?"

"You haven't fulfilled your purpose."

"That's not what you said."

"I lied," Lynx admitted. "You weren't meant to sacrifice yourself on the mountain. I was. You saving us from the hunters wasn't fulfilling your purpose. Our purpose is never for us, but to serve the gods and their will. You were meant to complete us, to be the last alive. To free the Eidolons from their prisons and liberate the world alongside them."

"Why do you keep lying?" Kestrel sneered.

"It's the truth. You can't leave here. They won't let you."

Kestrel pulled the trigger, and the gun jammed. He cursed. Lynx lunged at him and tried to wrestle the rifle away. He hit her with the butt of the gun, and they tumbled to the ground together.

The useless gun was abandoned as they grappled. They twined together; in the darkness, it was impossible to distinguish where one's body ended and the other's began—like a snake eating its tail.

Infinite devouring and unending death.

Lynx clawed at Kestrel's throat again, digging her sharp nails in— her favorite weapon. Cut off from air, his lungs sealed like a tomb, but he kicked and grabbed, trying to push her off. He felt around on the floor for the knife.

"You and I are the same. I've seen it in you," Lynx said as she pinned him down.

Kestrel saw the amber stone in her bolo tie gleam in the orange glow, its color cast across her face. Her eyes glowed orange and yellow, her teeth bared.

"I'm nothing like you," Kestrel muttered. Each word was painful, broken by his inability to take in enough air. He couldn't scream, even if he wanted to. A begging prayer rose within him—he was desperate for anyone to walk through the door.

"I see it in your eyes. There's hunger in you—the need to take, to find freedom. You desire so much in your life. That's why they chose you. You are ravenous, and your life before gave you nothing."

"No!" Kestrel grunted.

"Kestrel, don't be fooled. You were malnourished before. You have tasted and seen the wilderness, and I know you found it *delicious*. You hear them even now—calling you, clawing at your gut, scratching your mind. Satisfy your hunger. Give yourself to the gods."

Kestrel found the knife and thrust it into Lynx's shoulder, cleaving the socket. She released her hand and cried out as he blindly stabbed her body. She tried to fight back, but the slices silenced her.

Lynx rolled on the floor, and Kestrel sat on top of her.

"Now I'm free," Kestrel said with a smirk. "Go greet your death gods."

He plunged the knife into her chest, releasing a torrent of crimson from her arteries. Kestrel wished it were daylight so he could watch the life fade from her eyes. Lynx tried to speak, but only blood gurgled out.

Kestrel bent down and kissed her lips, licked up the pooling red liquid.

Follow your desire.

"Hello," Lynx sputtered as she stared at Kestrel.

The amber stone in her tie glinted in the darkness.

He bent down to smell the sweet scent of her dying body. There was a whisper on the wind, a little melody, the sound of shifting and becoming something new.

Devour, it said.

And he did.

The forbidden fruit was abundant, and there was no one to tell him to stop. So he ate of the tree, drank of its sweet juice, and felt his hunger dissipate. A smile crept on his face.

Kestrel felt at peace.

TWENTY-EIGHT
THE WAY OF THE RISING SUN

Kestrel sat in the corner of the room, waiting as Shrew scanned the area with a glowstick. Shrew gasped when the beam settled on him. He was covered in blood, drenched from head to toe, chewing on a kidney.

Kestrel laughed, gesturing toward the dead woman on the floor. "Eat."

Shrew moved the chair and bent down, the glowstick trembling. "What did you do?"

"What I was supposed to do. I *liberated* us," Kestrel said. "That's my purpose, after all. I couldn't let her live. She had to be stopped—you know that. She won't come back. I had to make sure of that."

"But did you have to do *this*?" Shrew asked.

"I was hungry."

"We're all hungry, but we shouldn't be doing this—eating people! That's why we were trying to escape. What Lynx, Hoatzin, and Caiman forced us to do in the woods was horrific. We did what we had to do to survive, but now we're free. We're on the way out. You were leading us out."

"We're free because of *me*. *I* saved us from her. The gods won't take us, and they won't become real. They'll stay up on the *fucking* mountain and rot." Kestrel spat out a piece of kidney.

"Hey, hey," Shrew hesitantly put his hand on Kestrel's knee, blood squishing between his fingers. "Let's get you back to the bunks. Gannet found the water line and got it turned on. Stoat found a propane water heater, and the tanks still have gas in them. They just finished their showers and are going to bed. Why don't we do the same?"

"But there's more."

"More?"

"To eat." Kestrel licked his lips. "I'm so hungry, and she tastes so good."

"No," Shrew said as he touched his hand to Kestrel's cheek. "Leave it be. She's gone. Without her heart, she won't be able to come back. None of the others will either. We're safe for now. Tomorrow we will get the cell phone working and get out of this place."

Kestrel nodded in forlorn agreement.

Shrew helped him up, stepping slowly to avoid slipping in the mess.

The air outside was bitter when it struck Kestrel's blood-speckled face. Shrew held him as they walked to the other building, little snowflakes rising and falling as if being conducted. Inside the bunk house, Gannet, Stoat, and Cottontail were fast asleep. They all looked so warm and peaceful, and Kestrel was proud of getting them this far.

Shrew led him down the back hall to the showers. The pressure was weak, but the water was warm; Kestrel stood naked and hesitant at the edge of the stream, which splashed onto the light blue tile floor. He reached his foot out, testing the water. Shrew stripped down and tossed his clothes on a bench. He put a hand on Kestrel's back. He shivered, turning around.

They stepped in together, the water washing away the blood

until they were clean. Soapy suds mingled with the crimson water, circling the drain, catching Kestrel's eye. He immediately began to cry.

"Hey, hey, hey," Shrew wrapped his arms around Kestrel and hugged him, his chin pressing into his shoulder.

"What have I become?" Kestrel whispered, filled with remorse.

"It will be okay." Shrew cupped Kestrel's face in his hands. "We'll make it out of this place and get the help we need. Don't you worry."

Kestrel finished his shower and dried off with thin, worn towels. Shrew sat on his cot and dried the rest of his hair. Kestrel laid down, tears staining his flat pillow. He raised up on his left arm. "Will you sleep with me?"

No response was necessary. Shrew moved his cot as close to Kestrel's as he could and filled the small gap with sheets and pillows, until it was one bed that could fit both of them.

Shrew wrapped an arm around Kestrel and kissed him goodnight.

Hours later, as the sun began to rise, Kestrel still hadn't slept. All he could think about was Lynx—her dead body lying in a room not far away, her flesh losing its plumpness, rotting and wasting away. He missed devouring her.

But he knew it wasn't right. Kestrel had fought against Lynx, Hoatzin, Caiman, and the others to be free from this, to stop the insanity—and now he was the one longing. He knew it wasn't something inside of him. He'd been through hell and back. Shrew's face flickered in his mind.

Help me, Kestrel thought. It might have been a prayer, but he wasn't sure whom he prayed to—certainly not the gods on the mountain. Maybe it was for Shrew—the one holding him, keeping him from the very thing enticing him. His tongue tingled at the thought of savoring flesh again.

"Cross," Stoat mumbled in her sleep.

Kestrel dismissed his cravings—pushed them far away, reminding himself of all the reasons it was wrong to dream of eating another person.

He once believed it, but something sinister had grown within him.

He had to get himself back.

Stoat shifted in her bed, catching Kestrel's attention. She muttered something, but he couldn't make it out. With the sun cresting in the distance and the windows filling with a warm glow, he finally drifted off to sleep.

It didn't last long.

The others woke up but felt no rush to get ready. There wasn't anywhere to go. All they needed to do was rest and watch the sunrise. A lazy morning was a gift they never expected to receive. There was no one hunting them anymore, but they still needed to get home and find themselves again. Kestrel dwelled on the fact that the gods might try to find another leader to gather more people until they could fully enter the human world. With a buzzing jolt, the overhead fluorescent lights began to sing and cast their artificial light upon them. Everyone looked up and marveled at the power.

"Morning," Shrew said hazily as he woke.

Kestrel tried to smile, but he felt drained. His body ached. He needed more sleep. Shrew was next to him, arm loose around his waist, like he was ready to restrain him if necessary. Was he really that much of a monster?

Once everyone roused from their cots, they hesitated, unsure of what to do first. Lynx had long commanded them, forcing them to carry out the various duties that upheld the thirteen, but now they were their own masters. Cottontail asked Gannet for breakfast and he obliged. Stoat went off to the toilets, and Shrew made their bed as if they would be revisiting the bunk.

Kestrel saw the cell phone bundled in the cord and bolted to it. The old matte plastic was worn thin by oily fingers, but it felt precious in his hand. He unraveled the charger and found the nearest outlet.

The gray screen blinked with a black logo before indicating it needed time to charge. Kestrel set it on the ground and sat down beside it, crossing his legs and staring at the phone. Shrew joined him, laying his head in the nook of his shoulder.

Waiting felt brutal.

Gannet and Cottontail brought over pouches of military food. Kestrel took one and began to shake it. He read the label: hash browns and bacon. It wasn't foul, but it didn't smell pleasant either. He wanted something he couldn't want anymore.

"You need to eat," Shrew said, urging him to try the food.

"I'm not really hungry."

"You need to eat normal food," Shrew said, setting down his food. He had French toast, which sounded better than Kestrel's. He put his hand on Kestrel's arm and pushed him gently to return to eating.

Kestrel stabbed the bits of bacon and ate them, getting them past his taste buds as fast as he could, swallowing hard. They weren't bad, but the *hunger* ate at him, begging him for flesh. He would have to fight his desire to consume, stave off the pain.

Or else.

The cell phone dinged, and Shrew's eyes darted to it. Kestrel grabbed it as fast as he could. The screen showed the time of day—something he hadn't known in ages—battery level, and signal. Two bars. Kestrel found saved contacts and scrolled through the list until he saw a name he thought could help them escape the wilderness.

Basecamp.

He hesitated. Did he want to leave? For so long he had wanted out from under Lynx, but now he could choose. His own free will. He could choose to feast again.

Kestrel pressed the button and confirmed the call.

It began to ring. Each toll felt like a century, a lifeline back to the old world. *Ring, ring, ring.* A new fear rippled through him—that no one would answer and they would have to try another number. He had no idea whom else to call.

Then someone answered.

"Hello?" the voice said suspiciously— a gruff woman's voice, quick and stern.

"Hi," Kestrel said, unsure.

"Who is this?"

"My name is..." Kestrel thought for a moment. "I don't know my real name. They call me Kestrel."

"How did you get this number?"

"It was in a phone I found on a hunter."

"Who are you?"

"We were taken against our will by a group wandering in the Hinterlands. We were led by a woman named Lynx. There were thirteen of us, but not anymore. We've been trying to find our way and return home, but we aren't sure where to go."

"We?"

"There are five of us. We escaped from the others."

"Do you know where you are now?" she asked.

"We're at an abandoned military camp on the east side of the mountain, I think," Kestrel said, then remembered Muskox's water bottle. "There was a milk jug with 'Waterford Farms' on the label. I'm not sure if that's near here, but I thought it might help."

"Okay, here's what you need to do."

She explained their next course of action. Kestrel listened carefully, taking mental notes, and gave verbal confirmation to the unknown guide. After a few minutes, Kestrel hung up the phone and looked to the others.

"What is it?" Stoat asked as she walked back into the circle.

"Someone is going to help us. She said there is a checkpoint south of the village, on the other side of the river. If we can make it there and cross, someone will come for us," Kestrel reassured them.

"We're going home!" Cottontail kissed the foot around her neck and bounced into Gannet's arms. He spun her around until she was dizzy, the two laughing and dancing together.

Stoat stood as silent and cold as a statue, staring off out a window. Kestrel saw the stain of distrust on her face.

"Let's get going!" Shrew bellowed as he stood up and stretched.

"How do you know you can trust them?" Stoat asked from the other side of the room. "That phone was taken from the hunters. It could be a trap. They could kill us as soon as they have us in their sights."

"They *were* trying to stop this," Kestrel admitted.

"We're getting out of here," Gannet said, beginning to pack their things.

"I think we should stay longer," Stoat argued.

Kestrel wanted to admit that he agreed with her on some level, but he couldn't. He had to put all this behind him as fast as he could. If not for him, then for Shrew.

"Stoat, we will run out of food soon. There isn't any here." Shrew sighed. He glanced at Kestrel. He nodded to Shrew, reaffirming his commitment to get out of the wilderness.

"Do you hear that?" Stoat asked, turning to the door.

"I didn't hear anything," Kestrel said as he followed her gaze. "We'll have my rifle and the handgun," he continued. "If it gets dicey, we can regroup and find another way out. This is our best chance for now. We're not *them*. The woman on the phone seemed surprised. I doubt they expected any of us to escape." Kestrel handed Stoat the handgun.

Dismissing Stoat's concerns, the others focused on finishing packing. She relented and gave in.

But Kestrel *had* heard the whispers and could feel his stomach yearning for more. He put a hand on his belly and tried to quiet it all.

"Are you still feeling hungry?" Shrew whispered as he put a hand on Kestrel's knee.

Kestrel tried to ignore the hunger pangs, but a tear rolled down his cheek. Betrayed by his own body in more ways than one. Shame tingled up his spine and grabbed him by the throat. Desire slithered through his veins, coiling in his stomach.

He felt like he wouldn't make it out alive.

"Here," Cottontail said as she turned Kestrel's hand over.

Kestrel mentally shook himself and saw the little girl standing before him. He opened his fingers. She took off the chain around her neck, placed her foot in his hand, and closed his fingers around it. Her small hand clasped his as tight as she could. The girl looked up at him with eyes too knowing for her young age.

"I want you to keep this," Cottontail smiled, a tooth missing. "My purpose was to give luck, so I hope it helps you. It'll be better. I promise."

Kestrel couldn't speak. It was too much. The bizarre foot, the little girl being braver than he was—reality sunk in. He had to get better. It was time to step into the light again, to cross back into the human lands and remember.

But remembering was the issue.

Who am I? Kestrel thought.

"Thank you, Cottontail," Shrew said, tossing her a wide grin when Kestrel froze.

The little girl smiled again and hopped away. Kestrel pocketed her foot with tears in his eyes. It was time to go. Kestrel patted Shrew on the hand and finished packing his things. They set out in a line. Kestrel, Shrew, Gannet, Cottontail, and Stoat—the last ones left.

Outside, the sun was bright and the world was soft with snowfall. The breeze was gentle. The earth seemed to sing with a long overdue welcome. Kestrel stopped as they gathered in the center of the village.

"We'll be there soon enough," Kestrel told them. "We head away from the mountain, go south for about an hour, then go east, the way of the rising sun. That should get us to the river."

"How do we know when it's been an hour?" Gannet asked.

Kestrel held up the cell phone. It was the first time they'd seen one in a while. He pressed a button and the time flashed on a gray-green screen. They all stared at the device in his hand.

Time was back. It felt so simple, but so powerful.

"We should get going," Shrew said. "They'll be waiting for us."

Gannet picked up Cottontail and put her on his shoulders. She clasped his head and leaned forward to balance herself while Stoat flung her backpack on. Shrew looked up at the pink sky.

Kestrel looked to the building across the way. He recalled the temptation just beyond the door. But the door was closed, and he had to keep it that way.

TWENTY-NINE

BEYOND THE RIVER

In a line just as before, the five walked toward the human lands with Kestrel at the lead. Their steps in sync, crunching the frost on the ground, their breath formed little clouds that vanished as quickly as they arrived. The sound of their footfalls lessened, deadened not by the ice beneath their boots, but by one person stopping their procession.

Kestrel turned around. Stoat stood alone, frozen like a statue, staring off at the mountain peak behind them. The group halted, turning their heads in order to look. Kestrel hurried to Stoat's side and touched her shoulder.

She didn't turn around.

He moved in front of her. She was transfixed, like someone had cast a spell on her, her eyes open wide but unmoving. She didn't realize Kestrel was there. She simply gazed up at the sacred mountain.

"Do you hear that?" Stoat muttered.

"What do you hear?" Kestrel asked, unwilling to admit he knew what she meant. It was the whispers, the ones he heard before—nothing more.

"It's *her*."

"Lynx?" Shrew suggested.

"Cross Fox," Stoat chuckled. "She's calling to me. I have to go."

"No, she's not," Kestrel snapped his fingers in front of her face. Stoat's eyes shot to his thumb and middle finger, her trance broken.

"She's calling me."

And maybe she *was* calling Stoat, but Kestrel knew she wasn't Cross Fox any longer. She was something else. He could hear the whispers on the wind, though they were strangely faint and stagnant.

"Let's go."

Stoat bowed her head but didn't resist.

Kestrel guided her back to the line, and she took her place. He considered putting her between Shrew and Gannet, but he let her have some semblance of autonomy.

There was an affliction among them, a disease. It was naive of Kestrel to think it could be cured by leaving the thirteen. The gods were still on the mountain, beckoning, spilling their blight into the earth, into those in their service. Everything imparted to them was a virus, altering their bodies. It was a sickness so potent it changed their very cellular structure.

It would be inside them forever—that was Kestrel's worry. But for now, they would walk on. Salvation awaited them.

An hour passed, and the party followed the sun to the east. Stoat had not stopped walking, but the few times Kestrel checked on her, she was walking slowly, turning to look over her shoulder, slowing her steps at the slightest sound. When Stoat noticed him watching her, she would catch up and keep pace.

Shrew caught up with Kestrel. "How are you feeling?"

"I'm hungry," Kestrel admitted. "I don't understand why I'm the only one who seems to be this way. Something is wrong with me, Shrew. It's not just that I can't remember my fucking name, but I'm starving and I need to eat. I'm different from the rest of you. I think I lost myself in these woods."

"Kestrel, Lynx lied to you. She manipulated and brought us all into this madness. It took me time to see that."

"But I doubted from the beginning!" Kestrel looked over his shoulder.

Gannet was intentionally avoiding eye contact while telling Cottontail a made-up story about a talking tree who was friends with a rambunctious squirrel.

"It takes hold of us in different ways. The lies, the hunger, the control. You were a victim just like the rest of us, even if you doubted from the beginning and planned to escape the moment you woke up. Even though Stoat manipulated and lied to you."

"The gods were real," Kestrel sighed. "From the beginning, I knew that Lynx was delusional, Hoatzin was insane, and Caiman was a deviant. All of them were monsters for doing what they did and forcing others to play along, but that's the thing I keep coming back to. It was real. The gods do exist."

"I'm not sure what to think about what we saw up there. It was unearthly, otherworldly—even unholy—but it doesn't matter. Yeah, the gods exist, but you still had a choice—we all had a choice—and you chose not to sacrifice yourself. We stopped them from destroying the world."

"Maybe."

"No, not maybe. We went all the way up the sacred mountain! You led us there. You had the gall and guts to get us to the top, and you led us out of there," Shrew said with a grin. "You didn't follow blindly or fall under their sway. You didn't listen to their siren song. You saved us all."

"Then why do I feel this pit in my stomach?" Kestrel asked. "Endless hunger for one thing. I tasted flesh, and now I'm starving. I don't want to be. I want to feel sick at the thought of it. It's wrong."

"We've all done horrible things out here. Things I would be ashamed to tell you. But I know you, Kestrel. I loved you before, I love you now, and I will walk with you out of this cursed wilderness."

Kestrel began to weep.

"What's wrong?"

"They were real. Lynx was right, I was wrong, and the others..." he trailed off. "They lost their lives to the death gods. They believed, and they were right. But they still lost their lives."

"But you didn't choose them or bow to the Eidolons. You didn't! They may have a will to carry out, they may try to whisper or shout commands at you, call you back to them, but you didn't give in. You didn't listen to them, and you didn't choose them. They exist, but you don't have to believe in them or follow their path."

Kestrel wiped a tear from his cheek.

"We will get through this together," Shrew said, holding him closer. "I won't let them take you from me again. You found me. I'll help you find yourself."

Kestrel wished a bit of the warmth in Shrew's heart would transfer to his own.

"What if they call out to me and I want to answer?"

"Then I'll hold you down until you drown them out. I'll keep you anchored."

"And what if we never remember?" Kestrel asked.

"Then we make new memories."

And that was that.

The trees thinned out the further down they went, and the air seemed thicker compared to the mountain altitude they were accustomed to. A roaring tickled their ears.

"The river!" Cottontail shouted. Her finger extended to the gentle curve of the stirring waters ahead. Foam formed over rocks, the water tumbling and churning, undisturbed by the veil of winter.

Kestrel, Shrew, and Gannet hustled down the old, unused road and exited the tree line. The land near the riverbank turned to muddy slush, the blades of grass worn down to almost nothing.

A thin edge of ice had seized the water's edge, the top frozen like a layer of glass. In the middle of the river, the water waged war with frost, crushing bits of ice from the mountain.

"We have to cross," Kestrel commanded.

Gannet made sure Cottontail was secured on his shoulders. Shrew tightened the straps of his backpack and quickly grabbed and squeezed Kestrel's hand.

Kestrel went to the bank and reached his hand into the water. It wasn't as fast as it appeared, but it was icy cold. He recoiled and wiped the frigid water on his pants before putting the glove back on.

"Let's wait until we see them coming. It's too cold for us to wait here, soaking wet until they rescue us," he told the others. He hoped the rescuers would arrive soon.

He looked up at the sun; it was almost noon. Stoat stood further away from them, her body turned toward the mountain, and her face scrunched in pain. She cupped a mittened hand to her ear.

"Do you hear her?" Stoat asked before turning to the others.

Gannet stepped closer to her, holding on to Cottontail with one hand and reaching out to Stoat with another. When he touched Stoat's arm, she turned around too quickly and thrust both hands against his chest, pushing him away from her. Gannet fell, and Cottontail toppled over onto the ground.

The little girl yelped in pain. Kestrel and Shrew ran to them, but Stoat held out the handgun Kestrel had given her. His folly struck him like a hammer to the gut.

Stoat kicked Gannet and picked up Cottontail by the arm. The little girl's appendage was covered in mud, her wrist turning red when Stoat twisted it. She pointed the firearm at Gannet, then Shrew and Kestrel. She stepped away, holding on to Cottontail.

"Let her go," Kestrel demanded. His rifle was on his back, but any sudden movement would be a mistake.

"I need to go back to her. She's calling me. I can't be without her —I can't leave. If we cross that river, we won't come back. They need us," Stoat said with a panicked voice. Her eyes darted around, sweat pooling on her hairline. "We have to go back to the mountain."

"No," Kestrel commanded.

"Stoat," Shrew said as he took a step forward, arms out. "Let Cottontail go. You're hurting her. We can talk about this."

Shrew shot a side glance at Kestrel, signaling.

"They need us!" Stoat screeched. "Cross Fox needs me."

We need you. The thought slammed into Kestrel's mind. It wasn't his own—it was static overlaid by whispers. Pain surged in his head. Kestrel pressed a hand to his forehead.

"We can't go back." Kestrel groaned the words through gritted teeth. He tried to follow Shrew's lead, but a pang railed through his mind. One step seemed impossible. Kestrel felt like he was going to fall over.

The gods were beckoning. Hunger called to him again.

Kestrel couldn't let them win. He had to reclaim every bit of himself, fight back, and remember who he was before. For himself, for Shrew, for Gannet, and for Cottontail. The Eidolons did not possess him, and they never would.

"Let her go," Gannet demanded as he sat up in the mud. His hands slid along the ground, smearing the earth.

"I hear her, too," Shrew lied. "Do you?"

Kestrel watched Stoat turn around sharply, her eyes fixed on the mountain peak far in the distance. The wind wrapped around them. He felt the power it carried and heard the whispers on the wind. Shrew stepped forward slowly as Gannet got to his knees and shifted into a lunge, ready to leap. Stoat took a deep breath. Kestrel watched Gannet and Shrew get in place.

"Cross Fox."

Gannet struck, knocking Stoat in the back, her hand letting go of Cottontail. Shrew scurried and picked up the little girl, shielding her with his body as they fled back toward the river. Kestrel waded through the fury hitting him, and found his way out.

Kestrel pulled the rifle off his back and aimed it at Stoat, but Gannet and Stoat were tangled together, fighting and rolling around in the mud.

"Gannet, let her go. I've got her," Kestrel shouted.

But Gannet wouldn't relent. His hatred for Stoat trying to take Cottontail made his fists pound with fury. Kestrel knew he wouldn't let her go. Limbs flailed as they rolled once more. Gannet tried to get the handgun out of her grasp, but Stoat held on as they struggled.

Kestrel ran to pull them apart, but a shot was fired.

Then another.

Gannet rolled on top of Stoat, the wound in his arm and side pocked bright red. Blood ran down his side as he fell over. Stoat pushed him off her, grabbed the gun, and stood up. Kestrel aimed at Stoat, but she had already drawn.

"You don't have to do this," Shrew said, hiding Cottontail's face in his shoulder.

Stoat fired without warning.

Kestrel returned the favor, and Stoat went down. The bullet pierced her skull, killing her instantly.

"No!" Shrew screamed.

The wind died down; only the roar of the river and the cries of a child could be heard.

Kestrel turned around to see Shrew hovering over Cottontail's body, her shoulder bloodied. The air smelled of mud and iron. Shrew took off his jacket, peeled off one of his layered shirts, and put his coat back on. He wrapped the shirt around Cottontail's wound and pressed tightly, tying the cloth in a knot on the back and whispering to her softly.

"Is she okay?" Kestrel asked as he ran to Gannet.

"It's just a flesh wound," Shrew yelled back.

"Cottontail!" Gannet struggled to get up, clasping his side with his good arm as he slipped in bloodied mud. Kestrel helped him up and tried to check his wounds, but he pushed Kestrel away and ran to the girl.

"It's okay, it's okay," Gannet repeated as he brushed her hair. Her little eyes were fading, her frown trying to flicker into a smile, her shoulder bleeding profusely through the shirt that Shrew had given her.

Kestrel stood above them all, took Cottontail's lucky foot out of his pocket, and held it up. He took it and, bending down, placed it around her neck. As if she knew what it meant, Cottontail smiled weakly before falling asleep. She had endured so much.

Gannet checked her breathing every moment, refusing to take his eyes off her, running his fingers through her hair, and singing a sweet lullaby. Kestrel walked with Shrew over to Stoat's corpse. The mark on her forehead from the bullet's impact bubbled ruby red.

"I'll take care of her," Kestrel said as he handed his rifle to Shrew and unsheathed his machete. His eyes watched as a droplet ran down Stoat's face, over the bridge of her nose, down to her lips.

He felt it—the enticing desire. Stoat might be sweet like Lynx or foul like Hoatzin. Maybe she was smoky, or salty, or tangy. He wondered how her ears tasted, how her thighs would rip and tear. Kestrel pulled himself together, letting the thought die as best he could.

There's no other way, he thought. This thought was wholly his own—no whispers from the gods. There was no other way. If Stoat was left here, the gods could bring her back to life like they'd done before.

Kestrel's stomach growled, and he began to weep. He put his unused hand in his pocket and felt something there.

"Let me," Shrew said as he put the rifle on his back and reached for the knife.

With a bit of hesitation, Kestrel let it go. Shrew placed a hand on his shoulder, then kissed Kestrel on the cheek and told him to turn around.

He obeyed.

Kestrel walked away, past Gannet and Cottontail, toward the river.

The current was moving, but near the banks, he found a patch of ice reflective enough to see himself for the first time in a long time. It wasn't who he expected. Kestrel thought he'd look different than before. He most certainly did.

Kestrel, Kestrel, Kestrel.

It sounded unfamiliar now, the wrong name he'd held onto for so long. It wasn't right. It wasn't him. He took off his feathered coat and knelt. His nose was long and sharp, his eyes narrow and piercing as he stared, and a feather was lodged in his hair. Kestrel took it out and offered it up to the wind, which gleefully carried it away.

He pulled his hand out of his pocket, grasping the object he'd found inside. The amber stone. It seemed so insignificant that one would never guess it had witnessed such atrocities. Kestrel turned it over and over in his fingers. In it, he could see another world, a reality where he'd never been out searching for Shrew and hadn't wound up here. Still another where he'd believed it from the beginning and sacrificed himself on the mountain, unleashing chaos into the world.

Kestrel threw the amber stone into the river. It plopped into the roiling waters and sank to its icy grave, never to be seen again if he had his wish. He stood and looked back up to the mountain. A gust of frigid air pummeled toward him, carrying the clarion call to return, but he ignored it and stepped into the water.

Kestrel shouted as the freezing water hit his skin. It felt like a painfully slow death at the end of the world. He knew he would be reborn—not of fire but of frost. He waded through the river, sharply inhaling when the cold pierced him.

Teeth chattering, he called to the others to follow as he climbed out on the other side. His soaked clothes froze to his skin, his entire body shivering, skin turning ghostly white. But he was beyond the river. In the distance, a military truck approached through the snow.

It was time to go.

The others noticed too and began to walk to the river's bank.

Kestrel wasn't sure if the gods were still on the mountain or if they had vanished into dust after the failed ritual. It didn't matter to him anymore.

He heard the grinding grunt of the truck engine, the wheels driving over what remained of the grass, and the sound of his friends —his family—crossing the river to meet him. Their life was theirs again.

Small details began to flutter around him. Flashes of a home, of the street he walked down with Shrew, of family and friends. Memories of long ago. All the little things that once were unimportant seemed so monumental now—a sunny day in the kitchen, a first date, the day his mother died, an old, snowed-in cabin for Christmas, a drink of champagne on their anniversary, the day Shrew lost his job.

His real name felt sweet on his lips as he said it out loud. Shrew couldn't contain his smile as he looked over to his partner. Wonder struck like lightning, a bolt across the neurons in his mind, firing and reforming the forgotten parts.

Kestrel remembered.

ACKNOWLEDGMENTS

Thank you to my father who encouraged me to follow my dreams. For that, I dedicated this book to him. I had a lot of options but I couldn't narrow it down to one phrase. How do you reduce what you wish you could say to someone who's passed down to a single line? So with encouragement from my publisher, the dedication became a poem of sorts–messy and complex in the way that grief is but simple in the end.

I wish he could've been here to see this day. I know he would be endlessly proud of me. He often told me so. Before his death he requested the first signed copy of my book so I signed a copy just for him and put it on my shelf.

A huge thank you to the entire team at Quill & Crow Publishing House for their contributions to this novel. To Cassandra, for taking a chance on me, guiding me through the publishing process, and your commitment to championing independent authors and creatives. I couldn't have done it with you.

To the editors–Lisa, Matt, Tiff, and Kayla–thank you for all the effort you put into polishing, perfecting, and publishing *Hinterland*. I don't know where I would be without your tireless work. I'm sorry I made some of you sick to your stomachs, but I'm secretly wearing that as a badge of honor.

Thank you to Alma, Stephanie, and Matthew for all the work you did to ensure *Hinterland* made it to the right audience. From social media to book stores to everything in between, your marketing prowess is unmatched.

For such a powerful and punchy cover, I have to give all the credit to Fay Lane. She understood my vision for the book and created a beautiful work of art for the world to see. I still can't get over how great the cover turned out!

Thank you to Julie Lew for reading the first draft of *Hinterland* and providing input on the manuscript. I'm sorry for making you sick to your stomach, too, but I'm glad you powered through. Her book, *The Wives of Henrick Hall,* is coming soon. Go check it out. Thank you to Kay, Ryan, Olivia, and Suze for their input on the title of *Hinterland.* In the end, the first one was the right one.

To all of my friends, thank you for always listening to me ramble about the latest book I'm working on. Your constant encouragement and support mean the world to me. A special thanks to Hannah Packard for letting me bounce ideas off you, giving me feedback, and pushing me to keep writing when things got difficult. To my cousin, Jake Spurgeon, for helping me think through various aspects of the novel and giving me marketing advice.

For the survivors of the doomsday cult, I'm thankful you left when the truth was revealed. It takes time to unlearn what we were taught but we're in this together. Don't give up. Keep going. Brighter days are ahead.

Finally, thank you to my readers. I do this all for you. I hope you enjoyed your journey into the wilderness and that you leave hungry for more.

ABOUT THE AUTHOR

Logan Spurgeon is a speculative fiction author originally from Houston, Texas. After leaving a doomsday cult, he received his MA in Theology and revived his lifelong passion for storytelling.

His debut novel, *Hinterland*, will be followed by *Sourwood* in March 2026 and *The House on Garnet Hill* in December 2026 (Quill & Crow Publishing House). His short story *These Flowers Must Bloom* can be read online at Thin Veil Press and his novella, *The Castle on the Inside*, is out now.

When he isn't writing, Logan can be found wandering around vintage stores, hiking, tending to his plants, or having deep conversations over food with friends. He now resides in Lexington, Kentucky.

THANK YOU FOR READING

Thank you for reading *Hinterland*. We deeply appreciate our readers, and are grateful for everyone who takes the time to leave us a review. If you're interested, please visit our website to find review links. Your reviews help small presses and indie authors thrive, and we appreciate your support.

More LGBTQ+ Horror by Quill & Crow

Sourwood, Logan Spurgeon

God's Own Country, Mathew L Reyes

The Wives of Herrick Hall, Julie Lew

www.ingramcontent.com/pod-product-compliance
Lightning Source LLC
Chambersburg PA
CBHW061801190726
48289CB00007B/2029